ashes

KATHRYN LASKY

PUFFIN BOOKS
An Imprint of Penguin Group (USA) Inc.

PUFFIN BOOKS

Published by the Penguin Group

Penguin Young Readers Group, 345 Hudson Street, New York, New York 10014, U.S.A.

Penguin Group (Canada), 90 Eglinton Avenue East, Suite 700, Toronto, Ontario, Canada M4P 2Y3
(a division of Pearson Penguin Canada Inc.)

Penguin Books Ltd, 80 Strand, London WC2R 0RL, England

Penguin Ireland, 25 St Stephen's Green, Dublin 2, Ireland (a division of Penguin Books Ltd)

Penguin Group (Australia), 250 Camberwell Road, Camberwell, Victoria 3124, Australia
(a division of Pearson Australia Group Pty Ltd)

Penguin Books India Pvt Ltd, 11 Community Centre, Panchsheel Park, New Delhi - 110 017, India

Penguin Group (NZ), 67 Apollo Drive, Rosedale, North Shore 0632, New Zealand
(a division of Pearson New Zealand Ltd.)

Penguin Books (South Africa) (Pty) Ltd, 24 Sturdee Avenue,
Rosebank, Johannesburg 2196, South Africa

Registered Offices: Penguin Books Ltd, 80 Strand, London WC2R 0RL, England

First published in the United States of America by Viking,
a member of Penguin Group (USA) Inc., 2010

Published by Puffin Books, a division of Penguin Young Readers Group, 2011

1 3 5 7 9 10 8 6 4 2

Bye Bye Blackbird
Lyrics by Mort Dixon
Music by Ray Henderson
© 1926 (Renewed 1953) by OLDE CLOVER LEAF MUSIC (ASCAP) /
Administered by BUG MUSIC and RAY HENDERSON (ASCAP) /
Administered by RAY HENDERSON MUSIC
All Rights Reserved Used by Permission

THE LIBRARY OF CONGRESS HAS CATALOGED THE VIKING EDITION AS FOLLOWS:
Lasky, Kathryn.
Ashes / by Kathryn Lasky.
p. cm.
Summary: In 1932 Berlin, thirteen-year-old Gaby Schramm witnesses the beginning of Hitler's
rise to power, as soldiers become ubiquitous, her beloved literature teacher starts wearing a
jewelled swastika pin, and the family's dear friend, Albert Einstein, leaves the country while
Gaby's parents secretly bury his books and papers in their small yard.
ISBN: 978-0-670-01157-5 (hc)
[1. Germany—History—1918-1933—Juvenile fiction. [1. Germany—History—1918-1933—Fiction.
2. Family life—Germany—Fiction. 3. Nazis—Fiction.] I. Title
PZ7.L3274As 2010
[Fic]—dc22
2009033127

Puffin Books ISBN 978-0-14-241112-4

Book design by Sam Kim
Set in Palatino
Printed in the United States of America

Dort, wo man Bücher verbrennt,
verbrennt man am Ende auch Menschen.

Where they burn books,
they will end by burning human beings.

—Heinrich Heine

about this book

The historical fiction you are about to read is set during one of the most tumultuous times in modern history, a time when it seemed that a nation lost its mind, and a tyrant, Adolf Hitler, became Germany's leader.

Here is what you need to know about the world in which the book's main character, Gabrielle Schramm, lived during the years 1932 and 1933 in Berlin.

Gabrielle was born in 1919, the year after World War I ended. Not only had the Germans been defeated during the war but the Treaty of Versailles required Germany to disarm, to give up large areas of territory, and to pay the victorious Allies back the complete cost of all losses and damages caused by the war.

The immense cost of this repayment imposed many hardships on the German people and helped lead to the collapse of the German economy. Bitter resentment saturated the defeated nation and provided fertile soil for Adolf Hitler to sow the seeds of hatred that led to the rise of Nazism.

The German state that emerged in 1919 was an attempt to establish a liberal democracy in a country that had previously been ruled by an emperor. It often became known as the Weimar Republic because it was formed at a national assembly that convened in the city of Weimar. The new German government was headed by a president, who was elected by popular vote. The parliament, or Reichstag, was also elected by popular vote. The president then appointed a cabinet, and a chancellor who headed up the government. The president had the power to dismiss the chancellor, dissolve the Reichstag, and call for new elections whenever he chose, while the Reichstag could force the resignation of any cabinet member by a vote of no confidence. Power struggles among the president, chancellor, and Reichstag made the new government potentially unstable, and it was also threatened from the start by conflicts between left- and right-wing extremists, and by economic hardship.

Hitler, a mesmerizing figure, exploited the instability of the government to orchestrate his own rise to power. He had joined the newly formed, deeply conservative German Workers' Party in 1919. After being arrested for a failed political coup, he decided to try to gain control from within the political system. Soon he started to gain popularity among the working classes by promoting extreme nationalism and promising to override the Versailles treaty. His party, renamed the National Socialist German Workers' Party, or Nazis for short, began to win seats steadily in the German parliament in the early 1930s.

In March of 1932, Hitler was one of four candidates for president. He came in second, behind the incumbent president, a war hero named Paul von Hindenburg, but no candidate won a clear majority. A runoff election took place in April, which Hindenburg won, but these two elections helped weaken the public's faith in the government.

By the time our story opens in the spring of 1932, the Weimar Republic was on its last wobbly legs. Hitler and his Nazi Party were determined to undermine the republic by using both the tools of the political system and violence. During the 1920s Hitler had created his own private army known as the *Sturmabteilung* or "storm force" (SA). Because they wore khaki shirts purchased from the German Army, they became known as the Brown Shirts. An elite group known as the *Schutzstaffel* or protective squad (SS) acted as Hitler's personal guard. The targets of SA and SS violence were primarily Communists and Jews. Hitler claimed in his book *Mein Kampf* that it was the Jews who were to blame for Germany's defeat in World War I. He also believed that the Jews and the Communists were united in a joint conspiracy to take over the world.

In April 1932, only four days after the runoff election, the SA and SS were banned by the Reichstag. It was hoped that this action would weaken the Nazi Party. But instead the effect was the opposite. The Nazi Party solidified and grew stronger.

Between June and December of 1932, the Reichstag was dissolved several times, making it necessary to hold new elections. Hitler was by this time was desperate to be named chancellor. Since the chancellor was supposed to be chosen from the party with the most seats in the Reichstag, Hitler needed the Nazi Party to do well in the elections, but a clear majority of votes eluded him. There followed an extremely confusing period of behind-the-scenes deals and double-crossing, during which the government seemed on the point of collapse, and martial law was threatened. Finally the frail President von Hindenburg was forced to name Hitler the chancellor of Germany, and he was sworn in on January 30, 1933. Although the republican system of government was officially still in place, practically speaking, Hitler was now in power. (When Hindenburg died the following year, Hitler took on the role of president as well as chancellor, giving himself the title of *Führer und Reichskanzler*—Leader and Chancellor.)

Terror and violence were quick to follow. Communists and Jews were not the only targets. The Nazi Party was also deeply suspicious of intellectuals, artists, and writers. Scientists, too, came under attack, especially Albert Einstein. His theories were labeled "Jewish physics." This was a derogatory term used by violently anti-Semitic scientists who were deeply suspicious of Einstein's general theory of relativity and many of the ideas that became the basis for modern physics. The campaign for "Aryan physics," which had begun before World War I, intensified after Einstein won the 1921 Nobel Prize.

Within days of Hitler becoming chancellor, laws were passed restricting freedom of speech and freedom of the press, and orders were issued for the confiscation of literature considered to be dangerous to the state.

This story is based on meticulous research, and all major historical events are described as they happened. Sometimes, for dramatic purposes I took some creative license with minor events, moving or revising them slightly. In such cases, I tried to stay true to the historical reality of the time. For instance, the speech of Hitler's that Gaby and her family listen to on the radio in Chapter 18 is actually created from an earlier speech given in a private club, combined with passages from Hitler's book *Mein Kampf*. However all the words are really his.

It is against this turbulent background that the story of Gabrielle Schramm begins.

prologue, chapter 1, chapter 2, and chapter 3

In 1914 my story begins. Without me. I had not been born yet. Not for another five years. But that doesn't really matter, for in truth this is not just my story. It might be similar to those of others who lived in Berlin at this time, but my story, like most people's, begins before I was born. The stage is set, so to speak. After all, the universe began billions of years ago, and who was here then? Not me, Gabriella Schramm. Not my parents. Not my sister. Not Albert Einstein. Yes, he is part of my story too, and part of the universe's story, for he was certainly one of its diarists.

Nineteen fourteen, then, is perhaps the prologue to my story. That was when my father went to observe a solar eclipse in southern Russia. You see, my father believes that light is affected by gravity. It is almost as if light has weight. At least, that is the way I like to think of it. So my father measures the "weight" of light. The eclipse of 1914 was supposed to help prove this theory. He hoped to use it to measure the way mass makes light bend. But the eclipse of 1914 was itself eclipsed by an even more meaningful event. The Great War broke out while Papa was in Russia, and he, along with four other scientists, was captured because he was from the enemy side—Germany. His captivity did not last long. The Russians released him and his colleagues within a matter of days. He went back to Germany, to Berlin, to the apartment on Haberlandstrasse, to Mama who would soon become pregnant with my older sister, Ulla, and to his lab at the university.

So that is the prologue.

The first chapter begins on the day I was born. May 29, 1919, less than a year after the end of the Great War. My father was not there that day. He was far away on a tiny island off the coast of West Africa, where he was finally able to photograph an eclipse. And in the moment of totality as it is called—those scant minutes when the stars closest to the sun could be seen—I was born.

The next several chapters of my story are rather boring. That is why I will start with Chapter 4. The first three chapters seem simple. I am born. I learn to walk. I learn to talk. "Clock" was my first word. I learn to read. *Winter Mouse* is the first book I read all by myself. I make summer visits to my grandparents' farm. My Opa dies. My Oma dies. The farm visits cease. I meet my best friend, Rosa Ebers, in kindergarten. When I enter third grade, Mama, a pianist, begins teaching piano lessons in our apartment and Papa gets promoted. He is soon chairman of the Department of Photo-astronomy at the University of Berlin. He writes important books and papers. Mama's roster of piano students grows as Ulla and I become older. Our apartment is painted a soft sky blue. Mama lets Ulla and me choose wallpaper for our bedrooms. I choose wallpaper with daisies that look like they are blowing about in the wind.

So that is it, three chapters in one paragraph. It might seem fast the way I tell it. But it wasn't. These milestones mark long, lazy interludes.

Now my father and my mother think we might be hurtling toward another great war. But it hardly seems like hurtling to me, because there is this underlying sense of dread. Accidents happen fast, unexpectedly. No time to dread. But not wars. There is time, and in my mind dread is slow. You first disbelieve or deny what might be happening. You look once, twice. You don't quite admit what you see. Time begins to slow, to bend.

It is complicated, bending time. But all you need to know is that one's perception of time is affected by gravity. I am in Berlin where the local time is 2:27 p.m. on May 30, 1932. Yesterday I turned thirteen.

Oh, I forgot to tell you one thing. My middle name—Lucia, from *lux*, "light" in Latin. I was named for the star-light my father captured on film the day of my birth. All of our stories begin in the stars. We are all made of stardust. Every single atom in our bodies and every living or non-living thing, not just humans—butterflies, horses, mice, flowers, bugs, me, and Adolf Hitler—all stardust, forged in the hot core of an ancient star. Or as Papa says, "Ninety-two elements and I'll bake you a universe. That's all it takes."

chapter 4

He had never seen dogs fight as
these wolfish creatures fought, and
his first experience taught him an
unforgettable lesson. It is true, it
was a vicarious experience, else he
would not have lived to profit by
it. Curly was the victim. They were
camped near the log store, where she,
in her friendly way, made advances to
a husky dog the size of a full-grown
wolf, though not half so large as she.
There was no warning, only a leap
in like a flash, a metallic clip of
teeth, a leap out equally swift, and
Curly's face was ripped open from eye
to jaw.

—Jack London, <u>The Call of the Wild</u>

1 did not hear Herr Doktor Berg's footsteps as he approached me. But his words dropped like chunks of cold sleet through the dry, stuffy air of the classroom. "And tell me, Fräulein, precisely how reading this *Call of the Wild* . . ." I had the book hidden inside my mathematics text. Doktor Berg cleared his throat noisily and then twisted his head about so he was actually reading the chapter title on

the right page, "'The Law of Club and Fang,' this particular chapter is called, I see . . . in this book by Mr. Jack London . . . Yes . . . Now, how might such laws help you with those laws that apply to solving quadratic equations?"

"So sorry, Herr Doktor Berg." I didn't look up but slid the novel out from the algebra book and put it on top of my desk.

"Would you care to interrupt your reading—briefly, just briefly—and go to the blackboard to give us a demonstration of what I was just speaking about? Solve the equation I have just written up there. "

"Uh . . ." I finally looked up and squinted at the blackboard. I had absolutely no clue as to what Herr Doktor Berg had just been speaking about. He bent over a little closer and whispered, "The special feature of the quadratic equation is that such an equation can and usually does have two answers, two completely different answers to just one tiny problem. Please show us this, Fräulein, if you can tear yourself away from *The Call of the Wild*."

I could hear a few giggles behind me—not from Rosa, of course. She sat across the aisle, and I knew she sympathized with me.

The problem, you see, was the unfailing politeness of Herr Doktor Berg. It would have been so much better if he had given me a *Watschen*, a good slap. But instead he used his tongue like a strop and his polite, mannerly phrases mysteriously acquired a razor sharpness. As I walked to the

blackboard to demonstrate the special feature of the quadratic equation, I felt as if my skin had suffered hundreds of
little cuts, each seeping thin threads of blood.

Herr Doktor Berg rocked back and forth on his heels
and addressed the class. "Perhaps Fräulein Gabriella does
not realize that literature can have many levels of interpretation, but can they all be simultaneously truthful? Whereas
in mathematics there is usually only one right answer, one
truth. But the oddity of the quadratic equation, indeed
its elegance, is that there can be two completely different
answers, each truthful."

I illustrated his point, quickly, neatly, precisely. It didn't
matter that I hadn't been listening. Papa had shown me this
stuff already. Such are the advantages of having a professor
of astrophysics as a father. At the blackboard I explained
that although both answers were "truthful," only one was
correct for the equation Herr Doktor Berg had written.

"And why is that, Fräulein?"

"Because, Herr Doktor Berg, if x equals ten or if x equals
sixty, either will make the equation into a true statement.
But x equals ten is the right answer in this case."

"Why?" Doktor Berg pressed. He paused and raised his
incredibly bushy eyes brows above his spectacles. "Why
can you not apply the second answer? Why is the second
answer like extra baggage?"

"Well, I guess because it is not reasonable for the particular situation you described when setting up this problem."

"Precisely, Fräulein." His eyes drilled into me. "It seems that although you have mastered the operations of demonstrating the oddities of quadratic equations, you have not mastered certain elements of real life, the real life of this classroom. You are cluttering it with your extra baggage. I think I need to help you out by collecting some of it. At the end of this period, you will kindly deliver to me the book you have been reading."

My heart sank. It was almost as if I could feel a little plop at the base of my rib cage. I was only into the second chapter and Buck the magnificent dog, half Saint Bernard, half sheepdog, had just watched as his best friend, the dog Curly, was killed, her face ripped off by a pack of huskies. What would happen to Buck? What would happen to me? This was the second book Herr Doktor Berg had "collected" (his word, not mine. I would have said "confiscated") from me since the beginning of spring term. Where could I find another one? A friend of Papa's had sent this one from Heidelberg when we couldn't find a German translation in Berlin.

The bell rang. School was over, but before I could get up from my desk Herr Doktor Berg was standing beside me. His hand was stretched out, ready to receive the book. I gave it to him. He made a small, snuffy sound high in his nose, took it, and began to leave. "Herr Doktor . . ." The words sounded more like raggedy tatters of phlegm in my throat. He turned around, clasping the book to his chest, and raised his eyebrows expectantly but said nothing. "Uh, Herr Doktor Berg . . . at the end of term, might I have the two books back . . . please?"

He blinked, his pale gray eyes unreadable behind the thick lenses of his spectacles. The lenses were divided not into two parts like Papa's but three parts. Three different focal lengths—one for reading close up, one for reading the blackboard, and one for distance, I imagined. Three different solutions for one problem—seeing. He blinked again, perhaps trying to fit me into a perspective, a plane. Perhaps not. I am not really that complicated. I just wanted my books back. But he said nothing as he turned and walked away.

chapter 5

He saw, once for all, that he stood
no chance against a man with a club.
He had learned the lesson, and in all
his after life he never forgot it.
That club was a revelation. It was his
introduction to the reign of primi-
tive law, and he met the introduction
halfway. The facts of life took on
a fiercer aspect; and while he faced
that aspect uncowed, he faced it with
all the latent cunning of his nature
aroused.

—Jack London, <u>The Call of the Wild</u>

Rosa was waiting just outside the main school door
to walk home with me. We lived near each other
in Berlin in a neighborhood called the Schöneberg, also referred to as the Bavarian Quarter, or the Jewish Switzerland. I was not sure about the Switzerland part.
Perhaps it was because many people who lived in our
neighborhood were well off, and Switzerland was considered wealthy compared to postwar Berlin. But the Jewish
part was more understandable. There were many Jews

who lived in the Schöneberg. Most were associated with the University of Berlin and the Kaiser Wilhelm Institute. I was not Jewish and neither was Rosa. But Papa was a professor of astronomy at the university and held an office at the Kaiser Wilhelm Institute for Physics. Rosa's mother, a widow, was a stenographer for the university. Her father had died when she was an infant. And ever since then her mother had worked in the classics department. This was very convenient, for Rosa got lots of help on her Latin homework from students in this department, and then I could get help from Rosa. I was not as good in Latin as I was in mathematics, but Rosa was lousy in math. It was a nice little deal Rosa and I had. She helped me in Latin and I helped her with math.

What Rosa was very good at was fashion. Fashion and movie stars. We were both mad for movies. Our favorite actress was an American, Joan Crawford. We'd seen her in *Montana Moon* and *Dance, Fools, Dance*. They didn't normally let children in to such movies without their parents, but Rosa's cousin Helmut was an usher at the Gloria Palast Theater. He let us sneak in. Now I was so excited because Joan Crawford was in the movie *Grand Hotel*, which had just come out in America. The movie was based on the book *People at a Hotel*, which I had received this past Christmas. It was written by one of my favorite authors, Vicki Baum. I had read it twice already. I had heard that Joan Crawford played the secretary. I was glad that Marlene Dietrich didn't get cast instead. Marlene was prettier in a way than Joan Crawford, but there was something a little scary about her, at least in the movie *The Blue Angel* when she sang that song "They call me wicked Lola." She was very daring—sexy daring. My parents and Rosa's mother would have died if they had known we'd seen *The Blue Angel*. We'd go to matinees, then yes, we would lie to our parents and say we'd been to get ice cream with friends, or we'd gone roller skating. We made sure to take our roller skates with us on the days we used that excuse. Clever liars we were.

Ulla, my older sister, had seen *The Blue Angel* a few months back, and Mama nearly had a fit about that. But Papa had just said, "She's a university student now, Elske. At eighteen she's old enough." Ulla got away with a lot just because she was a "university student." One thing she was not getting away with, however, was neglecting her studies. A university student is supposed to study. That is a reasonable expectation. Nor was she practicing her violin that much. Except for me, everyone in our family was very musical. The music gene "had taken a powder" with me, as my mother would say. That means it vanished. In any case Ulla was very musical. She hoped to go to the Vienna Conservatory, where Papa and Mama had gone, to study violin when she finished her program at the University of Berlin. Mama had performed in many concerts, but now she just taught piano. Papa, before he contracted infantile paralysis—they call it polio sometimes—as a teenager, had been considered a violin prodigy. But his bow arm became useless after his illness, for all the muscles in it had been affected.

Mama and Papa were very upset with Ulla when she started to practice less. At the rate she was going with her academic studies, her degree might be in doubt, as well as her chances for the conservatory. This had all started when she met Karl. When Karl became her boyfriend, Ulla was suddenly not so interested in her studies—German literature. Her marks had slipped. Karl was a student too at the university. He studied engineering. I didn't know about his marks.

Rosa and I were coming to the corner where we normally would part ways. But the day was lovely, end of May, and the air had more than a hint of summer.

"Do you have any money?" Rosa asked suddenly.

"Not much. Just a little. Why?"

"Helmut is working this afternoon. We could catch the last bit of *The Blue Angel* and then have a coffee at the Little. The movie would be free. Didn't you say you wanted to see it again? And we could share the coffee."

"I have enough for that."

We walked two more blocks to the tram. Ten minutes later when the tram pulled up to the stop in front of the theater, we saw not a neat, orderly line of people buying tickets for the next show but a sea of brown.

"*Schweine*," I muttered as I looked out the tram window.

"Hush! Gaby! Don't go calling them swine," Rosa whispered.

"Let's stay on for another stop," I said quickly. There was no way I was getting off that tram. Not with those *Schweine*. There were not enough bad words. *Scheiss-Sturm*, the Shit Storm. That was what Papa called Hitler's private army, the *Sturmabteilung*, or SA. There was also the SS, the *Schutz-staffel* that functioned as Hitler's personal guard and had been established some years before.

"Why so many all of a sudden? I don't understand," Rosa said.

"Look at the marquee," I said. "It's not *The Blue Angel* playing. It's *All Quiet on the Western Front*." I'd read the book. Papa said it was the best war book ever written. Very sad. Really antiwar. It was all about a young man, a soldier in the Great War. There was a lot of gory stuff about trench warfare—blood, dressing stations where the medics and doctors did field surgery, amputation of arms and legs. I didn't want to see the movie. I knew there would be parts I couldn't watch, and there definitely wouldn't be any glamour girls like Joan Crawford.

"But still, I don't understand," Rosa said, looking out the tram window at the SA in their brown shirts milling about under the marquee. It wasn't a march, really. The men did not seem organized. But why were they there at all? "I thought they were supposed to have been banned, but Mama went with her friend for lunch at Ciro's and she said it was all Brown Shirts in there. Suddenly it seems as if they're all over the city."

"I don't think it's all of a sudden," I replied as the tram pulled away from the theater. "Last night we were listening to the radio and heard about Brown Shirts breaking up a synagogue service on the east side of the city. And Papa said there was no way the ban could be enforced, and the Brown Shirts would come back twice as strong."

"Oh no," Rosa said, and slumped down in her seat.

"Does your mother say anything about the Brown Shirts coming into the university, to her department?" I asked.

"Mama's department? Why would they ever? It's so boring. Classics. Nothing's changed in a thousand years."

True, I thought. Meanwhile everything in Papa's department of astronomy and astrophysics was changing almost every month. New discoveries, new technologies for measuring light, the orbit of planets, the trajectories of astral bodies . . .

"Look!" Rosa said. "We're almost at the zoo. Let's go there instead of the movies. We can get off here and walk the rest of the way."

"Good idea." I loved the zoo. Much better than a movie theater on a sunny day. We got off at the next stop. Only a short two blocks to the zoo. The blocks were good for shopping, and we lingered in front of a fancy dress store.

"You see," Rosa said. "Shoulders—it's all in the shoulders." There were three mannequins all wearing daringly tailored outfits that were nipped in at the waist, with shoulder padding that lent a powerful look to a woman's figure. Feminine but with uncommon force.

This was the Rosa Ebers theory of shoulders. She believed that Greta Garbo, Marlene Dietrich, Joan Crawford, and all of our favorite movie stars had wonderful shoulders and they knew how to move them.

"Shoulders are much more important than the bosom." Rosa spoke with a great authority that seemed at odds with her round, freckled face. "And now see how they are taking shoulders into account." She was pointing at a mannequin with a long black skirt topped with a glittering silver jacket that looked slinky—like falling rain. "You have to have shoulders to wear that!" Rosa proclaimed. She began twitching her shoulders, right and then left, being careful to angle her chin just so. Her soft, springy brown curls bounced a bit. Rosa had me beat in the height and hair department. She was taller than me, and my hair was straight as a stick. I wore it in long braids that were more white than golden blond. Papa called them *Milchstrasse,* the Milky Way, because they were so bright.

"Ah, a pretty little vamp!" Someone laughed behind us. As I caught his reflection in the window, I felt a wave of nausea. A Brown Shirt. A higher-up one. Lots of ribbons and bars decorated his uniform. He was smoking a tiny dark cigarette. Or was it a cigar? I had never seen a cigarette this color. He was handsome. Angular jaw, very tanned skin, light brown hair. Just one feature ruined it. His eyes were like two tiny, dark, malevolent bugs, and they crawled over Rosa.

We grabbed each other's hands and started to run. His laughter followed us like tin cans tied to a dog's tail. The sound disappeared finally into the clank of the tram, the burble of conversation of the pedestrians, and the excited cries of children as they danced at the end of their mothers' hands in anticipation of the zoo. We said nothing about what the SA officer had said. To speak of it was to acknowledge it. We wanted to wipe those words and his image from our minds.

Finally we were at the zoo gates. Two stone elephants crouched in front of an ornate pagoda. We automatically went up and touched their trunks for good luck. This was not a tradition in a public sense, it was Rosa's and my tradition. We invented it. This time, I think we each gave the wrinkled trunks an extra pat. As soon as we passed through the gates we felt better. I liked the smell. The animal dung did not offend me. It reminded me a little bit of my Oma's house in the country in Austria, which was near a dairy farm. I liked the smell of real manure, not Storm *Scheiss.*

We spent the money that would have bought coffee on peanuts. It was more fun feeding the monkeys than trying to look grown up drinking coffee in a café anyway. We walked by the cage of an elderly lion, toothless now, with one eye filmy like my Opa's before he died. The lion keeper had told us he could not see anything really except maybe shapes and movement. Rosa and I had been visiting the lion for years. We believed he knew our voices. So we pressed up as close as we could to the cage and whispered to him. We were certain that once the lion had been beautiful. I had invented a life for him. In my mind, he prowled the savannahs of Africa a long time ago. He stalked through the long golden grasses, blending in so perfectly that his prey did not even know he was there until he was almost upon them. Then the gazelle, the eland, or the duiker would run. And Old Lion would begin to run like a golden comet come to Earth, stretching out sleek and fluid, devouring distance until he reached his prey. Now the lion keeper told us they only feed him mash with lots of vitamins.

In the *Raubtierhaus*, the house where the lions and tigers live, there was a photo studio where it was possible to have one's picture taken holding newborn cubs. There is a picture of me when I was four years old sitting on the sofa in the *Raubtierhaus* holding a cub. It was my birthday present. I had begged and begged for it. And this was when there was hardly enough money for bread, 1923, just a few years after the end of the Great War when every day the mark became worth less and less. One loaf of bread was said to cost five hundred thousand marks! But Papa worked out a deal with the photographer. In exchange for my picture, he supplied the photographer with some film from his own lab.

Rosa and I walked on. We looked for feathers shed by

inhabitants of the birdhouse. Our favorites were flamingo feathers, but we had no luck this day. We lingered. We didn't want to leave. It felt comfortable here with the smells of fur and manure, the slightly more acrid odors of the birdhouse. There was a playground at the zoo, but at thirteen, we had grown too large for the swings, the monkey bars, and the jungle gyms. We were truly at an awkward age. Too big for the playground, too young for the cabarets. Our shoulders were not broad enough yet for fashion, and we had no bosom to speak of. So why did that SA fellow look at us with his venomous insect eyes? And why had *he* made *me* feel dirty? He was the dirty one, I thought. He was crap. *Him, not me.*

chapter 6

Suddenly a change passed over the tree. All the sun's warmth left the air. I knew the sky was black, because all the heat, which meant light to me, had died out of the atmosphere. A strange odour came up from the earth. I knew it, it was the odour that always precedes a thunderstorm, and a nameless fear clutched at my heart. I felt absolutely alone, cut off from my friends and the firm earth. The immense, the unknown, enfolded me. I remained still and expectant; a chilling terror crept over me.

—Helen Keller, The Story of My Life

I turned onto our street, Haberlandstrasse, after I had said good-bye to Rosa. Did I smell rain? I wasn't sure. I closed my eyes and sniffed. This was a small experiment that I enjoyed doing after I had read—well, almost finished reading—*The Story of My Life* by Helen Keller. I say almost finished because it, too, by route of a mathematics book, had found its way into Herr Doktor Berg's hands. I had only one more chapter to go when it was confiscated, and I had become completely fascinated by this woman who had gone blind and deaf at such a young age—less than two years old—and who could not speak. She was locked in a dark, soundless prison until a teacher named Annie Sullivan came along and taught her what language was. The first word Annie taught Helen was "water." She spelled the letters W-A-T-E-R out with her finger in the palm of Helen's hand. *Water*, what an ordinary word. But at that moment it was as if those five letters illuminated everything for Helen. She describes her soul as awakening. She learned to read, to speak. She went to Radcliffe College in Cambridge, Massachusetts. She became an author. But what intrigued me the most was how she unlocked the world of sight and sound through her other senses.

So as I walked I ran my left hand over the hedge that grew alongside the sidewalk and just like Helen Keller, I tried to feel my way home. I did smell a dampness in the air—a slightly metallic odor. *Is it a storm, or am I imagining this?* With my eyes closed tight I could see bright, squiggly threads. Then suddenly I saw brown, that sea of brown uniforms. Those milling SA officers had invaded my mind's eye. *Was that the storm?* I squeezed my eyes harder, willing away the scene I had witnessed earlier in front of the theater.

This reminded me of retinal fatigue, which I knew about from Papa and his studies of light. It had been proven that if a person stared at an image on a white screen for about thirty seconds and the image was then removed, its negative afterimage could be seen briefly. It had been demonstrated that this was due to the overstimulation of color receptors in the eye, which could cause them to become "fatigued." Of course retinal fatigue happened immediately after an image had been removed and, luckily, I had not seen the brown shirts for many hours. But this was how I explained it to myself.

Suddenly I caught a sharp, acrid smell. Tobacco smoke, but not a cigarette, not a pipe. I instantly knew what, or rather whom, I was smelling. I smiled and kept my eyes shut a second longer, so sure I was right.

"Gaby?"

"Herr Professor!"

I opened my eyes just in time to see the ashes fall silently off the tip of Albert Einstein's cigar. "Papa said you came back just two days ago, right?"

Professor Einstein was both a colleague of Papa's at the university and a neighbor who lived just down the street from us. Of late he had been making many trips to the United States. Most often he visited CalTech, the California Institute of Technology in Pasadena, California, which was close to Los Angeles—and to Hollywood!

"I did indeed."

I scuffed the toe of my shoe softly against the sidewalk and felt the creep of color rising in my face. "And did you see the stars?" I looked up smiling. This was our joke, the professor's and mine. You see, near CalTech there is a huge telescope on top of a mountain.

Professor Einstein tipped his head up toward the sky. "Let me think. I saw Alpheratz. . . . I saw Sirius. . . . I saw Charlie Chaplin. I saw Mary Pickford. . . ." I must have wrinkled my nose. "And what's wrong with Mary Pickford? She's a beauty!"

"Did you see Joan Crawford?"

"No, not this time. Maybe next." He had removed the cigar from his mouth and now held it behind his back. His other arm was also behind his back. This was a favorite posture of the professor: his feet planted a half a meter apart, his hands clasped behind him, his shoulders rolled slightly forward and his face turned directly to me, looking with great intensity. But at the same time there was always something in Einstein's eyes that seemed to gaze beyond you, as if he glimpsed past the range of ordinary people to a distant horizon that only a seer could perceive. "But I promise you, Gabriella, that if I meet her I shall collect her autograph for you."

"Thank you, Herr Professor. I think she is so beautiful."

He shrugged his shoulders and snorted softly. "Not my cup of tea, but *chacun à son goût.*"

"That's French, isn't it? 'To each his own taste'?"

"*Bien sûr, mademoiselle.*" He smiled. His dark, slightly drooping eyes twinkled. "And when do you go to Caputh?"

"Soon. As soon as school is out." I couldn't wait to go

to our summer cottage on the lake near the small village of Caputh. The lake is formed by the Havel River that flows between Berlin and Potsdam to the south. Caputh is not even two hours from Berlin but it seems a world away with its fragrant pines and peacefulness. Papa always says Berlin is for working and Caputh is for dreaming. Einstein also dreamed in Caputh. His summer house was next door to ours.

"And we shall have ourselves a sail?"

"A race!" I replied.

"You always win." He cocked his head and attempted a look of regret.

"That's the idea!"

He laughed heartily at this, then took his hands from behind his back, jammed the cigar in his teeth, and began to speak around it as he pinched my cheek. "*Liebes Kind*, dear child, tell your papa, I saw Hubble and we talked more about that Andromeda discovery he'd made." He paused. "You see, the Lady in Chains . . ."

"The Andromeda Galaxy?" Einstein was referring to the myth of the princess Andromeda, for whom the galaxy was named. The spiral arms of the galaxy were said to be the chains that held her as a sacrifice for some monster.

"Yes. You know your Greek mythology, I see. Well, as I told your father, Hubble discovered awhile ago that she's moving away from us." He paused again. The ashes on the tip of his cigar were stacking up. "I was right about what that meant, there's no way around it. The universe is expanding."

"Oh," I replied. I was not going to contradict Einstein, but to me it felt as if the universe was not expanding. It felt as if it was contracting. Hitler, who had been born and lived most of his life in Austria, was now in Germany. The Brown Shirts that were his invention—beer hall brawlers protecting Nazi gatherings in Munich, busting up Communist meetings, desecrating synagogues—were now here in Berlin, in front of Rosa's and my favorite movie theater! Nothing was receding, as the theory of an expanding universe suggested. It was all coming together in a most awful way.

The professor walked on, a trail of fine ashes drifting down from the cigar.

chapter 7

The idea of authority, which they rep-
resented, was associated in our minds
with a greater insight and a more
humane wisdom. But the first death
we saw shattered this belief. We had
to recognize that our generation was
more to be trusted than theirs . . .
The first bombardment showed us our
mistake, and under it the world as
they had taught it to us broke into
pieces.

—Erich Maria Remarque,
All Quiet on the Western Front

Most of the apartment houses on our street
were gray and severe like caricatures of the
strictest schoolteachers. They stood ramrod
straight, but in spring their poker faces were softened a bit
by window boxes that spilled with frills of bright flowers.
Our building was not gray. It was the color of butter, and
an immense patch of ivy spread across the front. If I looked
at the ivy a certain way it reminded me of Peter Pan. Well,
not Peter himself, but his shadow. Nana the dog caught his

shadow when he leaped out the window to escape from the Darling family's children's bedroom. This patch of ivy that sprawled across the façade of our building was shaped exactly like a boy who is about to take flight. And our street number is 14, the same address as the Darling family's house, except of course the fictional family lived in London, England, and not in Berlin. There I can tell you the similarities ended. There was no dog that functioned as a nanny to take care of the children at 14 Haberlandstrasse. We had only a grim *Hausmeister*, the building superintendent and concierge named Herr Himmel, who lived in the basement. A sour fellow, he greeted all tenants no matter what time of day or night they arrived with a severe gaze. He kept track obsessively of every individual's comings and goings. I had no idea when or if he ever slept. There was something very predatory about his appearance. His head reminded me of an anvil—a flat top, concave sides that met in a long narrow vertical ridge in the middle with his eyes crowded close to the wedge of his nose, and a tiny little mouth pursed beneath the nose. The word *Himmel* means heaven, but he was certainly the most perfectly misnamed man on Earth, so Ulla and I called him Herr Hölle, or "Mr. Hell," behind his back.

"You are late from school, Fräulein, and so few books you carry. I suppose you are starting your vacation early. Your sister certainly has. Do you know what time she got in last night?"

"No, Herr Himmel," I said, and rushed by.

"Two o'clock in the morning," he called after me. "I don't know why parents tolerate this. Too liberal," he muttered to my back as I headed for the lift, gritting my teeth.

I let myself into the apartment, and instead of music, which I usually heard in the late afternoon, I heard voices. Mama's piano student must have canceled. Instead Baba was there. Baba was Mama's best friend from their Vienna schooldays.

"So, Elske, what am I to do? He was at the princess's party. First high-society event he's attended. People beg to get their names in the column. I have to mention him. He's news, but he's so loathsome!" I heard Baba say.

"Do just that. Mention him. Don't flatter him. Hah! *Der Führer*, they call him. The leader. But he'll be gone in six months." Then their voices dropped and they must have said something slightly risqué, for Mama exclaimed, "Naughty, Baba!" and Baba burst out giggling. When Mama got together with Baba, just the two of them, they definitely became less inhibited.

"Mama!" I called from the hall just to warn them.

"*Schatzi!* Treasure," Baba cried out as I came into the music parlor, where she and Mama were taking tea.

"Sit down, have some tea." Baba patted the place next to her on the sofa.

Baba was two years older than Mama. They had met in Vienna, where they both grew up. Despite what seemed to me like a big age difference, they had become fast friends. Baba reminded me of a pastry confection. Her hair, which she had styled daily, was like a puffy, golden meringue. Her skin was soft, and her cheeks were sprinkled with cinnamon-colored freckles that she covered up with powder at night when she went out to report on all the parties she attended. Going to parties was her job. She was the social columnist for the Berlin newspaper the *Vossische Zeitung*. My parents said that it was now the only newspaper worth reading. The others, they said, were just Nazi bullhorns.

"Where have you been?" Mama asked.

"Rosa and I went to the zoo." I plopped down in a chair and reached for one of the teacakes. The little cake was called *Schnecke* for it curled about like a seashell and had pale pink frosting. But actually it reminded me of Baba's ears, especially as there were little sugar pearls dotting it and Baba was wearing pearl earrings that day.

"Go wash your hands, Gaby," Mama ordered. "You've been to the zoo, for heaven's sake."

"It's not the zoo that is dirty," I muttered. Mama and Baba exchanged glances.

"Now, what do you mean by that, *Liebling*?" I was Mama's "darling," Einstein's "dear child," and Baba's "treasure." I was Papa's *kleine Zaubermaus*—little magic mouse. He would call me that as he patted my braids and whisper, "*kleine Milchstrasse*." I would sometimes remind him that mice did not have braids.

I was thinking about the Brown Shirts, specifically the one with the insect eyes who had called Rosa a little vamp. My expression must have betrayed my thoughts. Maybe it was because Baba was a reporter, but she was very perceptive. She immediately jumped to her feet. Her gray eyes looked frightened.

"You saw them, didn't you? The SA They're all over town this week."

I was reluctant to say anything about Rosa's and my experience, so I just looked down at my hands. I didn't want to acknowledge what had happened. It was so creepy. He was so slimy.

"But I don't understand it," Mama said. "Yes, I've seen them, too. They were officially banned in the emergency decree. What was it, six weeks ago? Hindenburg issued it."

"Phut!" A blast of contempt shot out from Baba's perfectly lipsticked mouth. "The Old Gentleman, he can hardly find his way to the toilet. Mark my words, he will lift that ban in a matter of weeks, maybe even days!"

Then Mama scratched her head and said in a low, dim voice, "Otto said they would come back stronger than ever if they were banned."

"The Old Gentleman" was the name that some people called President Hindenburg. It was a term that expressed a sense of affection mingled with despair. He had been our national hero, Field Marshal Paul von Hindenburg, a Prussian soldier called back into action at the advanced age of sixty-six when the Great War broke out. In 1914, early in the Great War, he had won a glorious victory at the Battle of Tannenburg against the Russians, and soon became supreme commander of the German forces. He was elected the second president of the new Weimar Republic of Germany following that war after the monarchy was dismantled and the kaiser, or emperor, Wilhelm had fled. Now over eighty-four years old, von Hindenburg had been forced by the circle closest to him to run for reelection as president against Hitler.

"But I just don't understand, Baba. The Old Gentleman won, just a month ago." Mama sounded almost whiny, like a child disappointed about not getting some promised treat.

"He's putty in their hands. Watch. He'll appoint that *Schwein*, pig, von Papen," she flashed a quick look at me. "Pardon my language, *Schatzi*."

The door of the entry foyer opened and slammed shut with a ferocious bang. We all jumped. It was Papa. We could hear him muttering and then a "Goddamn!"

"Otto!" Mama squeaked as if she had been pinched.

I could tell Papa hadn't known we were all sitting in the music parlor. He stood there, his right arm hanging loose as always, but it seemed now that even his right leg was about to collapse. In his left hand he held his briefcase.

"You're back early," was all Mama could say.

"Yes, pardon my outburst." He bowed stiffly to Baba and then to me and Mama.

"What happened?" Mama asked. Papa closed his eyes and shook his head as if trying to erase a terrible image. Mama ran to his side. She looked at me. "Gaby, pour Papa a little *Schnaps*."

"This is beyond *Schnaps*," he groaned, and sat down on the piano bench. He opened the piano cover and played a few notes with his left hand, mournful notes that seemed suspended in the air like fragments of a tattered sheet of music. He stared out the window.

He looked at Mama again. "I told you, Elske, they would come back twice as strong as soon as they were banned." He shut his eyes tight and continued speaking. "They came into my lecture today."

Baba, Mama, and I looked at one another. He did not need to tell us who. We knew. It was the Brown Shirts

"Goldman was guest lecturing," Mama said.

"Yes." Papa nodded.

Max Goldman was a physicist from Berne, Switzerland. Papa had invited him to the university to give a series of lectures to his graduate students and any others who wished to attend. "Jewish physics." Papa whispered the two words, then muttered, "Such nonsense. You know these people dare call themselves scientists, and yet they reject the greatest breakthrough in modern physics because it was Einstein— a Jew—who figured it out! Goldman was describing how his work had been influenced by Einstein's and . . . *aachh!*" Papa threw up his hands in disgust.

"Yes, I know," Mama said softly, shaking her head. She paused. "But what did they do? Did they stop the lecture?"

"No, but they tried to take down every student's name as they were leaving the lecture. It was impossible, of course, for there were just too many of them. And one more thing." Papa looked up from the keyboard.

Mama's mouth moved, but the word did not immediately come out. "What?" She finally said.

"One of my students arrived at the lecture with a bloody bandage on his hand."

"What had happened?" Baba asked slowly.

"Well," Papa said, running his left hand down the keyboard. There was a rippling of notes across the air. "It seems that this afternoon there was a matinee showing of *All Quiet on the Western Front* at the Palast on the Kufürstendamm. A number of SA were in attendance, and as soon as the houselights went down, the SA began shouting anti-Semitic slogans, throwing tomatoes at the screen, and then a few enterprising Brown Shirts released dozens of rats in the theater."

"The dwarf!" Baba raised a hand to her flushed cheek.

"Indeed, Herr Goebbels. It has his handwriting all over it. With Hitler's blessing, he is becoming the arbiter of all things cultural, all things Aryan, and of true German spirit. You can bet that *All Quiet on the Western Front* is considered un-German by these thugs," Papa said.

Baba sighed.

"Who's Goebbels?" I asked. The name sounded slightly familiar.

"Joseph Goebbels." It was the closest Baba had ever come to snarling as she said his name. "Leader of the Nazi Party propaganda unit. An expert in crafting and spreading lies. An artist, one might say, of distortion and falsehoods. Last night he was at the reception I attended. He was going on and on about the antiwar, unpatriotic tone of the film." She shook her head. "It's like I said, Elske. The Old Gentleman is crumbling."

"Oh, he already has. I heard it. Von Papen is to be chancellor. It will be announced tomorrow. It is a fait accompli," Papa said.

"Who's Papen?" I asked.

Papa sighed. "A member of the Reichstag, very conservative. He opposed the ban on the SA. Now he'll be sure and lift it if he is chancellor. It's all politics. Poor old Hindenburg, trying to please everybody and winding up pleasing no one, really."

"No wonder these Brown Shirts, these animals, are all over the place. They're just waiting in the wings for Papen to get the nod," Mama said. She grabbed my hand and held it tight. But her eyes, which were now growing shiny with tears, were looking at her friend.

"Baba, be careful."

Baba flicked her hand as if she were shooing a fly. "Oh, don't worry about me, Elske. Why, last night would you believe that when I was at that reception, I commented to that idiot Hans Thomsen—you know the fellow in the foreign office—I said, 'Your Führer must have a cold.' And he asked why. And I said, 'There he stands, ten feet from me and they say he can smell a Jew ten miles away. His nose must be out of order tonight.' They all laughed."

"Baba, don't be foolish! We are not laughing," Papa said sternly.

chapter 8

"That is not the truth. You do not
want to be alone—you're afraid of
being alone—I know you're afraid. I
know you. You were desperate, just
now, if I go away you'll be more desperate than ever. Say I am to stay
with you . . . say it."

Grusinskaya looked into the Baron's
eyes and began to speak in a feverish
voice. "I shall dance and you'll be
with me and then—listen—After that
you will come with me to Lake Como, I
have a villa there. The sun will be
shining. I will take a vacation—six
weeks—eight weeks. We'll be happy
and lazy. And then you will go with
me to South America—oh!"

—Vicki Baum, People at a Hotel

Nobody laughed for the rest of the evening. Indeed
dinner was a wretched affair—not just because of
the pork knuckles and potatoes, which was not
my favorite dish, but no one seemed to notice that I hardly
touched the food. The misery factor increased exponentially
when Ulla, who had already aggravated Mama and Papa

by arriving late for dinner, announced that once the university term was finished, she did not intend to go to Caputh, where we have our summer cottage. She planned to stay in Berlin. And the worst of all was that she simply announced this and did not ask permission.

"To do what?" Mama barked. "Be with Karl?"

"Well, I imagine I shall see him," she said nonchalantly as she passed the butter to me. Baba and I exchanged glances. Ulla's sauciness—no, her impertinence—was staggering. She was usually very respectful to Mama. "But I have a chance for a job."

"What?" Papa blurted.

"A job."

"Doing what?"

"Working at the Chameleon."

While all this was going on, our maid, Hertha, was slowly making her way around the table with a bowl of steamed potatoes. She was pretending none of this concerned her, but I could see she was listening and deliberately slowing her pace to get as much of the story as possible before going out of the dining room to the kitchen again.

"The what?"

"It's a sort of café, like the Romanisches." The Romanisches was a café thick with smoke and artists and writers arguing about politics and philosophy and everything under the sun—except it was always very dark in the Romanisches. No sunshine.

"And what else is it sort of like?" Papa persisted, trying to affect a calm demeanor despite the tremor that made his fork quiver in his hand.

"Well, it's kind of like a cabaret."

Mama's and Papa's faces froze.

"It's not that kind. It's not an erotic revue, no naked girls. It's political humor," Ulla said, examining her pork knuckle as if it were the most interesting thing in the world.

"Better it be naked girls," Papa thundered. "Political humor! What are they going to make of the Storm Sh—"

Mama gave him a sharp look and with a quick jerk of her head nodded toward Hertha. Mama did not like us discussing politics in front of Hertha. I was not exactly sure why.

Papa stopped himself before the word came out. Then, looking at Ulla with steady eyes that had turned ice blue, he said, "There is no such thing as political humor these days." Mama gave him another fierce look and once again nodded toward Hertha's back as she disappeared into the kitchen with the empty potato dish.

"Well, say what you will!" Ulla sniffed. "But I'll have you know that the *conférencier* happens to be Max Weltmann."

"What's a *conférencier*?" I asked.

Ulla gave me a withering look. "The emcee, the master of ceremonies. And Max Weltmann is known for his sharp political humor. Ask Baba—the *Vossische Zeitung* did an article on him."

Mama pulled herself up straighter. Her clear blue eyes drilled into Ulla. "Pray tell me, what exactly are you going to do at this place . . . this Reptilian."

"*Chameleon*," Ulla corrected, but she appeared relieved by the question. "I'm the bookkeeper!"

"*Gut!*" Papa slammed the table with his good hand. "Then you do not have to be there in the evenings. Books are kept during the day."

Ulla appeared occupied with poking at the potatoes on her plate. But I caught the look in her eye. I knew immediately that she did not plan to be at the Chameleon only during the day.

"I shall talk to Hessie about this," Papa muttered.

Ulla looked up in alarm. "Why do we always have to talk to Uncle Hessie? Can't we ever think for ourselves?" Uncle Hessie, or Count Erich von Hessler, was not our real uncle, but he was Papa's best friend. Uncle Hessie was very handsome, very rich, a diplomat, an art connoisseur, and an unofficial member of our family. Papa had first met him many years ago through Baba, who knew everybody in society because of her job as a social columnist for the newspaper.

"Ulla!" Mama scolded.

Papa threw his napkin down, jumped up from the table, and headed for his study. "I have a lecture to prepare for tomorrow, since Herr Professor Goldman was told in no uncertain terms by the SA not to show up tomorrow or there would be violence." Papa took a drink from his water glass. "And they call this a university!" His voice seethed. I sensed that now was not the time to say, "By the way, I met up with Professor Einstein and he mentioned that he was right about something he told you earlier. It seems that the universe really is expanding."

Hertha had waited discreetly in the pantry, not wanting to come in with the torte while we were in the heat of a family argument, I imagine, but within two minutes we had all scattered from the table. No one seemed in the mood for dessert. Baba left to catch a late party at the British embassy. Mama went to the music room to sort the pieces of sheet music she would need for the next day's students. Ulla went to get her books and her coat. The books were a cover, I suspected. I seriously doubted she was going to study. You see, I saw her tuck into her book bag a little suede pouch that had a tiny brush, lipstick, and mascara in it. Most likely she was meeting Karl someplace.

I *did* have to study. It was almost the last week of school, and final examinations began in two days. Latin was the first one. Fräulein Weigler had already told us that we would have to give commentary on the use of the predicate dative and the accusative in selected short passages. There would be five of these passages and we could choose three to translate from Latin into German, and then give commentary on them. There was sure to be one from Caesar's history of the Gallic wars and one from Seneca. I hoped that there would be one from Pliny the Younger's description of the eruption of Vesuvius.

So I went to my room with the best of intentions. I would start with the most arduous passage for me, Caesar's. I stared at it for half a minute trying to figure out this stupid accusative and dative stuff as I attempted to translate the Latin into German.

> When Caesar inquired of them what states were in arms, how powerful they were, and what they could do in war, he received the following information: that the greater part of the Belgae were sprung from the Germans, and that having crossed the Rhine at an early period, they had settled there, on account of the fertility of the country, and had driven out the Gauls who inhabited those regions . . .

Oh God, I hated this. I was going to have to call Rosa. But then I remembered that Rosa was out with her mother and grandmother. My eyes wandered to the mirror over my bureau. I needed a little break. What happened to those nice phrases we had been required to translate in beginning Latin? *"The maiden milked the cow by the well." "The centurion stood by the gates."*

I had stuck pictures, mostly cut from magazine pages, into the mirror frame, and under the glass top of bureau I had slid another dozen or so as well. Joan Crawford was there, of course. The largest picture was of Vicki Baum, my very favorite author. Vicki, like Mama and Baba, was from Vienna. Mama had not known her there, for Vicki was about ten years older than Mama. But Vicki was living in Berlin now, and Mama had met her through Baba. Mama said she was very beautiful. I had read almost all of her books. But *People at a Hotel* was my all-time favorite. It was through Baba that I got the information about the making of the movie and that Joan Crawford got the role of the secretary and Greta Garbo was cast as the ballerina. In Baba's words, or rather Baba quoting Vicki, "This is the role that will make Joan Crawford!" She was already made, as far as Rosa and I were concerned.

The picture of me with the lion cubs was next to Vicki's. One of the cubs died in its first year. It was sad to think about this. I had already lived a decade plus three years longer. If the cub had lived, she might have had her own cubs by now. Funny to think about how the time scale is so different for animals. I would imagine that I had at least another ten years before reproducing! Then I wondered how long Caesar had lived before he was murdered. I knew I should return to my studies. But I didn't. My eyes lingered over the pictures, especially one of Papa when he was about ten or eleven, before his illness, playing his violin—or Papa B.I.P. That stood for Papa Before Infantile Paralysis. Before he had to give up the violin, before the stars, before all that. You see, my Papa has had two lives.

Until Papa was fifteen, he studied violin at the Conservatory in Vienna. That was where he met Mama. She was studying the piano. In 1902, many people in Southern Austria were diagnosed with the disease known as infantile paralysis. Despite its name, infantile paralysis struck not only babies and children and teenagers, like my father, but grown-ups as well. My great-grandmother died of it. My mother's cousin died of it. My papa did not die, but his life as a violinist was finished. Mama, too, contracted the illness, albeit very lightly. There was no damage to her muscles or nerves. But for Papa, it was terrible. He said it was as if his life had ended at fifteen. He fell into a deep depression. His parents sent him to a small sanitarium that was more of a guesthouse than a hospital, run by friends of theirs. It was in the mountains. He was supposed to be taking the baths, thermal baths that were part of the therapy for people whose muscles were weakened by the illness. But he began hiking. His right arm was paralyzed, but his left arm and his legs were fine. It was in the clear air of the Tyrol, in the west of Austria, where there were no city lights to bleach the night, that he discovered the stars. He loved to tell the story of his time in the mountains when he discovered what he called "the other universe," the one made of stars and not music.

I can remember exactly the first time he told me the story. We had all gone to the Tyrol for a summer holiday and we were on a long hike. My legs got tired, but he promised me that if I completed the hike I could stay up very late and go on a "star hike" with him the next night. Just Papa and me!

It sounded so exotic, so un-babyish. I never got to stay up late. And that star hike was the first time I had heard the story. I always thought of it as a sad-happy story. I cried when Papa described to me the pain of the illness, how his right arm began to lose strength and wither, how it soon became so weak he could not draw the bow across the violin strings. But then there was his discovery of this other universe!

Papa said it was the stars that saved him. I imagined him on some mountain peak at night, a moonless night, the kind all astronomers love, when every constellation burns with a silver radiance, and I saw my father listening for some kind of far-off music. It was the music of light, the music of the night's soul. Music, Papa said, is the most abstract of all the arts. And light is like that too—elusive, fragile, fleeting. So on that night, his bow arm dead at his side, he began to play the strings of darkness. Soon he bought a modest telescope and with it he found first the single notes, then the chords, and finally the melody within the harmony of the sky.

After a few months at the sanitarium he returned to Vienna and quickly finished his secondary school studies at the Adolphus Wilhelm Gymnasium, then passed his *Abitur* examinations to enter the University of Vienna. When Papa returned he and Mama began to really fall in love, although they had met years before through music. But it would be a few years before they married, because first he went on to Cambridge University in England, where he enrolled in

Trinity College, the same college where Sir Isaac Newton had studied.

But Papa, like everyone else who studied physics at Cambridge, including Arthur Stanley Eddington, his favorite professor, was fascinated by Einstein's work on the theory of general relativity. The professor knew that Einstein needed just one thing to validate his theory, and that was to be able to prove that gravity affected light. General relativity predicted that when light passed near something massive, its path should bend. Einstein had calculated how much the mass of the sun should bend starlight passing near it. But to show he was right, you would have to be able to see the light of the stars right next to the sun. For this, an eclipse was needed. Thus began Papa's first work in refining the techniques, the film, and the lenses of the camera that could gather the incontrovertible evidence that gravity bent light.

So next to the pictures on my dresser of Vicki Baum and Joan Crawford and me holding the cub and Papa playing the violin B.I.P., there were a dozen or more prints of Papa's photographs of stars. The one picture that was actually bigger than that of Vicki Baum was my birthday picture, taken on May 29, 1919. I knew all about that night, but perhaps not the way one would expect. It was not the events on Earth surrounding my birth here in Berlin, but the celestial happenings my father was observing from that island off the coast of West Africa that became the background narrative of my birth story. The picture on the mirror was not an image of me but of the sun being swamped by the moon so that only a fiery halo was left floating eerily in the sky. The predicted totality—the time of the complete eclipse of the sun—had been a period of 410 seconds, almost seven minutes, which is quite a long eclipse. But bad weather had set in with a blanket of roiling clouds. The seconds were shaved away. For 400 of the 410 seconds the eclipse could not be seen because of the clouds. Then in those final seconds the skies cleared. Six pictures were taken in all during those last ten seconds. There were two pictures that proved that indeed the mass of the sun had pulled the light of the stars toward it. The deflection of the light, about 1.61 arc seconds, matched Einstein's projection and thus his theory of general relativity was validated.

When Papa returned to Berlin and met me for the first time, he looked at the birth record and insisted that I must have been born during those same ten seconds.

I realized I had to stop this daydreaming, or night dreaming. "Back to the Gallic Wars, Vicki!" I muttered, looking at her picture. But then I thought of the dessert none of us had eaten. I knew I had better hurry out to the kitchen, because Mama always let Hertha take any leftovers home for her mother and the elderly aunt with whom she lived.

When I got to the kitchen Hertha was packing up a slice of the torte.

She looked up. "You want some, Gaby?"

"Well, I was hoping, but . . ."

"Have a piece. There is plenty for me to take home." She went to the cupboard and got a plate. "Some milk?" She turned around to ask me.

"That would be nice, thanks, Hertha."

I sat at the kitchen table on a stool. Hertha settled across from me with a mug of coffee. "So your mama and papa are worried about Ulla?"

"That and everything else." Almost as soon as I said it, I realized I probably shouldn't have, for "everything else" was politics.

"*Aachh!*" Hertha made a scolding sound in the back of her throat. "They shouldn't worry about everything else. Just Ulla."

I kept my eyes on the torte and mumbled into the crumbs as I cut it with my fork.

"Well, they do," I said softly.

"What is your papa so worried about?"

I felt my heart beating loudly in my chest. I couldn't look up.

"Well, the Brown Shirts, for one thing."

Hertha leaned across the table. She patted my hand. "Oh, they're just rambunctious boys. And they want to get these Communists. The Communists are bad, Gaby. You don't remember how awful it was. You were a little girl in the twenties. I didn't work for your family then, but even they were poor. No one escaped, believe me. Maybe not as poor as many, not as poor as me and my mother and her sister, but they were. Every week the price of the simplest things like eggs, milk, bread, was five or six times more than the week before. Sixty marks to buy what ten marks had bought a week earlier!"

I knew she was right. The money had become outrageously inflated, worth almost nothing. One had to spend it immediately because it would be worth even less the next day. I had seen a picture in a scrapbook of Papa taking a knapsack stuffed full of bills for a loaf of bread, because all the money he needed would not fit in his wallet.

Hertha lowered her voice to a conspiratorial whisper. "And the Communists will make it even worse than it was back then. I am sure. But now I think there might be a chance for things to get better."

I withdrew my hand from hers. I couldn't quite believe what I was hearing. "You think there's a chance with Hitler?"

"Maybe," she said almost gaily.

"Hertha, don't say anything to Mama and Papa about this."

"Oh no, I wouldn't."

"So why are you telling me?" I couldn't help ask.

She looked at me almost dreamily. "Because you are young, you are not set in your ways, and maybe you don't understand how hard it is for people like me."

I pushed the plate away. I wasn't hungry anymore. There was so much I wanted to say, so much that crowded up in my mind, but the thoughts became tangled as soon as I began to even try to say anything. I knew that Hertha was a sweet, gentle person. I knew that she liked my parents a lot. She had said time and again that they were the most generous people she had ever worked for. But if Hertha felt that Hitler was good for Germany—Hertha who was not a fanatic—how many others might feel the same way?

chapter 9

O Dearest, canst thou tell me why
The rose should be so pale?
And why the azure violet
Should wither in the vale?

And why the lark should in the cloud
So sorrowfully sing?
And why from loveliest balsam-buds
A scent of death should spring?

And why the sun upon the mead
So chillingly should frown?
And why the earth should, like a grave,
Be moldering and brown?

And why it is that I myself
So languishing should be?
And why it is, my heart of hearts,
That thou forsakest me?

—Heinrich Heine,
translated by Richard Garnett

My Latin examination was on June 3. I did fine. Not as well as Rosa, who achieved a dazzling 14 out of 15, but I got an 11. Anything hovering around 12 was OK as far as I was concerned.

The next day, sometime during our history exam, the Reichstag, the German parliament, was dissolved. Bella, the class wit, joked that at least there wasn't time for this bit of history to be included on the final exam. I would soon lose count as to how many times the Reichstag would be resurrected and dissolved over the next six months. The day after the history exam was the class picnic, with ice cream. And on June 14, school let out for the summer holiday. It was our last day at our old school building. When school resumed in September, Rosa and I would move to a different building, where the older students of the gymnasium attended classes. It was still the same school, but we would have different teachers. Because this building was closer to the library, we would be allowed to go there during our fifteen-minute break.

I had hoped that Herr Doktor Berg would return my books on that last day of school, but he did not. Two days later my family, minus Ulla, would leave for our cottage in Caputh.

Papa was still worried about Ulla staying behind. On the very day we were to leave, I had just finished packing my books and summer clothes for the trip, so I was in the living room reading the newspaper. There was still hours before the car was to arrive to take us. The Kaiser Wilhelm Institute always sent a car to take us to Caputh. This was a special perk of Papa's membership. Mama was giving her last music lesson before the summer break and Papa was talking to Uncle Hessie about Ulla. Hessie was once again reassuring Papa that the cabaret Chameleon was not such a bad place. Neither Papa nor Uncle Hessie had noticed that I was in the room when they entered, as I was swallowed up in the large wing chair reading. I was small for my age, and times like this was when it paid off.

"*Lento! Molto adagio,*" Mama kept telling her student, a rather intense young girl named Lotte who was trying to play the Moonlight Sonata. "Slow it down. What's the rush? We want to feel the moonlight. *Molto adagio!* Very slow. *Molto adagio!*"

As the conversation continued, Uncle Hessie seemed uncharacteristically irritated with Papa. He was losing his usual cool demeanor. I heard him raise his voice slightly, which was rare for a man like Hessie. He was a count by birth and like so many extremely sophisticated people, he was always very calm, cool—fizzing with ideas but rarely rattled. That morning, however, he was rattled. He stood with that old Prussian rectitude in his stylish three-piece suit and wing-collared shirt, and fingered the large knot of his tie. Papa always looked rumpled next to him, but I now saw color creeping above the collar of Uncle Hessie's shirt.

"Honestly, Otto," Uncle Hessie groaned in that languid way the very rich and stylish have of speaking. "How can you be concerned about a cabaret when that complete idiot Papen, who looks more like a billy goat than a chancellor, is proposing that unemployment insurance be scrapped? He is focused on the most extreme right-wing ideas and

he's slandering all social democracy as bourgeois liberal-
ism that is morally undermining the *Volk*. Do you know I
lost count of how many times he used the word *Volk* In his
address? When he says *Volk*, he does not mean people. He
means exactly what the Austrian corporal means. Aryans,
not Jews, not negroes, not *degenerate* artists, as Hitler calls
most creative people."

Papa gave a short, harsh snort. "And of course along
with the degenerate artists, there are the degenerate scientists."

"Yes, I heard one does not need to be Jewish to practice
Jewish physics apparently."

"Certainly not—am I Jewish?" Papa said. "And yet guess
what they call me and Heisenberg?"

"What?" Uncle Hessie asked.

"White Jews, because we subscribe to Einstein's work on
relativity."

Werner Heisenberg was a physicist and a colleague of
Papa's who taught at the University in Leipzig. He was very
handsome! I'd seen him once when he came for dinner. He
had invented something called the uncertainty principle,
which was much too hard for me to understand.

"By the way, speaking of artists, have you heard Vicki
Baum has already cleared out of town?" Uncle Hessie asked
Papa.

At this I jumped up from my chair, where I had been
reading Baba's column in the newspaper. "That can't be! It

says right here in Baba's column that Vicki Baum was in attendance at the Italian ambassador's party."

Papa turned to me. "*Kleine Zaubermaus*! What are you doing here, little mouse? You are a magic mouse tucked in there so small we didn't notice. You're supposed to be helping Mama pack for Caputh. We are leaving this afternoon."

"That ambassador's party was two nights ago, *Liebchen*, darling," Uncle Hessie said. Being called "darling" by Uncle Hessie was preferable to being called a magic rodent by my father. They both meant well, however.

"Now, stop reading about parties and go help Mama," Papa ordered. "She wanted you to go down to the garden and put in the pansies where she is taking out some of the begonias, or something like that."

At that moment Mama walked in, having finished with her music student.

"Gaby, I told you I needed your help with those begonias. I have others to replace them. Come on, we need to get down to the garden. You should have started yesterday."

My mother was the unofficial and unpaid gardener for the small courtyard garden behind our building. Hausmeister Himmel knew nothing about plants, and I was certain that any flower would wither immediately from his touch. But Mama, whose fingers could coax the most beautiful music from the piano, could also wheedle flowers from the most deficient, poorest soil imaginable. Papa said Mama could make a flower grow in ashes. And Mama would always say, "Ashes are part of the carbon cycle, aren't they, dear? You should know that, Herr Professor Astronomer."

Mama actually used ashes from our fireplace to fertilize the garden. She collected ashes from the four other families in the building as well. They were only too happy to contribute. For in the spring through summer and well into fall, the flowerbeds of our courtyard were a continuous pageant of color. In spring the pansies flourished, in addition to the dozens of bulbs that Mama had planted some years before and replenished every fall. Come June the roses were climbing the stucco walls of the garden and would bloom throughout the summer. There were neatly shaped boxwood hedges that Mama "coiffed"—her term for pruning—with long shears into geometric designs. In the center of each design she planted great bursts of candytuft, nasturtiums, and all varieties of annuals, which she changed every year. Her imagination seemed limitless.

She had now decided that the begonias clashed with the candytuft, or maybe it was the nasturtiums that clashed with the begonias. In any case, I was to help her dig these flowers up and we were going to transport them to Caputh and replace them with pansies. All this had to be done before we left, and I had completely forgotten that it was my job. So I went out to the garden and began digging up the begonias. I carefully placed them in a carton and took them to the lobby to load into the car when it arrived.

My mother tended this garden as much for the tenants

as for herself, especially Professor Blumen and Frau Meyeroff, who were the oldest people in our building. The professor had to walk with two canes because of his arthritis, but he really enjoyed sitting in the garden in nice weather. Frau Meyeroff was at least ninety-five and in a wheelchair. The two of them spent endless hours enjoying the garden. They had no summer home to go to in the country as we did.

Of course, in Caputh there was another, even bigger, garden in which Mama grew vegetables and flowers in what Papa called a "merry chaos." No intricate geometry of boxwood hedges, just all sorts of country flowers tossing their heads in the winds off the lake. Great tangles of sweetpeas clambered up trellises made from twigs. Pumpkins and squash swelling to golden rotundity rose like bulbous mountain ranges. She grew at least three or four different varieties of berries—gooseberries, raspberries, and even cloudberries, the latter of which everyone said could only be grown in Scandinavia. Well, my Mama grew them. All summer long we would eat from the garden and hardly ever go to the market for food. A fishmonger came by door to door all summer and Mama could call the butcher for deliveries of meat. We had already made a trip to Caputh three weeks before to do the planting. So when we arrived, there would be several rows of lettuce ready to pick, as well as radishes.

By the time I came back from the courtyard garden with the trays of the begonias that had offended the color scheme,

I expected that all would be ready for us to go to Caputh.

"But Mama, you see it all works out for the best," Ulla was saying.

"It is not for the best that you flunked your exam!"

"Ulla flunked!" I gasped.

Ulla turned and gave me a withering look. "Yes, I flunked my literature exam. This is not the end of the world. I'll just retake it in three weeks. I'll study very hard. So it's all for the best that I am staying here."

"Did you flunk it so you could stay home?" The question just popped out before I could stop it.

"Don't be an idiot!" she snarled.

Mama was now shaking her finger at both of us. "Gaby, you stay out of it. Ulla, make yourself useful and call up to find out where the car from the Institute is."

But Mama and Papa did not seem that upset about Ulla flunking her exam—perhaps because it was not so bad compared to the rest of the day's events, which I had apparently missed while I was in the gardening digging up begonias. You see, almost as soon as Uncle Hessie left, Papa turned on the radio. It was blaring with the news that indeed the SA was back in business! And not just the SA but the SS that Himmler headed. The Old Gentleman, Hindenburg, now truly a puppet of von Papen, had lifted the ban on the SA and the black-shirted, *Schutzstaffel*, or SS.

If these events seemed to some to happen quickly, to stack up on top of one another with a frightening speed in the space of a single afternoon as we waited to go to Caputh, to me there was this awful slowness as if we were marching, dragging inexorably but steadily toward doom.

That afternoon as we waited for the car, I called Rosa twice to say good-bye and figure out exact dates when she could visit me at Caputh. She said that her mother was as worried about Papen as she was about her grandmother who had recently been diagnosed with a heart condition.

There is an old notion that when a person falls from a great height, his or her life flashes before him in the seconds of the fall. But I don't believe that "flash" is the right word. I believe it is a long, drawn-out affair. Think how slowly those seconds must seem to pass as every scene of one's life and its inevitable end are perceived. *Lento! Molto adagio.*

chapter 10

Once I said to myself it would be a thousand times better for Jim to be a slave at home where his family was, as long as he'd got to be a slave, and so I'd better write a letter to Tom Sawyer and tell him to tell Miss Watson where he was. But I soon give up that notion . . . .

So I kneeled down [to pray]. But the words wouldn't come . . . It was because my heart warn't right; it was because I warn't square; it was because I was playing double. . . . I was trying to make my mouth say I would do the right thing and the clean thing, and go and write to that nigger's owner and tell where he was; but deep down in me I knowed it was a lie, and He knowed it. You can't pray a lie—I found that out.

—Mark Twain,
The Adventures of Huckleberry Finn

By now it was late afternoon and we were ready. Our bags were downstairs, including half a dozen boxes of books—mostly Papa's, but some were mine—and at least two boxes of Mama's music. There was a hamper of food so we wouldn't have to go out and buy anything for our first night's dinner. I was just planning a third good-bye call to Rosa when Papa came up and said he needed to call the office at the Institute again. The car that was supposed to pick us up had still not arrived despite Ulla's earlier call, when the person she spoke with said it would be right over. It wasn't a long drive to Caputh—an hour in light traffic. Hertha had already left on the train that morning to prepare the house.

Papa dialed the phone number and was speaking to someone from the Institute. He nodded into the receiver while Mama stood by listening, trying to make out the entire conversation from his end.

"Yes. Problems you say? Did the car break down, Frau Hagen? Not that you know of, eh." He turned to Mama, shrugged his shoulders, and opened his eyes wide as if confounded. "Well, can you connect me with Professor Haber, kindly." There was a long pause and Papa grimaced. I noticed a ruddiness flush his cheeks. "Not available, you say," he snapped. Mama sighed. "All right. Thank you for your efforts. Good-bye." He slammed down the phone.

I could tell that Papa was really upset. I couldn't help but wonder if the car not coming was something to do with "Jewish physics."

Just the two words "Jewish physics" seemed crazy enough. Now, after Papa's talk with Uncle Hessie, there were two more words: "white Jew." I didn't quite understand these terms. Papa was a gentile scientist and member of the Institute, but it seemed as if there were just as many Jewish members as gentiles—Einstein, Max Born, Lise Meitner, Fritz Haber. And yet it wasn't as if Papa looked at gentile stars and Einstein looked at Jewish stars. Stars were just stars. And Lise Meitner studied isotopes. Were there Jewish isotopes that she studied and gentile ones that Max Planck studied? I knew there were scientists at the Institute that Papa said might look at things this way. Philipp Lenard was one, I think. I had heard Papa say that Lennard was very critical of Einstein's approach to relativity, which he claimed "offended common sense."

In the end, the car from the institute never came, but good old Uncle Hessie sent his own Mercedes Benz and his chauffeur, Marcel. Hessie followed in his super sport touring car, the SSK Count Trossi model. Since he was helping transport us to Caputh, he would stay a few days with us at the lake. He came often throughout the summer.

We said good-bye to Ulla, who promised to call every other day. It all felt a little odd to me. This would be my first summer ever at Caputh without Ulla. We shared a bedroom at the lake cottage, and she joked that I could have it all to myself and keep it as messy as I wanted. Ulla was a lot neater than I was.

I got to ride with Uncle Hessie, which was much more fun than going in the big Mercedes, and it was big. The model was called the Grosser-Mercedes 770 and it seemed

like a salon or parlor with its gray upholstery and little silver rosebud vase. But the SSK sports car was made for a
jolly good time. The top came down and Uncle Hessie and I
both got to wear goggles. That's how fast he drove!

"There is a scarf in the glove compartment for your hair
if you want it." He reached over and popped it open. I took
out a peach-colored chiffon scarf with flowers on it.

"Oh, it's beautiful!"

"Do you know who that belongs to?"

"Who?"

"Josephine Baker."

"No!" I exclaimed. Josephine Baker, the American singer
and dancer, was one of the most famous entertainers in
Europe. I had heard that Uncle Hessie was very, indeed *very*
good friends with her. Although just a few years before she
had danced in an infamous nude revue, she somehow was
not considered just an ordinary, vulgar chorus girl. She had
become a symbol of erotic Berlin and yet was never considered crude. Naughty, yes. But lewd? Smutty? Never! That
was most people's opinion, including Baba's. But I doubted
Mama and Papa had ever gone to see her. Einstein had—
with his wife, Elsa, no less! But I could hardly believe that
I was about to wear the scarf of the Creole Goddess, the
Black Pearl. Those were nicknames that celebrated Josephine
Baker's exotic beauty.

"Are you sure she won't mind?" I asked as I finished tying

it over the straps of my goggles. I felt fabulously glamorous.

"No, of course not. She left for Paris three years ago and swears not to come back until the little corporal and his 'naughty boys,' as she calls Hitler and the SA, are gone."

First Josephine, now Vicki, I thought. *Who's next?*

We headed south, down the wide avenue of the Aschaffenburger Strasse. But we had only gone a block and were at Bayerischer Square when I heard Uncle Hessie sigh. The leather seats of the sports car were so deep that I could not quite see what had provoked this sigh. I rose up a bit to tuck my knees under me just as Hessie began to slow the car. Like sludge running from a river's mouth, hundreds of SA were moving through the street. I didn't know how our car would get past them—traffic had nearly come to a complete stop. Flags with swastikas stippled the air. It was a parade! The men wore high black jackboots to the knees. Above the top of the boots, their brown pants flared absurdly so that it appeared as if the men had wings attached to their hips. No wonder they called the stiff-legged march *der Stechschritt*, the goose step. They looked like a bunch of stupid geese coming down the street. As we got closer to the parade, the stomping boots were deafening. It was as if the pavement groaned beneath them.

"Not to worry, *Liebchen.*" Hessie patted my knee. I scanned the spectators on the sidewalk. Their faces were wreathed in some sort of anticipation. I couldn't help but remember Hertha's words: "Now there might be a chance." Was this why they were cheering? This chance they all anticipated. The rambunctious boys, as Hertha had called them, were thickening into knots on the streets.

We soon had to halt, as many of the Brown Shirts seemed to have broken away from the parade formation and were now wandering through the street. Some of the geese appeared quite wobbly and I could see they carried beer steins.

"*Mein Gott!* Are they drunk, Uncle Hessie?"

"As I said, not to worry, dear." He patted my knee again.

A young, smooth-faced SA approached the car with his friend. He slapped the hood hard with his hand. His eyes were sliding about in a frightening way. A string of foam from the beer threaded down his chin.

"So you like my car!" Uncle Hessie said brightly.

"Yes, yes!"

"Won't find a red Commie having one of these, will you?" Uncle Hessie said. The fellows were obviously drunk, and I sensed that the situation could turn ugly in a split second. Maybe Uncle Hessie was pretending to share their opinions. I knew he'd never really say something like that.

"*Nein, nein!*" the SA trooper replied.

"But maybe a Jew," said his friend. He cocked his head at Uncle Hessie.

"Ah, maybe a Jew," Uncle Hessie said. "And if it's a Jew,

I would sell it to him. Perhaps you've heard of the PAW."

I had no idea what the letters PAW stood for.

"PAW?" The man wiped his mouth on his sleeve.

His friend, who was not quite as drunk, leaned forward. "PAW. Yeah, I think I've heard of that."

I was beginning to get a glimmer of what Hessie was up to. He was going to use these louts to get us through the blocked street with nothing nasty happening.

"Of course you have heard of it, my good man!" boomed Uncle Hessie. "Prussian Auto Works. I am the president." I blinked. Hessie wasn't the president of anything. He had never worked a day in his life. He was now slapping his motoring coat as if searching for something. He reached for an inside pocket. "*Aachh!* Left my card at home. But hey, would you boys like a ride?"

"A ride?" The seriously drunk one staggered.

"I know you're not quite in shape to drive, but hop on the fender, boys. I'll give you a ride to the next intersection."

They did, and so we made our way through streets jammed with SA, two Brown Shirts clearing a path for us, one on each forward fender like hood ornaments, waving and shouting their disgusting slogans about death to Jews, Communists, and on and on, and then breaking from the slogans and lurid rants to join in the scattered choruses of the SA's favorite song. It was called the "Horst Wessel Song" and was being broadcast more often on the radio recently.

Die Fahne hoch! Die Reihen fest geschlossen!
SA marschiert mit ruhig festem Schritt.
Kam'raden, die Rotfront und Reaktion erschossen,
Marschier'n im Geist in uns'ren Reihen mit.

Die Strasse frei den braunen Bataillonen.
Die Strasse frei dem Sturmabteilungsmann!
Es schau'n aufs Hakenkreuz voll Hoffnung schon Millionen.
Der Tag für Freiheit und für Brot bricht an!

The flag high! The ranks tightly closed!
The SA marches with a firm, courageous pace.
Comrades, shot dead by Red Front and Reaction,
March in spirit within our ranks.

Make the streets free for the brown battalions.
Make the streets free for the SA man.
Already millions are looking to the swastika full of hope.
The day of freedom and bread is dawning.

The two SA men slid off the car when we arrived at the next intersection. Hessie pressed on the accelerator and shifted into a higher gear. His face was grim. From the corner of my eye I could see the small throb of a pulse beating in his temple. Neither one of us looked back. There was a sign indicating the direction to Potsdam and thus Caputh. We were going out of Berlin, to the country, away from all that, the brown sludge of the flooding river, the stomp of jackboots. There was still beer slobber from the SA men on the roadster. Hessie drove faster as if to dare the wind to clean it. The landscape flowed by. I put my head against the back of the seat and tipped my face up toward the sun. *I am going away.* I kept telling myself. *I am going away!*

I briefly wondered what Herr Doktor Berg had done with my books, if he had read *The Call of the Wild.* I was just about to ask Hessie if he could get me another copy when I heard his rather high but sweetly scratchy voice carrying above the rush of the wind.

> Pack up all my care and woe.
> Here I go, singing low
> Bye bye blackbird.

I knew these lines. They were from a very popular American song. Josephine Baker had brought it to Berlin and it swept through the city from the cabarets to the fanciest parties, to Mama playing it on the piano when she and Papa had dinner guests. I loved this song. I looked over at him and he winked at me. I joined in.

> Where somebody waits for me.
> Sugar's sweet, so is she.
> Bye bye blackbird.

No one here can love or understand me.
Oh, what hard luck stories they all hand me.
Make my bed and light the light.
I'll be home late tonight.
Blackbird, bye bye.

If only I could have driven to the ends of the Earth with Hessie singing all the way, the peach chiffon scarf fluttering at the edges of my face, looking though the amber-tinted goggles as Germany slid by.

chapter 11

My darling, we sat together,
We two, in our frail boat;
The night was calm o'er the wide sea
Whereon we were afloat.

The Specter-Island, the lovely,
Lay dim in the moon's mild glance;
There sounded sweetest music,
There waved the shadowy dance.

It sounded sweeter and sweeter,
It waved there to and fro;
But we slid past forlornly
Upon the great sea-flow.

—Heinrich Heine,
translated by James Thomson

"Look! Why don't they trim their sail?" Uncle Hessie looked toward the small sloop perhaps one hundred meters to our starboard side. It was the morning after our arrival in Caputh. We were out on the lake early to sail. The boat Hessie was looking at with the floppy sails was Einstein's *Tümmler*, which means "porpoise." Professor Einstein was at the tiller and Papa was his crew. I was at the tiller of my boat. Like Einstein's, mine was a sloop, single-masted, same class—a "snipe"— fourteen feet in length. My boat was called *Ratty*. People always teased me because it was such an ugly name. But it was the nickname of River Rat, one of my favorite characters from one of my favorite books, *The Wind in the Willows*, who just loved to mess around in boats.

At the moment we were not simply messing about but racing. I was the captain and Uncle Hessie was my crew. I was dressed in my old gymnastic culottes, *Hosenrock*. I looked at *Tümmler*. Papa wore a straw hat, but Einstein wore a handkerchief on his head knotted at the corners into a square. It looked ridiculous. I had told Papa that he must never wear a knotted handkerchief. It was so old-man-looking and silly, too. We were becalmed, but there was a riffle of wind where they were. Einstein and Papa were not paying attention, though.

"Idiots! *Dummköpfe*," I muttered.

"Well, why don't they sheet in and take that wind?" Hessie muttered.

"I'll tell you why. They are too busy gabbing about the universe to see what's happening on this little lake. Their heads are not in the clouds—they're in the exosphere, the ionosphere. They are thinking about interplanetary gases and God knows what, but not this wind that we are about to catch! Get ready, Hessie. Here it comes!"

It was just a slight breeze but Hessie was ready. I kept

my eyes glued to the two little ribbons called telltales I had
tied to the wire stays of the mast. I had detected a slight
quiver, then a flutter. I pushed the tiller a bit to bring *Ratty*
just a sliver closer to this nearly phantom wind. When the
two ribbons were streaming parallel to the sail I knew we
would be at the proper angle to the wind. In another half
minute they were. Gently Hessie trimmed the sail. Soon we
were sliding by *Tümmler*.

"Auf wiedersehen!" Uncle Hessie called, and tipped his
crisp white yachting cap to Papa and Einstein. We won the
race.

It was later the next morning when I saw Hessie coming
down the hall with his valise from the guest bedroom.

"Uncle Hessie!" I hissed from the door of my bedroom,
which I had opened just a crack. "Come here!" I peeked out
and beckoned him with my finger. He set down his valise
and with exaggerated tiptoeing came over to the door.

"What's up, *Liebchen*? A plot? A secret romance?"

"Don't be silly. It's just that—well, I'm a little bit worried."

"What about?" He looked genuinely concerned.

"You, Uncle Hessie."

"Me?"

"Yes." I sighed. What had happened in Bayerischer Platz
when we left Berlin seemed like a million years ago, even
though it was only two days before. "I'm worried about—"

I hesitated—"well, you know when we left Berlin and those awful SA fellows came up to the car and how you told them you were the president of that . . . that . . ."

"That made-up company?"

I nodded. He crooked his finger under my chin and lifted it a bit. There was a look that was almost like mist in his hazel eyes, one part wistful and one part mournful, perhaps. There is a word in German that means to feel a bit of each of these sentiments. The word is *nachtrauern*. And I had never in my life seen that feeling in Hessie's eyes, but I did now.

"Don't worry, *Liebchen*. Those fellows were too drunk to remember anything." He sighed. "And all this will be over soon. It's a passing thing, a fashion."

It was so like Uncle Hessie to view all the world through his scrim of style, fashion, and taste. "*Kleinbürgertum*—the petty bourgeois—the lot of them, KB," he muttered. To be KB was not good in Hessie's book.

"Baba says they are barbarians, *Barbaren*."

"How alliterative!" Hessie exclaimed, and bent down to kiss my cheek.

"Don't make jokes. Hertha's not KB," I blurted out.

"Hertha?" He was puzzled. "What does Hertha have to do with any of this?"

"I'm not sure. But she said to me a few weeks ago, before school let out that . . . well . . . she thought that . . ." I squeezed my eyes shut trying to remember her exact words. "She said that the Communists will make things worse and she felt that there might be a chance for things to get better with Hitler."

Hessie's eyes darkened. He seemed to almost shrink a bit. His shoulders dropped.

"And Uncle Hessie, Hertha wasn't drunk like those louts. She was just . . . Hertha."

"She's tired."

"Tired? What are you talking about? Do you see the way she buzzes around this house cooking, cleaning, helping Mama in the garden?"

"She's tired of being poor."

"But she has a good job with us."

"It's more than that. She's proud. She is tired of being a loser. Germany lost the war. Our country has been humiliated by the Versailles treaty. And there are some people who, how shall I put it . . . they want a scapegoat, someone to blame. Jews, Communists. If they can blame someone, if those people are punished, then everything will be all right again."

"But Hertha's not like Herr Himmel, our *Hausmeister*. He's mean. He's horrible. He worships Hitler, I am sure."

"Oh yes, Herr Himmel. You are probably right about him, and you're also right about Hertha. She is nothing like Herr Himmel. But you have to understand, Gaby, that you don't have to be mean to hurt." I bit my lip slightly, a habit I had when I was thinking hard. "Complicated, isn't it?" Hessie said.

"Yes," I said softly, looking down at my bare feet. But

then I had a sudden thought. I jerked my head up. "Uncle Hessie, how many Herthas are there in Germany?"

He shook his head wearily, then turned and went back down the hall to fetch his valise.

We quickly settled into the summer rhythms of our lake house in Caputh. I slept late. Mama and Papa were nice about that. Some parents made their kids get up early and go swimming in the ice-cold morning water of the lake, or do calisthenics, like the Rudemeirs two cottages down. Not Mama and Papa. Everyone got to do what they wanted, including Ulla who had stayed in Berlin. It was a holiday. Oh, except for one thing. I was the designated mouse hunter. We set traps at the end of summer and when we came back, after the winter, we emptied them. But invariably we would forget where we had put some, and a smell would begin to emanate. I was famous for my sensitive nose. Mama said I should be a *parfumier* and blend scents for perfume manufacturing.

But mouse work occupied only the first few days at the beginning of the summer. After that I got to do just what I pleased, which was sleep late, sail, swim, or fish. Papa and I both loved to fish from the end of our pier. There were lake trout, something we called grubbies that were a kind of small salmon, and silver bass, which were not quite so common, but delicious. We had fish for dinner four nights out of five.

* * *

When I was not sleeping late, sailing, swimming, or fishing I would read. In Caputh I could read my books not stuffed into my school textbooks. I read them "naked" as I thought of it—wherever and whenever I pleased. Mama even let me read at the breakfast table and during lunch and sometimes during dinner if there weren't guests. I read everyplace—the hammock, the bathtub, the ice-cream shop in the village—everyplace except on my boat *Ratty*, for one really must tend to business on a sailboat, even when not racing. I sometimes wondered about the two books Herr Doktor Berg had confiscated from me. I hoped he hadn't lost them.

For Mama, doing as she pleased meant practicing the music she never got to teach to her students. She loved early music that was made for the virginal, a musical instrument similar to a harpsichord but invented in the Middle Ages. Of course her second greatest pleasure was working in the garden. She would often work out there late into the evening, if there was enough moonlight. She called these times her stealth attacks on garden invaders. Like some kindly witch, she would steal out into the night with her strange potions—diluted laundry bleach, squashed garlic, baking soda, and something called elixir of bergamot. Apparently it worked wonders in vanquishing aphids, one of the worst garden pests. Mama was not dependent only on chemical warfare, however. She was a strategist as brilliant as any general or statesman. Forget von Hindenburg and his triumph at Tannenburg. She was more of a Bismarck, the superb diplomat-engineer who united Germany through political maneuvering and war. She figured out strange alliances between plants and insects. Put nasturtiums next to tomatoes and the flowers will drive off aphids. Grow basil near asparagus and get rid of the beetle that devours the stalks.

Papa's garden in the summer was the night sky, unpolluted by city lights. He especially relished the moonless nights. He had several telescopes that he would wheel out onto the lawn to gaze at this night garden that bloomed with the ancient brilliance of stars embedded in other galaxies, of planetary nebulae, those last dying gasps of gas blown off from withering stars. When it was cloudy, Papa would go over and have an evening smoke with Einstein.

One morning a few weeks into the summer I went fishing hoping to catch a silver bass but instead only got a half dozen of the little grubbies. I was walking up from the lake to the back kitchen door to deliver the catch so Hertha could clean the fish when I heard the sound of the radio. The announcer's voice crackled through the screen kitchen window into the calm of the morning.

"Street gangs, apparently including some SA members, went on a rampage. . . ." There was a temporary blast of static, but then the voice resumed clearly. "Last night, destroying a large part of the Jewish section . . ."

I stopped and listened. Through the screen window I could see Hertha calmly preparing a pie crust. I knew it was a pie crust simply by the rhythm of her shoulders as she rolled out the dough.

"The blaze, thought to have been fueled by petrol, was so hot that the fire brigades could not get close enough without great risk for several hours. . . ."

I simply could not walk into the kitchen at this moment. I set the fish on the wooden worktable where Hertha usually cleaned them and began to gut them myself. I had seen Hertha and Papa do this countless times. I had always thought myself too squeamish to slit open their bellies and scoop out their intestines. *Get over it*, I told myself. The newscaster finished his report on the synagogue and then moved on to a report about the Frankfurt beer festival. I slit the pale pink belly of the first fish, scooped out the swirl of intestines, and threw them into the trash. I glanced through the window at Hertha. She was still crimping the edges of the pie. I could tell by the look of fierce concentration on her face. Her pie edges were always perfect.

We had no guests for dinner that night, so I brought two books to the table. We were having the grubbies I had caught and cleaned. These were always cooked whole, and then it was up to each person to fillet his or her own fish by removing the bones from the split body.

"Your fish is getting cold," Hertha said. "Here, I'll fillet it for you while you read." She whisked my plate away. I looked up from my book.

"Oh, thanks, Hertha," I replied. My eyes followed her. She was standing at the sideboard, deboning my fish. She had earlier thanked me for cleaning the fish. I hadn't told her why I had stayed outside and done it; that I couldn't enter the kitchen as she calmly rolled out the pie crust and listened to the news. Maybe she hadn't been that calm. Maybe I would have appeared calm to someone watching me gut the fish. But the question I had asked Hessie was still scraping at the back of my mind. How many Herthas? It seemed somehow an unfair question, I told myself. She was just Hertha—sweet, kind, always ready to help.

"What are you reading, little mouse, two books?" Papa asked.

"Yes, *The Adventures of Huckleberry Finn* and this book of Heinrich Heine's poetry."

"How can you keep them straight?" Mama asked.

"Well, that's sort of the point," I replied.

Mama blinked. "I don't understand. You want to be confused?"

"Not confused, really. You see, I have a theory about reading."

"Yes?" Papa said leaning toward me. Now he was interested. He loved theories.

I took a bite of the fish, chewed, and arranged my face

into a thoughtful countenance. I really was thinking. I had already worked out the theory but I was not quite sure how to explain it.

"You see, I think it is good to read two books at almost the same time. One funny and maybe a bit raucous." I tapped on the cover of the Huckleberry Finn book. "And one romantic." I tapped on the poetry book.

"*Zucker und Gewürze*, sugar and spice, *rauh und glatt*, rough and smooth," Papa said.

"Yes, exactly." I nodded. "And in August when Rosa and I go back to the gymnasium, we will spend a lot of time first term on Heine's poetry. So we are both reading to get ahead this summer."

Mama now nodded approvingly. "Oh yes, I remember Ulla reading all that when she had Fräulein Hofstadt for literature. I guess you will have her, too." A worry shadowed Mama's eyes. I knew she was thinking now of Ulla and hoping she would pass the exam she had failed. But no one said anything. Ulla had been a top student at the Kaiser Wilhelm School.

"Oh yes!" I couldn't wait to enter what I thought of as the upper realm of the gymnasium in the new building. Although it was all part of the same school, the move seemed to signify so much. The Kaiser Wilhelm School had introduced some new educational theories, and it was in the upper levels where the classes started to feel different.

Fräulein Hofstadt was said to be the best literature

teacher in the entire school. She was so beautiful, and I had heard that she often gave little parties in her classroom. Heinrich Heine was one of her favorite poets, and Ulla said that she gave a party on his birthday. But most exciting was that Fräulein Hofstadt's class always put on a play under her direction. When Ulla was in her class they did a play by Friedrich Schiller, *The Maid of Orleans*, about Joan of Arc. Ulla's friend Marta played Saint Joan. So Fräulein Hofstadt loved Heine and Goethe and Schiller—all the great German writers.

"But how do you think Fräulein Hofstadt will take to Mark Twain?" Papa asked.

"Oh, we won't read him in class," I replied. "I'm not sure how she'd like him."

"A bit rough for her, maybe?" Papa asked.

"Maybe, but he is so funny!"

"And more complicated than one might think, if I recall," Mama offered. "He can surprise you."

"Heine never really surprises me," I said

"Surprises can be good," Papa said.

And bad! I suddenly thought as Hertha came in with a bowl of applesauce, still thinking of how calm she seemed as she listened to that horrible news on the radio. Was it possible that she had looked upset and I just hadn't noticed? *She's just Hertha,* I kept telling myself. It was quickly becoming an annoying refrain in my head.

•   •   •

At least an hour or more after dinner that evening I came out and lay in the grass, looking up at the Milky Way that stretched like a cobweb across the sky. Papa was out there with his big telescope. I brought a pair of binoculars but preferred to view the stars with my naked eyes. Professor Einstein nearly stepped on me as he walked over from his house.

"Put it out, Albert," I heard Papa say, referring to Einstein's cigar. Its glowing tip polluted the blackness, and this was a precious nearly moonless night. Only a scrap of moon floated like a sliver of a fingernail above. Our house was darkened, all the lights having been extinguished except for a very small one for Mama's piano that shone only enough to illuminate her music. She was playing now. The notes spilled out of the window and, weaving through the air, found a new harmony with the light breeze off the lake.

Despite Einstein nearly stepping on me, I soon realized that these two men with their heads in the exosphere had not noticed me, or perhaps Papa had simply forgotten I was there. Now Papa was adjusting the scope for Einstein and saying something about how with the powerful telescope at the observatory one could easily see the blue tinge of Rigel in Orion's belt.

"Can't you see it?" Papa asked.

"Not really, Otto."

"I know it's not easy. Close your eyes. Look away from it . . . now come back," Papa instructed. Papa was right—it wasn't easy to see the stars' color. But it was not impossible. At first all stars look alike—little points of white. But if one learns to be a very careful observer it is possible to distinguish some of the colors of the brighter stars. Papa was an expert at this.

"Aah, yes . . . and so you think that with the right kind of cameras . . ." Einstein asked.

"And film," Papa said.

"Yes, and so you could refine the data on the absorption lines?" Einstein's voice brimmed with excitement. I had no idea by this point what they were talking about. Something to do with the spectral class of stars, which was a way of sorting stars based on their temperatures and had some relation to color. But as for absorption lines, I was clueless.

"Yes, yes. But you know with the way things are going." Papa sighed

"Oh, God . . . that fool Lenard again! I heard. Though I try not to hear."

"Oh, it's not just Lenard. A lot of *völkisch* talk. People in the department are getting very, you know, *völkisch*."

I pricked up my ears. What had once been a perfectly nice, reasonable word had become tainted. It was almost as if a bad smell clung to it. The word *Volk* meant simply "folk." And *volkstümlich* meant something rather like "folksy." The word conjured up images of cuckoo clocks, boys in lederhosen, and pretty girls with braids wearing dirndls. But suddenly it seemed as if the word had been corrupted. When it was seized upon by the Nazis, it became equated with all that was pure German and pure Aryan.

Papa had explained to me that actually "Aryan" was another word that had been corrupted by the Nazis. Originally it had referred to people who spoke a language from Northern India, but the Nazis gave it a new definition—of pure northern European, not Jewish, descent. Quickly the broken cross, or swastika, an ancient Indian symbol, became a symbol of this purity. I never realized how powerful a graphic arrangement of lines could be. It was strangely hypnotic.

These days the words *Volk* or Aryan almost automatically conjured up the image of the swastika. Two perfectly decent words were ruined.

So when Papa said people in the department were getting *völkisch*, I became very interested. I prayed I could continue to listen and they would not realize that I was a scant few feet from them in the grass. I suddenly was beset with itches and imaginary ants crawling up my legs, but I didn't move a muscle. They had lowered their voices. I had to strain to make out the words.

"CalTech . . . next March?" It was Papa's voice.

"God willing . . . but this fellow Abraham Flexner from Princeton . . ." Einstein replied.

Wisps of conversations floated over me.

"No . . . I'm considering giving it up . . . but I still have Swiss citizenship."

Had Einstein given up his citizenship? He was no longer German? I tried to listen harder. My ears almost hurt.

"But, Otto, did that SA fellow who came to your office really demand that your secretary turn over the notes from the London conference?"

"Yes, that was the one that Goldman and Eddington . . ."

"And then they broke up the lecture?" Einstein sighed deeply. "It's going to be a military dictatorship. . . . I am starting to think that it is inevitable. That it's not a question of if but when. . . ."

Their words wound into the night, mingling with the ancient light of the stars. Einstein nearly stepped on me a second time when he left. Papa was peering through his telescope again and did not hear him. Soon Papa left as well. If he had known I was there, he had forgotten completely.

How much simpler the rest of the universe felt compared to this small part here on Earth. I picked up my binoculars and turned them toward the night sky that was puddled with light, adrift with shoals of stars. What were we, I thought, but a speck in an insignificant galaxy, among countless galaxies with millions perhaps billions of stars.

Once when I was very young Papa accidentally dropped a half kilo bag of sugar on the floor, and it split open. Before he fetched the broom to clean it up, he got down on his knees and swept the sugar into a pinwheel pattern. He called me over to kneel beside him.

"Imagine, Gaby, that this whole mess"—he gestured

toward the sugar that was all over the floor—"is the Milky Way, our galaxy. Now this part here"—he drew with his fingertip a very small circle around some of the granules—"this lot is our solar system, and . . ." He took his Swiss Army knife from his pocket and pulled out the tiny tweezers. He tried to pick up one little granule of sugar. It was impossible, of course, because the points of the tweezers weren't fine enough. "Well," he said with a sigh, "you get the idea. Our Earth is just a little speck of sugar riding this sugar swirl that is part of an immense sugar sea. And actually," he added, "to be really accurate, numerically accurate, I would need maybe an additional five thousand half-kilo bags of sugar to give you a more precise model of our galaxy."

I thought of that swirl of sugar on the kitchen floor from years before. How could Hitler cause so many problems? I put down the binoculars. The scrap of moon had slipped away, making the dark even darker and the stars even brighter. They scorched the blackness with their fire. Ninety-two elements to bake a universe and one madman to blow it up?

chapter 12

All of a sudden, bang! bang! bang!
goes three or four guns—the men had
slipped around through the woods and
come in from behind without their
horses! The boys jumped for the
river—both of them hurt—and as they
swum down the current the men run
along the bank shooting at them and
singing out, "Kill them, kill them!"
It made me so sick I most fell out of
the tree. I ain't a-going to tell ALL
that happened—it would make me sick
again if I was to do that. I wished
I hadn't ever come ashore that night,
to see such things.

—Mark Twain,
The Adventures of Huckleberry Finn

"Yes, yes, Frau Blick, I've got your order right
here." The scent of cinnamon swirled through
the air. I was in line at Steinhoff's Bakery in
Caputh. The baker was known for his cinnamon strudel.
Mama had sent me to get a half dozen strudel plus a ring
cake called a *Gugelhupf*. There were three people ahead of
me in line.

"Frau Blick, you want some fresh *Mutti Brötchen*?" *Mutti Brötchen*, or Mama's bread, were the white rolls that the bakery was famous for. They were named after Herr Steinhoff's wife, whom all referred to as *Mutti*.

"These are the last of the fresh batch." He nodded at the bin for day-old bread. "I'm sending yesterday's up to the Jew house on the lake. She don't know no difference."

I froze. There was only one Jewish house on the lake. It was Einstein's. I wanted to say, "She does know the difference." Elsa Einstein came from a very old and refined family and, as Mama always said, she knew how to set a table, which meant she entertained beautifully.

I looked around the bakery to try and see if anyone else seemed shocked or disturbed, but their expressions were unreadable. I didn't know what to do. My first instinct was to flee the shop, but Mama had put in a big order and I was to pick it up. Steinhoff's was the only baker in town. Baba was arriving for a couple of days' visit and some neighbors were coming for dinner.

"What can I do for you, *mein kleiner Schatz*?" It was my turn. I swallowed. And looked down at my sandals.

"My mother's order, please."

"Oh yes, of course, sweetie." He turned and shouted into the kitchen, "Frau Professor Schramm's *Gugelhupf*!" Then he turned to me again. "And I believe some strudel, too, she ordered. Right?"

"Yes, sir."

As he wrapped up the strudel, he smiled at me. "Ahh, what a pretty little thing you are with your blond braids. I always say"—he turned to another customer who was looking in the pastry case—"that this little one reminds me of the *Volkspuppen*, you know the sunflower dolls for the *Sonnenblummenfest*. You should wear a dirndl for our sunflower parade."

"I hate parades," I muttered, thinking of the goose-stepping and drunk Brown Shirts I had seen when Uncle Hessie and I left Berlin.

"You what? Naw. The *Sonnenblummenfest* parade is one of the oldest folk parades of the region. You could be our sunflower princess with those blond braids."

"Put it on Mama's charge," I said and, taking the boxes of baked goods, I left the shop. *Parade! Never!*

First the perfectly good word *Volk*, then parades, and now even braids. Me a perfect sunflower princess, a *Volksprinzessin*. What would be ruined next? I must tell Mama, I thought, that we cannot buy from Steinhoff's anymore. There was a bakery in Potsdam that wasn't far, and I vowed that I would never ever eat another bite of Steinhoff's *Mutti Brötchen*. No more rolls. Fresh bread had in a matter of seconds turned rancid. Like Huck, I guessed I wished that I'd never come ashore.

"Your mama and Frau Blumenthal are down by the lake," Hertha said as she took the bakery goods from me. I must have looked at Hertha oddly, for she immediately said. "Is something wrong?"

"No, nothing." But in fact I wondered if there had been a slight edge, a sneer perhaps, in Hertha's voice when she said Baba's very Jewish-sounding last name. Was I going crazy? Imagining things all because of that horrid man Steinhoff? It wasn't fair of me to put Hertha in the same boat, was it?

I rushed upstairs to change into my bathing suit from last summer. I was saving my new one for when Rosa came to visit. We had bought them together earlier in the spring. But first I got the scissors from Mama's sewing basket. I went into the bathroom and looked at my face. All right, so no one would mistake me for Joan Crawford, but did I really look like *Volkspuppe*? A folk doll? I looped my braids onto the top of my head and attempted the infamous shoulder twitch that Rosa had so easily mastered. I squinted a bit, partly to look sexy, but partly so I could see myself more clearly. Mama was right. She said I had to get glasses before the start of the new term. Glasses would certainly diminish the folk-doll look, even if they would not enhance the Joan Crawford one. I let my braids drop and picked up the scissors. First I cut the left one off and then the right one. I blew a stream of air out through my lips making a blubbering sound. I felt better. More fit. Fit for anything except a parade!

After I got into my bathing suit, I ran straight out of the house across the lawn and jumped into the water. It felt wonderful. My head felt light and free. No slimy yellow snakes flopping about. Mama and Baba were floating on big rubber tires.

They were gabbing their heads off as usual. Baba was talking about a party that she had gone to that week, the Press Ball, and how someone named Magda Goebbels had worn an "atrocious" gown. "Absolutely atrocious, my dear. Fake silk. You'd think with how much Hitler admires Mussolini that she could go to Italy—Como—and get herself some fabulous silk. That's the best silk, of course, from Como. But no, she looked like a strumpet. She had better shape up, because they say that her husband is going to be made top minister in the Nazi Party. Joseph Goebbels will be the most powerful man next to you-know-who."

I dived like a *Tümmler*—the animal, not the boat—around Mama and Baba and then I began to swim under them, tickling their toes. They were giggling and yelling.

"Don't splash, naughty girl! She swims like a fish, that one!" Then there was this terrible choking sound, followed by a big splashy plop.

"Elske! Elske!" Baba screamed. Mama was spluttering and coughing. "Gaby! Gaby! *Was im Gottes Namen . . . ? Dein Haar!*" Yes, my hair, what, in the name of God, was I thinking? What had I gone and done?

"I decided I need a new hairstyle, Mama."

"That is not a style!" Baba said, her eyes bugging out of her head. That was true. I had been in such a hurry to cut off my *völkisch* braids that I had not even bothered to undo them. I had just chopped each one off at the scalp. Needless to say, there was probably a certain, well, a certain asymmetry. That was actually an understatement. In the back my hair felt as short as a boy's, but on the sides it hung down in tatters. The tatters were the only remnants of my *völkisch* braids, which my parents for the rest of the summer would treat like a holy relic.

"What ever possessed you?" Mama asked. She and Baba had immediately gotten out of the water and insisted I follow them up to Mama's and Papa's bathroom, where they would try to salvage the remnants of the hair left on my head.

"I'm not sure you want to know," I said.

Mama glared at my reflection in the mirror. "Of course I want to know! What happened?"

So I told them the story of what had occurred at the bakery.

"That fool inspired you to cut your hair?" Mama was aghast.

"Don't use the word 'inspired' with him, Mama. He's hardly an artist, even if you do like his strudel," I shot back.

"We'll never go into the shop again. I won't buy a crumb of his lousy *Mutti Brötchen*," she fumed.

Baba sighed heavily. "I agree you shouldn't patronize the shop, but that will hardly bring Gaby's hair back. Send her down to Berlin and I'll have Monsieur Marc try and do something with it." She extended a finger toward a stubby hank that stood out at the top of my ears.

"Oooh!" I cried gleefully. I had never been to a real hair-stylist in my life.

"She can come with me when I leave," Baba said.

"No!" Mama and I both said at once. Ulla and Karl were arriving two days after Baba left, and I really wanted to see Ulla. I knew it couldn't quite be like old times, since she would be with her boyfriend, but we could still sail and fish together. Ulla was better at fishing than I was.

"All right," Mama said, "when Karl and Ulla leave, I'll send her down with them. Karl is driving. She can get her hair cut and see the eye doctor, too." I felt as if I were a package of damaged goods being shipped off for an assessment, like an automobile that had had an unfortunate collision— could the chassis be straightened out? The dents hammered out of the fenders? And oh yes, a new windshield please! But at the same time, I felt terrific. No more folk-doll stuff for me. If I couldn't be Joan Crawford with my glasses, at least I would never be a *Volkspuppe*. I might appear slightly intellectual. Maybe I'd start a new style.

Later that afternoon when Papa came back from an errand and heard of the amputation, he ran upstairs and looked at the box with the braids that Mama had rescued from my waste bin. Then he stood on the landing holding them, groaning and whimpering as he looked at the gold streaming through his fingers, not quite believing that alas they were separated from the head on which they had grown.

"Milchstrasse . . . Milchstrasse . . . Warum, warum . . . die kleine milchstrasse?" The little Milky Way had been chopped off. I felt a bit bad then because in Papa's mind these were not the braids of some little folk doll that celebrated the sunflower festival in September, they were braids of starlight. But in the end they were *my* braids, and I figured I could do with them as I pleased, and if that meant cutting them off, I would. Papa did keep them, however. He folded them into thin layers of tissue paper, and Mama stuck them into a dresser drawer where they kept their freshly pressed handkerchiefs.

And for the rest of that summer it seemed like at least once a day each of my parents would run their fingers through my bangs or the hair on the back of my head where the braids had been, trying to hold on to what was once there—the gold that was now just stubble.

chapter 13

I love this white and slender body,
These limbs that answer Love's caresses,
Passionate eyes, and forehead covered
With heavy waves of thick, black tresses.

—Heinrich Heine,
translated by Louis Untermeyer

"A personal request," I said when we sat down at the table the night before Ulla and Karl arrived.

"What might that be?" Papa asked as he put some cauliflower, which I hated, on my plate.

"Can we not talk about my hair when Ulla and Karl come this weekend?"

"Of course," Mama said. "What makes you think that would be a topic of conversation?"

I rolled my eyes.

"I don't know. Just don't bring it up, OK? Because with Karl coming and all, I just think there are more interesting topics of conversation, that's all." The election was one topic. However, I didn't say so.

The Reichstag had been dissolved just before we left for Caputh, and new elections were coming. Would Hitler and the Nazi Party gain seats? That was all anyone was talking about on the streets of Caputh.

But Mama and Papa did not say much about the election or the happenings in Berlin. In the last two days, my braids' amputation seemed to command more attention. Was this a kind of denial on their part? *Let's not talk about Hitler. Let's talk about Gaby's hair instead. I think it's grown a little bit. Don't you think so, Otto? And oh yes, too bad about Hitler. So maybe he will gain a few seats in the coming election, but wasn't he just a passing fancy?*

No, they did not really say all that. They just refused to talk about Hitler at all.

"*Mäusi*, your hair!" Ulla exclaimed. I had run out the back door as soon as I heard the car drive up. Of course I should have known that no one would have to say anything about my hair. It would be the first thing Ulla would notice.

"What did you do?"

"What does it look like I did?" I exclaimed.

Karl laughed hard at this. It made me like him. I had only met him once or twice when he came to the apartment to pick up Ulla, and he would only stay a minute or two. Karl had blond hair, nearly as blond as mine, but his eyes were a very dark gray. It was odd but they seemed opaque, maybe overcast like a sky with weather moving in. But he had a nice mouth and he laughed a lot, and he had a quick dimple that animated his face.

Although Ulla's hair was exactly the same as always, she looked in some way changed to me. I wasn't sure what it was. She carried herself differently. There was a languorous motion to everything she did, as if she was beyond getting too excited, beyond rushing. It was almost as if she had arrived at some milestone and was deeply confident, satisfied with herself. And it wasn't simply that she had indeed passed the examination she had flunked earlier. This went far beyond achieving a high mark—although she had done rather spectacularly and earned a 14 out of 15.

"Guess what, Gaby?" Karl asked.

"What?" I was pleased that he had directed a question to me right away.

"When we drove through the center of town, we saw that the movie *Emil and the Detectives* is playing."

"It is? I can't believe it. I haven't seen it."

"Let's go!" Karl said.

"Oh, Mama, can I?" Mama had just come around from the garden and to greet them. Her face was streaked with dirt.

"Sure, you can go." She laughed. "Pardon my filthy appearance, Karl. I've been pulling weeds. They grow so fast once midsummer approaches."

"There's a matinee tomorrow afternoon. We checked. I told Karl how much you loved the book," said Ulla.

Emil and the Detectives was one of my favorite books ever. The movie had come out last year but I had missed it in Berlin because I had measles. It's about a young boy, Emil Tischbein, who is robbed when he falls asleep on a train. Through very clever means, he and his friends manage to catch the robber.

By dinnertime Mama was cleaned up and in one of her prettiest summer dresses and Papa had put a cornflower in the buttonhole of his lapel. I wore a pair of trousers that I thought looked sort of like something Joan Crawford would wear, and had done what I could with my hair, which was not much. I was hoping the dinner might distract from any comments on my appearance. I had for the first time all summer caught not one but two silver bass.

Hertha brought in the platter with my extraordinary catch all decked out with parsley and thinly sliced lemon.

"Silver bass, how delightful," Ulla remarked. "Delightful"—what kind of a word is that? Before she would have exclaimed, "Silver bass! *Wundervoll*, fantastic!" But now she seemed beyond such embellishments that marked unbridled enthusiasm. Instead she showed just this modest, cool note of appreciation. It irritated me a little bit. She knew how hard silver bass were to catch.

But at least there was no conversation about my braidless condition. At one point I thought we were veering a bit close, so I quickly changed the subject.

"How is your job? Are you making lots of money?" I asked Ulla.

"Some," she answered.

"Well, there are the tips," Karl said. Ulla shot him a warning glance.

"Tips?" Papa said suspiciously. "Since when do book-keepers get tips."

"When they find an accounting error. I prefer to call it a bonus," Ulla said brightly.

"What was the error?" Mama asked.

"It was regarding the delivery of the cigarettes and cigars that the Chameleon sells. The vendor had been shorting us."

"Good for you," Papa said. "Always pays to be vigilant."

"I should have thought to bring Professor Einstein some of the cigars. I think they are the kind he smokes, and I'm sure they would have included them in my bonus."

"Professor Einstein is here in Caputh? Goodness!" Karl said. He was clearly impressed, none of this nonchalant "delightful" business. There were true exclamation marks in his voice.

"For now, at least," Papa said. I was surprised by Papa's answer. Professor Einstein always spent the entire summer in Caputh. Just like we did.

"Otto, whatever do you mean that he is here 'for now, at least'?" Mama asked. "Oh, is this the thing with Princeton?"

"What's Princeton?" I asked.

"A university in the United States," Papa replied.

"And you said, Otto, that this Flexner fellow came all the way here to Caputh to visit Albert? He's with this Princeton school?" Mama asked.

"Yes."

"Princeton is near New York, right?" Mama asked.

"Yes. I think it will suit him—if he goes. They have founded a new institute," Papa said.

"What kind of institute? Like the Kaiser Wilhelm?" I asked.

"Not exactly like the Kaiser Wilhelm."

"Do they want him to go there for good, forever?" I asked.

"I have no idea," Papa said. He appeared uncomfortable discussing this.

"Oh, they'll probably pay a great deal to get the famous Professor Einstein, I would think," Karl said.

"I don't think it would matter to Einstein, nor would it matter to you, Otto. You physicists are all alike." Mama laughed as she spoke. She turned to Karl. "They are not necessarily practical. They don't concern themselves with money. Einstein will just be out there in the woods, thinking. He won't need much."

If he went, he would be away, I thought. Far away. It sounded romantic to me. Just the word "Princeton"—like some little kingdom in the wild. I sort of wished Papa could go there, and that he would take me, too. But CalTech might be more exciting. Closer to Hollywood.

•   •   •

After dinner Karl, Ulla, Papa, and I played croquet—Papa and Ulla against Karl and me. Karl and I won. Then, as it became darker, Papa brought out the scope and gave Karl a tour of the heavens. After the star tour, Papa yawned and announced that he was turning in. He gave me a look that seemed to say I should go to bed too, and then suggested that Ulla and Karl might want to take a walk. The message was more than clear. I was being sent to bed so the young lovers could have a moment to themselves. So I went up to the bedroom that Ulla and I shared. Karl was to sleep in the guest bedroom. It would be nice to wake up in the morning and not see the bed all flat with its covers undisturbed, but lumpy, the summer quilt rising and falling slightly with the rhythms of Ulla's breathing.

But when I woke up once during the night, I saw that the bed was as flat as ever. I couldn't fall back to sleep, and I'm not sure how long I lay there in the dark. Finally I heard Ulla and Karl's footfalls on the steps. When Ulla came into the bedroom, I could smell something—the lake. I knew without seeing her that she was all wet.

"Ulla! You went swimming?"

"You're not asleep?"

"I was, but then I woke up a short time ago. But you went swimming, didn't you?

"Yes, it's so hot tonight."

I turned on the reading light by my bed for a moment. Her hair was soaking, but her clothes seemed dry. "What did you wear to swim in?"

"Oh, I went in my twinset," she said casually. A twinset was a camisole and undershorts. "I'm going into the bathroom to change right now." She went to the closet and got her robe and pajamas. When she came back from the bathroom, she crawled into bed.

"So what do you think of Karl?" Ulla asked.

"He's nice. Very nice."

"He's wonderful." She sighed into the night.

"Are you in love?"

"I think so," she said, a little chuckle in her voice.

It wasn't long before I heard her soft, even breathing. She was sound asleep, but not me. I still couldn't sleep. I had to get up to go to the bathroom. When I got there, I saw Ulla's twinset spread out on the towel rack. It had dripped and made a small puddle on the floor. My first thought was how could it be wet enough to make a puddle but not soak the blouse or skirt she had been wearing? I forgot about peeing and picked up the camisole from the rack. For some reason I held it up to my nose and gave it a good sniff. It didn't smell like lake water at all. The lake had a distinct odor, perhaps from the algae or the water lilies that clogged one end of it. As I listened to the soft *plip* of the water drops on the tile floor—*plip . . . plip . . . plip*—the truth dropped into my mind.

Ulla didn't wear these swimming. She swam naked! She swam naked with Karl!

Tap water! She'd soaked her underwear in the sink when she realized I was still awake, and the swimming in her twinset story wouldn't work if the twinset wasn't wet.

For the rest of the night, that was all I thought about—Ulla and Karl swimming naked in the lake, their white bodies slipping through the bronze-colored water. The pale gold sunfish slipping between their legs, the tendrils of water lilies lacing through their hair, entwining their torsos.

Ulla was a living Heinrich Heine poem.

chapter 14

The pitifulest thing out is a mob;
that's what an army is—a mob; they
don't fight with courage that's born
in them, but with courage that's borrowed from their mass, and from their
officers. But a mob without any man at
the head of it is beneath pitifulness.

—Mark Twain,
The Adventures of Huckleberry Finn

Dear Rosa,

So much to tell! I just got back from the
movie *Emil and the Detectives*. It was good,
I think. Could hardly concentrate because I
went with Ulla and Karl. And guess what?
They've done it! Not in the movie theater.
They were just holding hands during the
movie, but I couldn't help thinking about
what I had figured out the night before. You
see, Ulla said that she went swimming with

Karl. Which she did. But through my excep-
tional skills of detection—Emil has nothing
on me!—I discovered that they had gone
swimming naked. I figured it out, or rather I
sniffed it out, just by the scent of tap water in
her twinset.

She had soaked her underwear so I
would believe that she hadn't gone swimming naked. She thought she could fool
me. But hey, I didn't just fall off the turnip
wagon. They weren't trying out for the 1936
Olympics out there in the lake! I know that
swimming naked together doesn't just mean
swimming naked. They were doing more.
They were doing *it*!

I can't wait to see you. I'm coming back
to Berlin for an eye doctor appointment and
to get my hair fixed. That's another long
story. Too long to tell now.

Love,
Gaby

There was something else that was not too long to tell
but too complicated, even more complicated than swimming
naked together. But I didn't know how to explain it to Rosa.
The weather had been perfect and after the movie it

seemed too early to go home. Karl suggested that we go to the Birkenwald, the Birch Grove. It was a beer garden. And now in the first week in July, the peak of summer season, the garden was packed with holiday merrymakers. Karl ordered a lager for himself and one for Ulla, and a lemonade for me. And then he ordered the special wurst plate that had three different kinds of sausage, including my favorite, the *Bierschinken* with chunks of ham and chestnuts. It was a perfect lazy summer afternoon. Easygoing, everyone cheerful in the beer garden as if no one had a care in the world. Karl offered me a taste of his beer, which Ulla scolded him for but in a teasing way.

"Ulla," Karl said, "she's almost a young lady. I bet your parents give her *Glühwein* at Christmas."

"They give me butter grog. It's even better than *Glühwein*. Not so sweet." I thought maybe that made me seem more sophisticated.

"Of course." Karl laughed. The dimple flashed. But his eyes never changed. "And even stronger with a shot of rum."

At this moment I was very happy. I looked around. The people were all rosy, some a bit sunburned. Everyone was talking and laughing. A fresh breeze from the lake stirred the birches, their pale green leaves filtering the sun to cast an embroidery of golden light on the tables.

The waitress had just delivered our platter of sausage when I heard a very pure voice rising from the burble of talk and laughter. It was a singing voice as clear and liquid as the lake. A hush fell upon the crowd as the voice grew stronger, more beautiful, and sang with increasing passion.

> *Es braust ein Ruf wie Donnerhall,*
> *wie Schwertgeklirr und Wogenprall:*
> *Zum Rhein, zum Rhein, zum deutschen Rhein,*
> *wer will des Stromes Hüter sein?*

> A call roars like thunderbolt,
> like clashing swords and splashing waves:
> To the Rhine, the Rhine, to the German Rhine,
> who wants to be the stream's guardian?

It was coming from behind us, and everyone turned around to see who was singing. Others began to stand up and join in on the refrain.

> *Lieb' Vaterland, magst ruhig sein,*
> *Fest steht und true die Wacht am Rhein!*

> Dear Fatherland, put your mind at rest,
> Solid and staunch stands the watch on the Rhine.

Mama had told me that the song "The Watch on the Rhine" was an old patriotic anthem popular during the Franco-Prussian War more than sixty years ago and also during the Great War. The lyrics called for Germans to rush to defend the Rhine against France, to ensure that no enemy set foot on the shores of the river. It had become very popular again lately. The Nazis had brought it back. They sang it at their rallies, and it was on the radio frequently. In the new history textbooks we used last year there was even a piece about the composer and why he wrote it. The Nazis were not thinking of the Franco-Prussian War, but of the Great War and the Treaty of Versailles that had cheated Germans out of their land, their money, and their honor.

The young singer's voice sailed out above the noise of the crowd.

I had to scramble up onto the bench so I could see who the voice belonged to. The singer was now standing on a bench too, so he could be heard and seen above the crowd. I finally spotted him, a young man, his hair almost as blond as mine. *He could be my brother . . .* I thought, *except . . .* My eyes traveled down from his chiseled face. There was a Nazi armband on his sleeve. I looked around, and everyone was singing now. Their faces had changed, no longer reflections of blithe summer, but glazed with expressions of mindless rapture. I looked down at Karl, who had encircled Ulla's shoulders with one arm and my waist with the other. His face, too, was glazed as he sang and at last his storm-sealed eyes sparkled. And Ulla? She was not tall enough to see the singer's armband, but she tipped her head back just far enough to look up and see Karl's handsome face, and then she began to sing softly as well.

chapter 15

Robert Cohn was once middleweight
boxing champion of Princeton. Do not
think I am very much impressed by that
as a boxing title, but it meant a lot
to Cohn. He cared nothing for boxing,
in fact he disliked it, but he learned
it painfully and thoroughly to counter-
act the feeling of inferiority and
shyness he had felt on being treated
as a Jew at Princeton.

—Ernest Hemingway, The Sun Also Rises

Princeton! The word jumped up from the page.

"Baba, I've heard of this place, Princeton." I looked up from the chaise longue where I was reading.

"Eh?" Baba said. She was at her desk, typing. Baba was the fastest typist ever. She could type at least one hundred words a minute, according to Mama. She could not hear me over the clack of the typewriter where she was working on the next day's column, so I repeated myself.

"Princeton?" She turned around to look at me. "Very fine university. Lots of fancy people go there."

"Jews?"

"Not many." Bewilderment swam in her eyes. "*Schatzi*, darling, what are you . . . oh no!"

"What's wrong?"

"You're reading my copy of *The Sun Also Rises*?"

"Yes, I just started it. I like the way this fellow writes." I closed the book but kept my finger in the place and looked at the name. "Hemingway."

"Oh dear!"

"Don't look that way, Baba. Are you scared or something?"

"No, *Schatzi*, it's just that it is a bit . . . sophisticated."

"Sophisticated? You mean there might be sex or something?"

"Let's just leave it at the 'or something.'" Baba sighed.

I laughed.

"Baba, he must be your friend—this Ernest Hemingway. He autographed the book to you. I can see it says, 'To my dearest Baba,' but what's the rest?"

She picked up the book and read the inscription. "'To my dearest Baba. More martinis at the Ritz, etc! What a babe! Ernest.'"

Baba blushed. Then she began to sputter. "I just . . . I just think there might be some things you might not understand in the book."

"Don't worry, I'll ask you if I have any problems."

An absolutely pained look crossed her face.

"Yes, *Schatzi*, ask me. Perhaps not your mama."

"Not to worry. I'm a fast reader. I'll have it finished by the time I leave."

It was mid-July, and I was staying at Baba's apartment for a few days. After the terrible event at the Birch Grove beer garden, in which only I among that crowd seemed to have suffered, I came home and went straight to my room. I was supposed to go back to Berlin for a few days with Ulla and Karl that Monday. Mama of course wanted me to have my hair styled, and I was to go to the eye doctor to be fitted for spectacles. Now I couldn't wait to get away. It was even hard for me to get through the rest of the weekend with Ulla and Karl. I tried to call Rosa on the telephone before I left, but there was no answer. I wanted to talk to her about what had happened.

It was as if in a few weeks between the episode in the bakery and the one in the beer garden my idyllic summer world had crashed in on me. It reminded me of what I felt when Rosa and I saw the awful SA man with the crawling insect eyes on the Kurfürstendamm that day we went to the zoo. I felt contaminated by the beer garden, by the people who sang "The Watch on the Rhine," and more especially by Karl and Ulla. Although Karl did not wear an armband, I could see that there was something not right with him even if she couldn't. But I wasn't sure how to tell her this. And would it help? Perhaps love had made her blind.

The plan had been for me to drive back to Berlin with

Karl and Ulla and stay with Baba. But I didn't want to drive in the same car with them, so I pretended to be sick on that Monday morning when they left. I was quite an expert at faking illness. I pretended a sore throat, and the night before I started talking in my scratchy-throat voice. So instead of going back on Monday I was permitted to take the commuter train by myself on Wednesday, once I had "recovered." It wasn't a long ride—less than an hour. Baba met me at the station in Berlin. I was looking forward to staying with her. I always had fun with Baba, and she said that she would take me to some tea parties and maybe even a luncheon, but first I would have my hair cut and get some proper clothes. I had arrived in a summer pullover top and my culottes with little else in my small valise, much to Baba's horror. But Mama had written a bank draft for Baba so she could buy me some new clothes. I refused to take cash, reminding Mama that this was exactly how Emil in *Emil and the Detectives* had met with disaster when he fell asleep on the train and was robbed. The moral of the story, and the last line of the book, was Emil's grandmother shaking her finger and saying, "Never send cash. Always use a money order."

Monsieur Marc at the Salon de Paris, who was no more French than I was but affected an accent that he thought sounded French and claimed to have learned haircutting from some famous Parisian coiffeuse, gave me a wonderful haircut. It felt as if I were wearing a sleek little cap. The best part was my fringe. No longer did my bangs just hang squarely over my eyebrows, but they had been cut at an angle so that they swept to one side.

"Charmante! Charmante!" Monsieur Marc kept exclaiming, rising on to his tiptoes as he snipped away the final uneven tatters and sculpted what remained into a gleaming golden cap that was snug as a ski hat on my head, but much more stylish. When Baba came back to pick me up, she slapped her hand against her pink cheek exclaiming, "Adorable! You look like a little gamine. Now we must find a suitable dress for the luncheon and the tea tomorrow."

From the hairdresser we went to Baba's office at the *Vossiche Zeitung* so she could deliver her column. A man with a green visor and black sleeve protectors to keep his sleeves clean from the ink rushed out of his office.

"Baba, a call came in. Can you squeeze in a reception this evening? Countess von der Gröeben's entertaining in Charlottenburg. They say the Empress Hermine will be attending." He crooked both his index fingers into to the air when he said the word "empress." Many people, including Baba, referred to Kaiser Wilhelm's second wife, Hermine Reuss, as the Quotation Empress, for as the second wife, who married him after he abdicated, she had never officially been the empress of anything, but she insisted on her title being recognized. Apparently no one liked her much. They felt that she was a fraud.

"*Mein Gott*, Wilfried!" Baba sighed. Wilfried was Baba's editor. "Yes, of course. At least they have a good chef. You'll like the pastries, Gaby." She turned back to Wilfried. "So, anything else?"

"Rumors that Papen might be laying the groundwork for Hindenburg to receive"—he dropped his voice—"the corporal."

"Yes, I caught wind of that. Mammi called and said that she's heard Papen might have to start preparing him to meet the Old Gentleman." Mammi was an old friend of Baba's and an invaluable source for gossip.

"'Preparing him'?" Wilfried said.

"Yes, Hitler's an uncouth barbarian. His parlor decorum leaves something to be desired. Trying to picture him sipping tea with Hindenburg strains the imagination."

"Yes, well . . . bound to happen. What with the July thirty-first election coming." Wilfried sighed and shut his eyes tight. The green visor cast a sickish wedge of light over the top half of his face.

"Well, Gaby." Baba sighed. "Quite a week you arrived for. We'd better go straightaway and buy you some clothes and get you rigged out. Some social life we have here in Berlin. You might be seeing history in the making."

"Let's hope not," Wilfried said. His expression was flat.

As Baba and I approached the shining brass door of the Wertheim Department Store in Leipziger Platz, I noticed two SA men posted at the entrance. One stepped forward and said to Baba, "Do you know that this is a Jewish-owned business?"

Baba blinked then drew herself up to her full height, which was not much, but she certainly no longer reminded me of a pastry puff.

"Do I know? Of course I know. I dated both the Wertheim brothers." The SA officers' mouths dropped open. Baba sailed through the door as if she were Field Marshal Hindenburg himself, fresh from the glorious victory at Tannenburg. I cast a glance over my shoulder as I followed her. The SA officers were still looking at her in wonder. I wouldn't have been surprised if they had saluted. You see, they were trained to respond to great displays of authority, and Baba, despite her small stature, had a bearing that could on occasion be considered indisputably authoritarian.

We went immediately to the dress department on the third floor, where a lady in a black dress with an elaborately arranged handkerchief pinned to her bosom glided up to us.

"May I help you ladies?" She seemed pleased and relieved to see us, for the floor was empty of customers. There was an eerie silence.

"Yes, we need a dress or two for this lovely young lady," Baba said. "She is expected to attend a reception this evening at the Countess von der Groeben's and then tomorrow we shall need something for a luncheon and a tea at the Adlon." I looked at Baba. "Oh yes, and I nearly forgot, nothing sailorish." I had warned Baba that at the age of thirteen I was too old for those babyish sailor-suit dresses that people often put their children in beyond a reasonable age.

"She's not in the navy, after all," Baba said good-naturedly. "We don't even have a navy." Then, under her breath, she whispered, "God willing."

I knew what Baba was thinking. After the Great War, one of the most important terms of the Treaty of Versailles was that Germany disarm. No armies, no navies, no air force. Neither the SA nor the SS was in fact considered an army. They were just the staff guard, or *stabswache*, of the Nazi Party.

The saleslady began to bring out dresses. In a fancy store like Wertheim one did not simply shop off the racks.

"Too dirndl-ish," I said when she held up one with lacings up the front and a frilly, square-neck collar. "No pinafores!" I announced as she brought out the next. "But it's very pretty," I added when Baba gave me a sharp look. "I don't want bows, either," I leaned over and whispered to Baba when the lady went back to fetch more dresses.

Finally the saleslady seemed to understand my taste. She came out with a soft gray dress in what Baba called a "crepe georgette" fabric. It was cut on the bias, at an angle to the grain of the fabric. I could tell this immediately by the drape, for the skirt fell beautifully, at least on the hanger. And luckily when I tried it on in the dressing room, it fit perfectly. It was the most grown-up dress I had ever worn.

I just loved it, and both Baba and the saleslady marveled at how becoming it looked on me.

"All right! That is perfect for the reception this evening at Countess von der Groeben's. Now for tomorrow, something transitional. Perhaps a little suit with a jacket to be worn at luncheon and then the jacket removed for the tea."

"I have just the thing, Madame," the saleslady said.

This time it only took one try. The saleslady was back with a slim, willowy blue dress with what was called a gored skirt that flared just slightly and a cropped jacket. "Cropped" apparently meant chopped, as in chopped off just above the waistline. Baba worried that it was a bit too old-looking for me. But the saleslady kept saying, "*Nein nein* . . . look at that chic hairdo she's got." Then another saleslady came over and clapped her hands together and said, "*Oh la la!*" So Baba succumbed. I was so excited. I couldn't wait to get home to change into my new clothes for the reception.

As soon as we walked in the door of Baba's apartment, the telephone was ringing. Baba rushed to answer it.

"Ah, Rosa! She will be thrilled to hear from you. . . . Yes . . . she's right here."

I *was* thrilled.

"What? Your grandmother? Is she all right? . . . Did you get my letter? You'll read it when it gets there, but I have so much to tell you!" I lowered my voice so Baba wouldn't hear.

Rosa and I made a plan. I would stay over at her apartment on Saturday, when her mother stayed upstairs with her grandmother, and then she would return to Caputh with me the following day.

The newspaper sent a driver to pick up Baba and me for the reception at the Countess's home in Charlottenburg, one of the very fancy suburbs west of the city center. In the car Baba reviewed with me the cast of characters I was about to meet.

"Now, I'll introduce you as my best friend's daughter, and how about I say you are my summer assistant as well? You'll meet everyone, since everyone wants to get their name in my column. Be prepared to look and listen. I'll need descriptions of what they wear, where they've been, fashionable spas they've visited, cabarets they've attended, and the like. So you must be my extra eyes and ears, Gaby. You remember the pictures I showed you at the news office today?"

I nodded.

"Well the countess is obvious. She's eighty-five, but her wits are as sharp as anyone's. She has impeccable manners. Her hair is an unfortunate tint of violet, but that aside she is charming. The Quotation Empress is really quite vile. She will do anything to get her husband reinstated as kaiser. Let's see now, who else? Well, I showed you the news clippings with the pictures of Magda Goebbels—a real beauty, but she doesn't know how to dress. Let's hope her husband's not there. Really an obnoxious man. Oh, but the Americans! Let's hope there are lots of Americans—they are wonderful. Percy Black and Sherwood Eddy. Wonderful sportsman, Percy, very handsome. And the latter, Sherwood, a wonderful humanitarian. Brilliant speaker. Slightly bald." Baba's running commentary on the beautiful, the powerful, the rich, the mighty, the fakes and the imposters, the greedy and the stupid went on nonstop until we arrived. I was so excited. I was going to a very sophisticated party in a very sophisticated dress. I didn't feel thirteen, I felt at least fifteen and maybe even sixteen!

The countess's house was grand. It looked like a palace. With its gray stucco, which matched my dress, and all sorts of decorative plaster, it reminded me of a wedding cake, except of course for the color. As soon as we walked in, people rushed to say hello to Baba. She led me over to meet the countess.

"It is so nice to see a young face," the countess said graciously as she nodded at me. Then with a twinkle in her bright blue eyes she continued, "And with a bit of a sunburned nose, I see. Have you been having a fun beach holiday?"

"Yes, madame." I curtseyed as Baba had instructed. "At Caputh."

"Ah, Caputh! Did you see my dear friend Professor Einstein there?"

"Yes, Madame, he lives next door."

"Oh, how delightful, and who did you say this charming girl's parents are?" she said, turning to Baba.

"Her father is the astronomer Otto Schramm."

"Ah yes, of course! Astronomer, not astrologer?"

"Astrologer?" I almost gasped.

"Yes, my dear." She had a tinkly laugh. "Did you not hear that Herr Hitler employs one by the name of Hanussen? Yes, Jan Hanussen. Hitler's favorite prophet." She lifted her chin sharply. "Ah, the empress!"

An imposing woman had just arrived. She wore a sash that ran diagonally over her shoulder and down the front of the bodice with several medallions and jewels. I tried to remember as many details of her dress as I could so I would be able to help Baba with her column. I understood exactly now why Baba and many others called her the Quotation Empress. No real empress would bother outside of court with all that imperial frosting.

"Your Highness," the countess said loudly, "how good of you to attend my little gathering." The countess, dressed chicly and simply in an elegant gown of chiffon with three strands of pearls, was an eloquent statement in contrast to the encrusted "empress."

"Now, I have been told, Your Highness, that your sympathies are with the National Socialists. Is it true that His Majesty has made a donation to Herr Hitler's party?"

The Quotation Empress stood perfectly still. A deathly

pallor turned her face as gray as my dress. She did not answer the countess's question, and it seemed as though an ominous silence descended upon the room. The countess finally broke the long silence. "Oh, do have some champagne. I think it's awfully good. Veuve Clicquot, of course!"

Almost immediately waiters appeared with new trays of filled champagne flutes. There was the clink of glasses as guests wished one another well and a cheerful fizz of talk as conversations were resumed.

The next afternoon found us first at a luncheon and then at a tea at the Adlon Hotel, Berlin's fanciest. Baba knew all the people there, starting with the doormen, then the concierge, the waiters, and of course the manager. I felt quite stylish in my blue gored dress. I had removed the jacket after the luncheon as Baba had suggested.

"*Guten Tag*, Frau Blumenthal," they all said as we passed by.

"My God, has this place turned into the Kaiserhof, or what?" Baba muttered. The Kaiserhof was the official Nazi hotel where Hitler always stayed when he was in Berlin. The brown sea of SA men milling about in the enormous lobby of the Adlon Hotel was punctuated by the black uniforms of the SS officers. Many seemed to be sporting a little smudge of a mustache in the style of Hitler. Some called it the toothbrush mustache, for it was no bigger than the clump of bristles used for brushing one's teeth.

"Oh dear, that dreadful man!" Baba whispered. An officer was making his way toward her. He stopped right in front of her and bowed. "Count Helldorf, what a surprise," she said, attempting levity. Perhaps I was the only one who detected a slight strain in her voice.

"Ah, no surprise, madame. I'm here for the tea. Yes, and my wife's over there." He nodded. "She is wearing a Worth gown, direct from Paris."

"Ah! How elegant!" Baba exclaimed. "There is nothing like French couture, particularly Worth. So goes our watch on the Rhine!"

I nearly gasped. What in the world had Baba just said? Was this a joke she was making? A very dangerous one, if it was.

"Are you suggesting, madame, that my wife is less than patriotic because she crosses the Rhine to buy French couture?" He turned around to the few people who were standing nearby and had overheard this exchange. "Don't tell me that now the Versailles treaty forbids not only arms but fashion."

"I am not suggesting any such thing at all, dear Count, but rather that in matters of fashion there are no borders. It only requires taste, sense of style, and well, of course, money. Now, let me alert the photographer from my newspaper that a picture must be taken of your wife and I shall get the details of the dress from her myself. It's silk faille, I believe."

The count chuckled now. "Oh, that is woman's business. I wouldn't know such things. Please go ask her."

Baba whisked me away as I marveled how she had averted what could have been a real disaster. Her fingers dug into my arm.

"Idiot," she murmured. "All of them. These Nazis, they worm their way into everything." She had lowered her voice and was whispering behind the small notebook she carried. "According to my sources, who shall go unnamed, Helldorf is one of the worst. He's responsible for all sorts of Jew baiting. I'll bet you anything he was behind those two SA in front of Wertheims."

Baba stopped as we made our way to a bay in the lobby, where a long table had been set up with several immense silver tea urns and tiered platters of pastries. Several people, including many SA and SS officers, were gathered around the table balancing teacups on saucers with petit fours.

"Look at them all. And to think six months ago when they were banned they didn't dare wear their uniforms in public. Now they're a virtual sea of brown and black, and their ladies all decked out, most of them atrociously except the few who crossed the Rhine into France for French couture!"

Countess Helldorf approached us, and Baba put a big smile on her face.

"Ah, Countess Helldorf. This is not Charles Worth

but . . ." Baba was scanning the countess up and down with admiring eyes.

"No. House of Lanvin. Whoever said it was Charles Worth?"

"Your darling husband. But what do husbands know?" Baba laughed gaily. "I must get your picture." Baba turned. "Fritz! Fritzi, over here." She waved to a man who carried a Leica camera with a coiled wire attached to a folding fan flash.

"Ah, look happy!" Fritzi said to us. "Say *Zweibeln*." *Zweibeln*—onions? But it did make one's mouth stretch into a smile. So we all laughed and the flash fired and a galaxy of light burst in front of me. For a few seconds there were no Brown Shirts, no black-clad SS. Just white exploding light. It was as if the sky was falling down.

chapter 16

We see men living with their skulls
blown open; we see soldiers run with
their two feet cut off. . . . We
see men without mouths, without jaws,
without faces. . . .

—Erich Maria Remarque,
All Quiet on the Western Front

"Is the 'E' right side up or upside down?"

"Upside down I think."

"All right, now tell me the lowest line on the chart
you can read?"

"F-E-L-O-P-Z-D."

"And now is that sharper or not?"

I was at the ophthalmologist's office, Dr. Feininger's. He
was Papa's eye doctor, too.

"Well, my dear, the good news is that you are not nearly
as nearsighted as your papa, but he seems to do pretty well
even so with his stargazing. However, you do need to wear
spectacles for reading, especially in school for seeing the
blackboard. So now you get to do the fun part and pick out
a pair of frames. My assistant will help you."

It wasn't that much fun, for the selection was very limited. I could have spectacles with no frames, just the glass lenses. Or I could have ones with silver, gold, or black thin wire frames. The shape could be round or rectangular. Rosa had come along to help me decide. She loved my haircut and of course had come up with the perfect fashion touch.

"You must wear scarves around your neck. Scarves will set off the shape of your head with this new hairdo. Very chic!"

I had protested that it was too hot to wear a scarf. But Rosa shut her eyes tightly as if she had delivered this lecture a thousand times. "On occasion one has to suffer for beauty. What's a little heat?"

All I could think of was the famous dancer Isadora Duncan, who a few short years back had died when her long flowing scarf was caught in the wheel of an automobile. That was suffering. It was a story that had entranced Ulla, and since I was always captivated by anything my older sister was interested in, I started reading all the news stories about her too. It had all the elements of drama and tragedy that engaged us. But it was a high price to pay for glamour.

Rosa and I looked at the spectacles in the case. "There would be more of a selection," I whispered, "if I were missing an eye." The case next to the one with the spectacles contained a huge variety of glass eyes. It was well known that Dr. Feininger carried the best glass eyes in the city. After the Great War it was said that nearly one-fifth of the returning soldiers were amputees or had lost some body part: arms, legs, and eyes. Yes, many had lost eyes. One saw these maimed veterans of the war in the streets all the time. In Dr. Feininger's window he still had a sign, now almost fifteen years after the war ended, that announced that he provided reduced rates and easy, no-interest payment plans for war veterans.

The assistant came out and I began trying on different frames. It was a lot easier than choosing my two new dresses. I settled on black wire frames with round lenses.

"You don't think I look too owlish?" I asked Rosa.

"No. Not at all. Intelligent but not birdlike. *Très chic.*"

The spectacles would be ready by the time school started. We had just walked out the door when Rosa screamed, "Watch it!"

A splatter of red paint accidentally hit her legs. Two thuggish looking young boys were crouched by the curb. They laughed and took their paint can and started running. On the wall of the building they had painted a swastika.

We knew about the painting squads, gangs of roughnecks who went out at night defacing Jewish businesses and public buildings with swastikas and signs that screamed WE WANT HITLER or HEIL HITLER. But I had never heard of them doing this in the day.

"In broad daylight!" I exclaimed. "I can't believe it."

"Why not?" said a woman walking by with her schnauzer on a leash. "He's a Jew doctor."

Rosa and I turned and looked at each other in dismay.

The boys were thugs, but this lady was well dressed. She wore a hat with a veil and white gloves. She could have been my mother or Rosa's, out to meet a friend for lunch at Ciro's. It seemed like she should know better, but beneath those nice clothes I felt she was as thuggish as the boys. Once again I thought of Hertha rolling out that pie crust so calmly while the radio blared the news about the destruction of the synagogue. How many Herthas are out there, and how many well-dressed ladies who would never think of leaving their houses without their gloves and veiled hats, but who think that with Hitler there might be a chance? Or, as Hessie said, how many are tired of being losers, feeling shamed by the Treaty of Versailles, and desperately need someone to blame—Jews! How easy.

On the way back to Rosa's apartment we stopped at mine so I could pick up some books Mama wanted me to bring to Caputh. I told Rosa I would find some turpentine to get the paint off her leg.

As we approached our building I suddenly remembered that I would have to see our concierge, Herr Himmel—"Mr. Hell."

I had hardly reached the front stoop of our building when he slithered out. "Ah Fräulein Gabrielle—back from summer holiday so soon."

"No, Herr Himmel, I'm just here to pick something up. I am going right back to Caputh." I didn't feel he merited the details of my staying with Rosa. But of course, how could I not have anticipated he would want to share some gossipy details with me?

"Well, I guess you're too young to keep an eye on that sister of yours. Not that it would do any good."

One eyebrow hitched up, and his eyes slid down and to one side in a suspicious glance. The left eye seemed to crowd even closer to that vertical ridge of his anvil face. But there was something different about his appearance.

"Ah!" His eyes were suddenly merry. "You noticed!" He touched the bristly smudge under his nose, the toothbrush-shaped mustache just like Hitler's. And just like those men at the tea Baba had taken me to.

"Noticed what?" I said, and rushed through the door.

"I don't think your sister has spent an hour here all summer." Rosa stood in the middle of the living room and looked about. There was indeed a strangeness as we entered the apartment. Even though Ulla was living there, Mama had covered much of the furniture in the parlor and the music room with summer drapery cloths to protect it from dust and sun. It was as if the air itself had not stirred since the day we all left.

"Didn't she ever open a shade or a curtain?" I whispered. The entire apartment was swallowed in a dim half light. The whole reason Mama had put on the covers was so Ulla would be able to open the shades. I didn't understand. I went into the music room. Ulla's violin case was on a table covered with a thick layer of dust. I ran a finger over it, making a trail across the top. She couldn't have opened it or practiced once all summer. *So much for Vienna*, I thought. Her audition for the conservatory would be coming up in the fall. If she didn't practice, I didn't know how she would get accepted.

Corners and bookshelves dissolved into murky shadows. The only signs of life were in Ulla's bedroom. Clothes were tossed about carelessly. If Ulla was living here at all it must have been mostly in the bedroom, I thought. I went into the bathroom. Rosa came in a minute later.

"What are you staring at?" she asked

I looked around at her slowly. "He's spitting in our basin."

"What are you talking about?" Rosa said, confusion swimming in her eyes.

I nodded toward a toothbrush I had never seen before. "That's his."

"Whose? Karl's?" she asked.

"Yes, who else's?" I snapped. It was as if all the anger that had been pent up in me about Karl and Ulla suddenly sprang up.

I hadn't told Rosa yet about the beer garden. I was ashamed. At first I had wanted to tell her, but then I realized I didn't want anyone to know how I felt about what I saw, not even Rosa. It was one thing talking about them having sex, but the beer garden was something else. What if she didn't think it was so wrong that Karl joined in the singing? It was, in a way, a perfectly innocent song about a nation that had lost a war to its perpetual enemy, France, decades ago, merely vowing to keep a watchful eye on the Rhine. It was not a song of hatred. And yet just as the perfectly good word *Volk* had been transformed and begun to acquire a loaded meaning, so had the song "The Watch on the Rhine." There were undercurrents of vengeance, a veiled threat of domination. Ulla had sung the song, too. But Ulla hadn't been standing on a bench like me. She had been too low to see the swastika on the young singer's sleeve. Maybe she hadn't really noticed that sparkle in Karl's eyes. And if she had, maybe she hadn't thought anything of it. But I had.

"Let's get out of here," I said.

"Gaby, what is it?" Rosa asked.

"I don't want to talk about it."

I went into the music room and got the books that Mama wanted. We left before I could even look for the turpentine.

We didn't talk all the way back to Rosa's apartment building. Then I began to feel a little guilty about my mood and how short I had been with her.

"Look," I said, "why don't we go to the movies tonight."

"Helmut doesn't work at the theater anymore."

"Oh no! Too bad." I noticed a funny look cross her face. "What is it?"

"I was going to tell you earlier but it seemed like you didn't want to talk about your sister."

"What? Tell me."

"He's working at that cabaret where she is the bookkeeper—the Chameleon."

"You're kidding!"

"No! And he can get us in."

"Into a cabaret?"

Rosa nodded.

"Oooh!"

"Want to go tonight? He said we can sit way in the back and watch the show. It's supposed to be very funny. We can go out late. Mama's staying over with grandma two floors above us. She will never know. They always are in bed sound asleep by ten."

"I absolutely want to go! What'll we wear?" I knew that my beautiful new dresses were not right for a cabaret.

"Leave it to me, your fashion consultant. I'll figure out something."

chapter 17

Do you know the land where cannons are
in bloom?
You don't? You're going to!

—Erich Kästner,
"Do You Know the Land Where Cannons Are in Bloom"

"Look at her! Look at that skirt, it's so short. You can see her bottom," Rosa said. It was Ulla's bottom!

"Nothing compared to what you're going to see onstage," Helmut said. He was the maître d'. He wore a cutaway jacket much fancier than his usher outfit at the movie theater, and his job mainly was to seat people and direct a waiter to take their drink orders.

Rosa and I were tucked into a tiny table in the farthest corner of the Chameleon. We were both wearing dark berets, black stockings that Rosa had borrowed from her mother's bureau, and dark skirts of her mother's that, with the help of belts and pins Rosa had refashioned to make shorter and a bit tighter. Over this we wore long, loose, jacket-style sweaters that buttoned down the front. We didn't look exactly fashionable but we didn't look like schoolgirls, either. We dissolved into the shadows, and Helmut promised us that Ulla would not see us. But we certainly saw Ulla. She was dressed in a very short skirt with black net stockings. She wore a sparkling sequin halter top. Her hair was piled up high and had a white plumy feather sticking out. She wore absolutely tons of makeup.

"I wonder how she keeps the books in that getup!" I muttered. She, of course, was not keeping books at all. She was the cigarette girl, passing through the tables with a tray that was filled with packs of cigarettes to sell to the customers.

"She actually does do the bookkeeping in the morning." Helmut seemed at pains to somehow show us that Ulla was more than a scantily clad purveyor of cigarettes.

I shrugged. "Makes no difference to me," I said, trying to appear detached. But it was a little disturbing thinking about how she had lied to all of us. I mean, even if she really was keeping books, it was still a lie of omission. She conveniently left out the scanty costume part.

"And as I said, you'll soon see that there are many girls with less clothing," Helmut said, perhaps trying to make me feel better about my half-naked sister.

I shrugged again but said nothing.

The lights dimmed now, and there was a metallic smear

of cymbals crashing. A spotlight struck the center of the curtain. The master of ceremonies, Max Weltmann, peeked out from behind the curtain, almost shyly.

"This is his style," Helmut leaned over and whispered to us. "He always delivers his opening monologue partially hidden. But he is very funny, quick . . . he has a sly wit."

"Ladies and gentlemen—a poem, if you please, about the glories and glitter of lost wars, but triumphs none the less. This poem, set to music, is by Erich Kästner."

"Erich Kästner?" I gasped. "The same?"

"Yes, the author of *Emil and the Detectives*!" Helmut replied.

This is going to be fun! I thought. A clarinet began to play, and Max Weltmann's voice looped out into the smoke-curled darkness of the cabaret.

"Do you know the land where cannons are in bloom? You don't? You're going to!"

The song went on to describe business executives in their fine suits, but beneath, they wore soldiers' armor. To me, it all seemed to be a sly reference to the growing belligerence and military spirit in Germany.

When he finished singing the crowd roared its approval. But I was astonished. I looked at Helmut.

"You're right. He is sly. That was . . ."

"Subversive? Is that the word you're looking for?"

"I guess so." For the whole poem that Max Weltmann had sung was a parody of one of the most famous poems in the German language that everyone knew, a song sung by Goethe's Mignon. To use these almost sacred lines as a humorous ditty sung in a cabaret was truly subversive!

I thought back on my last three days in Berlin: There were the two SA men at the department store, then the "empress" at the countess's reception who was said to contribute money to the Nazi Party, followed by Count Helldorf at the tea, and finally the thugs painting the swastika outside Dr. Feininger's office. I glanced over at Ulla. She was on the other side of the room. Suddenly her risqué costume didn't bother me in the least, nor the fact that she had lied about parts of her job. In fact, it seemed rather courageous of her to be working in this subversive club.

"Do SA officers come here?" I asked Helmut.

"Not very often. And if they do, half the time they don't get what Max is saying."

"Oh good lord, look at that!" Rosa nudged me. The curtain had risen to reveal a dazzling human replica of the Brandenburg Gate, Germany's patriotic symbol, which was located just west of Berlin's center and one block south of the Reichstag, at the beginning of the avenue Unter den Linden. The gate seethed triumph and was the embodiment of all that was glorious in German history. On its top was the quadriga, the four-horse chariot that was raced in the ancient Olympic Games, with the goddess of victory driving it.

The replica also had a quadriga, but there was one difference: The goddess driving it was completely naked, as were her attendants, except for a few strategically placed leaves below their waists. Helmut had been right. Ulla in comparison was as well clad as an Eskimo on a dogsled run.

Though this was my first-ever cabaret experience, I had a feeling that what Rosa and I were seeing was the most slyly anti-patriotic show in Berlin. One didn't have to listen that carefully to the lyrics of the song to see that they mocked Germany's obsession with military power. And the words certainly hinted at the mounting militarism with that line about the land where the cannons bloom. I looked over at Ulla, who was just now selling a pack of cigarettes to a bearded gentleman. As she walked away from him, I could see her face quite clearly. I could see creases at the corners of her mouth as she smiled. Little crinkles of pleasure at her new independence perhaps, her new daring life in this subversive café? A small curved line punctuated each corner of her mouth like quotation marks. But Ulla, unlike the Empress Hermine, was no quotation girl. I felt a sudden twinge—pride. I was proud of her working here. But did everyone realize how subversive this was? Did Karl?

We didn't stay long. But part of me wanted to remain, wanted to tell Ulla that I thought her working here was not bad even if she wore a skimpy costume and did more than just keep the books. I wanted her to know that I understood the sophisticated humor of Max Weltmann. But I thought, not now. Later. Her boss might get angry that her little sister and her little sister's friend were hanging about. So Rosa and I walked out into the night. Although it was late, it was not very dark. It was the kind of night filled with the fuzzy gray light that Papa found maddening. Warm and humid rags of mist floated up from the river Spree.

We had turned down an alley when suddenly Rosa grabbed my arm. Directly ahead was a gang of young men with paintbrushes.

"Another painting squad!" I whispered. We turned to go the other way, but now behind us, seemingly out of that gray mist, three more figures appeared.

"Hello, Fräulein." One boy had already dipped his brush into a bucket he had set down, and he began painting the first arm of the swastika on a brick wall. "Want to help?"

We shook our heads. "We have to get home," Rosa whispered hoarsely.

"*Nein*, sister," another boy said, coming up and pulling on a curl of Rosa's that stuck out from under her beret. "You ain't going no place. I think you need to help the Führer."

"He doesn't need our help," I said softly.

Yet another boy came up, a taller one. "Come on, Egon. Let 'em go. They're just kids. We got a lot more work tonight."

Egon took a step closer. His eyes were like blue slits. His skin was as gray as the night air. His face looked like a mask, the mouth a slot. It was as if there might be another face behind this one. "Say it, sister."

"Say what?" I asked.

"Say it!" The others pressed in on us.

The slot opened to reveal square yellow teeth with large spaces between them. And then the arm shot out, the palm flat. "Heil Hitler!" The two words tore the darkness. Rosa's arm and mine immediately sprang upward.

"Heil Hitler," we called. The words stumbled out of our mouths. And we ran into fog-thick air of the Berlin night.

chapter 18

> That was morality; things that made
> you disgusted afterward. No, that
> must be immorality.
>
> —Ernest Hemingway, The Sun Also Rises

I am standing naked now in the murky light of the alley.
Scraps of fog swirl around me. I try to grab something,
anything, to cover my chest, but the mask in front of me,
suspended in the mist, just laughs, opening its mouth wider and
wider until I can see all the square yellow teeth.

"Heil Hitler!" it screams, and the words ricochet from the slot.
The mask's slit eyes stretch open and become round holes. One eye
suddenly pops out. I watch transfixed as it hits the pavement and
begins to roll toward a storm sewer.

"Meine Auge, my eye, meine Auge, my eye. Meine Gla-
sauge! My glass eye!" The mask contorts in fear, not rage. Like
a baby it wails. I want to comfort it as one would a toddler with
a broken toy. I want to pick it up and cuddle and kiss it. I am so
ashamed.

I woke up from my nightmare shocked and trembling. I
looked over at the twin bed where Rosa slept. I hoped I had

not cried out. I wondered if Rosa was having nightmares too. We had not talked about the incident in the alley when we got home, and except for one time, neither Rosa nor I would ever mention that night again.

We had taken baths when we returned to Rosa's apartment. Luckily there was no sign of her mother. She was still upstairs at Rosa's grandmother's apartment. But now I wanted to take another one. I felt dirty. I wondered if it would wake Rosa up if I ran the water. The bathroom was down the hall. She might not hear it. I decided to try.

As I lay in the cool water of the tub, I wondered about my dream. Why was I naked in that alley? Was it something to do with the naked girls in the cabaret? But their nudity hadn't seemed bad when I saw them onstage in that living tableau of the Brandenburg Gate. It didn't seem dirty or shameful, just clever, although I would never want to stand up that way on a stage or even wear that scanty little skirt of Ulla's. Why in the name of God was I always feeling ashamed?

When I got out of the bathtub, I went into the parlor of the apartment and found a piece of writing paper. I began to list those terrible moments in recent weeks when I had felt dirty or shameful. Thus began my Diary of Shame. At this point it was just a piece of paper, but when I got back to Caputh I planned to copy it into a notebook.

The first item was the day on the Kurfürstendamm when the SA officer had called Rosa a vamp. He hadn't called *me* a

vamp, and yet I felt ashamed for some reason. The second—
well, here is my list.

1) SA officer on Kurfürstendamm
2) Beer garden in Caputh when boy sings "The
   Watch on the Rhine"—K's eyes
3) U doing it with K
4) K's spitting in our basin; K's toothbrush
5) "Heil Hitler" in the alley; alley dream. Paint
   squad boy

And after the list I wrote this: *I feel as though I am seeing
things I shouldn't see. I feel that somehow I have stumbled into
the wrong place, the wrong world. I am a peeper, a voyeur. . .*

Rosa came back with me the next day to Caputh. She was
going to be able to stay for a while. This was good news
for Rosa and me and also for Rosa's mother, who would be
busy taking care of Rosa's grandmother.

We took the noon train from the Alexanderplatz station. The train was always packed with people during
the summer, and that day was no exception. We were in
Caputh in time for lunch. Before we even walked into the
dining room, I heard a voice, a high, shouting, strained
voice. It was Hitler on the radio. When we came in, I saw
that Uncle Hessie was there. No one greeted us, as they
were all listening intently to the radio broadcast. Papa

raised his finger to his lips. Mama had a grim look on her face. I went up to kiss her.

"Hardly good for the digestion," she muttered, nodding at the radio.

"Unfortunately our radio seems to be able to pick up a station we don't ordinarily get."

"Which station?" I asked.

"It must be from southern Germany, near Munich or maybe even Austria. He's so popular there. I doubt Berlin would put him on . . . at least, not yet!"

"Shush! Elske," Papa said.

"Nothing new here. Heard it all before," Hessie said in a scathing whisper.

Rosa and I sat down. Hitler's voice was so loud that even the water in the glasses seemed to tremble.

"Can't we lower the volume?" Mama hissed at Papa. She was clearly angry at Hitler for dominating our lunch. Mama thought mealtimes should be peaceful affairs; she never liked to have the radio on when we were eating. Papa held up a finger as if to say just a minute more. Now the voice was almost screaming.

"That conclusion is forced upon us if we look at the world today: We have a number of nations which through their inborn outstanding worth have fashioned for themselves a mode of life which stands in no relation to the living space—the Lebensraum—which in their thickly populated settlements they inhabit." Then there was a staticky sound, obliterating his shrill voice. Mama

was about ready to jump up and turn off the radio when the broadcast became clear again. I noticed that the door to the kitchen was open just a crack and I could see a narrow slice of Hertha's face. She was so still, it was if she was hardly breathing.

"In an era when the Earth is gradually being divided up among states, some of which embrace almost entire continents, we cannot speak of a world power in connection with a formation whose political mother country is limited to the absurd area of five hundred thousand square kilometers. . . . We must hold unflinchingly to our aim . . . to secure for the German people the land and soil to which they are entitled to on this Earth."

I caught another glimpse of Hertha. A slight smile played across the wedge of her face just as Hitler spoke of securing the land for the German people. I felt something turn in my stomach.

Papa now jumped up from the table and turned off the radio.

"Thank God, Otto!" Mama exclaimed.

"I knew it, Hessie. What did I tell you?" Papa sat back down. His eyes were hard. I had honestly never seen such bitterness in my father's face.

"Knew what, Papa?" I asked.

"Lebensraum, living space. He goes on about it constantly in *Mein Kampf."*

Hessie picked up his napkin and patted his lips almost primly. Then he carefully put it back in his lap. "I hate to tell you, Otto, but businessmen like those in Düsseldorf love Hitler. Who do you think arranged the Düsseldorf speech?"

"Who?" Papa asked.

"The steel magnate Thyssen, and Krupp, and many others. They are all financing Hitler. They think he's good for business."

"Fools." Papa nearly spat in his soup plate.

"But what does he mean by living space? He doesn't think there's enough room?" I asked.

"Exactly," Papa replied.

"Hmmm . . ." I said, studying my napkin. Then I looked up and smiled. "Why doesn't he go talk to Professor Einstein?"

"Why in heaven's name?" Mama said.

"The universe is expanding. There's definitely room for everyone," I replied.

At this they all burst out laughing, even Papa.

It had been raining when Rosa and I arrived in Caputh, and it continued for the next few days. Papa seemed distracted during this time. He went over to Einstein's sometimes as often as twice in one day. On the morning before Hessie went back to Berlin it was still raining, and I saw Hessie and Mama hunched under an umbrella, taking a lakefront walk. I think maybe Mama was telling him something—worries about Papa, the university maybe, Jewish physics. I wasn't sure.

The rain was a great disappointment not simply because swimming and sailing were out of the question but also because Rosa and I were eager to wear the new bathing suits we had bought at Wertheim earlier that spring, which we thought were quite glamorous. Rosa's was a wonderful aquamarine and mine was a deep pink. Most bathing suits were rather dreary colors. Ours were not the usual flannel or cotton but were made of a very sleek material and with shoulder straps that could be let down for tanning if the sun ever appeared again. But because of the bad weather we pranced around in them inside the house. Papa, who had to test some film, even took a picture of us scampering around on the lawn when the rain let up one day. We looked a bit idiotic, for it was cold and we were hugging each other to keep warm. Professor Einstein was off to one side in the picture, laughing at us.

Mostly during this rainy spell Rosa and I devoted ourselves to preparing for the new school term. We were excited about the new curriculum, the library, and most of all about Fräulein Hofstadt.

"You know," I said, "Ulla told me that Fräulein Hofstadt likes to give surprise quizzes where we have to stand up and recite a passage in class."

"Really?" Rosa said.

"Yes."

"Oh dear, I'm terrible at that."

It was a dismal afternoon when it was not, as the expression goes, raining cats and dogs. Instead, it was a softer rain, which I called raining kittens. I looked out the window and saw no promise of the sun.

"We might as well start practicing. I think I could do part of 'The Old Dream.' That's a pretty simple poem of Heine's."

"Try it," Rosa urged me.

"Well, first I have to get *The Sun Also Rises* out of my head, since Heine is very different from Hemingway." I had finished it, but Baba lent me her copy, and I had started to reread it. I closed my eyes tight. "All right, I'm ready."

"I'll count to three, then you can start," Rosa said.

"This isn't a track meet, Rosa. I'll just start.

"The old dream comes again to me
With May night stars above,
We two sat under the linden-tree
And swore eternal love.

"There!" I said.

"That's it?" Rosa exclaimed.

"It's the first stanza. That really wasn't too hard. The trick is to find a poem with a really simple rhyme scheme. Then it's much easier to memorize."

Rosa and I decided to try to memorize at least ten passages or poems. I still kept rereading *The Sun Also Rises*.

It was a very sad book. Something had happened to Jake Barnes in the Great War so he couldn't do it with a woman. That must have been what Baba meant when she said "Let's just leave it at 'or something'" in reply to my comment "You mean there might be sex or something?"

The problem was that Jake was in love with Brett Ashley, but she couldn't fully love him back because she liked sex so much. All this made me think a lot about Ulla and Karl. I liked Jake. And it was not just that I liked him more than Karl, I suspected that in the long run despite his wounds, maybe Jake was more of a man than Karl.

chapter 19

He who joyfully marches to music rank
and file, has already earned my contempt. He has been given a large brain
by mistake, since for him the spinal
cord would surely suffice. This disgrace to civilization should be done
away with at once.

—Albert Einstein,
"The World as I See It"

The sun finally peeked out. The air cleared, and yet there always seemed to me a point around the end of vacation when summer grows slightly stale. The July thirty-first election hadn't helped the mood. Hitler gained a few seats in the Reichstag, just as we'd feared. Rosa and I were both anxious to get back to school. School seemed safe somehow. Nonetheless, the sunny weather justified wearing the new sleek bathing suits, so we went out sailing in *Ratty*. Our intention was to sail to a nearby beach and actually go swimming in these new suits, causing what we imagined would be a wild sensation.

There was very little wind, and our progress toward the

beach was achingly slow, so we began to practice reciting our Schiller and Heine verses in anticipation of Fräulein Hofstadt's class. We were both determined to make the highest marks. The sails flapped languidly, and the day was very hot. We drifted in toward the public beach hoping the water would get shallow enough for us to drop our anchor and swim. From off the shore the beach looked like an encampment, for there were clusters of the huge wicker beach chairs with their hooded tops that people could rent. It was customary for the families on German beaches in the holiday season to fly their city flag. So there were of course several from Berlin, and a couple from Leipzig and Dresden, as well as some from Frankfurt. In addition to the wicker encampment there were sand castles, and they too were flying flags.

The scene looked so festive and cheerful it took Rosa and me a minute to actually register what we were seeing from our gently rocking little vessel. A breeze suddenly sprang up, and like some terrible rash we could see amidst the city flags the *Blut und Boden*, the blood and earth colors of the swastika, its broken arms in their deadly right-hand spin snapping in the fresh wind. In front of one cluster of wicker beach chairs, half a dozen children, young enough to wear no clothes, were marching about with their arms raised toward the sky, crying in their singsongy little voices "Heil Hitler." Then a mother came out from under the hooded beach chair. She was large—very tall and fleshy. Her skin was a coppery rose color from a summer of beach tanning.

She had stuck a small Nazi flag at a jaunty angle in the coronet of white braids that were wound on top of her head. She picked up a naked child, put him on her shoulders, and began leading the march. He took the flag from her hair and started waving it. The woman's voice sailed out across the beach as she sang the opening lines of the "Horst Wessel Song."

The flag high! The ranks tightly closed!
The SA marches with a firm, courageous pace.

Yes, the flag is truly high, I thought, as I saw the little naked boy atop his mama's shoulders.

"Don't drop the anchor," I said to Rosa. Rosa turned to me. Her eyes were grim, and then she looked back toward the beach. I saw her shoulders drop and she shook her head ever so slightly in disbelief.

At just that moment a teenage boy's face broke from the water's surface not five feet from the bow. Rosa and I both gave small yelps.

"Don't leave, girls. I'll tow you ashore!"

"We don't want to go ashore," Rosa called back in a steely voice.

I pulled the tiller toward me, *Ratty* caught the breeze, and we slipped away. Now, this was the odd thing: When the teenage boy surfaced, I saw in my imagination the face of the singer from the beer garden. But Rosa saw another face.

"Those square yellow teeth." That was all she said. And that was the only time the incident in the alley in Berlin with the painting squad was ever referred to by either one of us.

We were reluctant to land on any of the other beaches, and for the rest of the afternoon we sailed aimlessly about until the sun set and we made for our dock at the cottage.

The incident on the beach became the next item in my Diary of Shame, which was now listed in an old, unused notebook of Mama's she let me have.

1) SA officer on Kurfürstendamm
2) Beer garden in Caputh when boy sings "The Watch on the Rhine"—K's eyes
3) U doing it with K
4) K's spitting in our basin; K's toothbrush
5) "Heil Hitler" in the alley; alley dream. Paint squad boy
6) Baby Hitler naked on mother's fat shoulder

And then I wrote this in my diary: *The beach looked like a medieval encampment. But am I looking back in time, or forward? Papa looks back through his telescope and seeks out ancient light. Am I looking through the wrong end of the telescope?*

That night the sky was very black, and Papa was happy. The dark, after all, was his element. He would rise like those animals who prowl the darkness—the raccoon, the owl, the bat. Stalking the night sky he hoped to untangle the stars' light and thereby their histories—where they were born, how they die. Rosa and I lay in the grass and watched the flow of the night. Around me were other creatures of the darkness—the firefly with its flickering incandescence, a whippoorwill with its cry. If I listened closely enough, could I hear the fluttering wings of a moth desperately seeking a house light? Not in our house. Our house was darkened.

His cigar was extinguished but I smelled the tobacco in Einstein's clothes as he approached. A fresh breeze brought the scent of sweetpeas. Mama was in the garden, barefoot. That was how she liked to work on hot summer evenings. She wove in and out of the merry chaos, putting the tomatoes, now heavy in their summer ripeness, on stronger stakes, untangling the snarl of pumpkin and squash vines in their inexorable scrambled march across the ground. August was just beginning. Everything was growing rotund, near to bursting in its lusciousness. Even the moon was now ripening, much to Papa's chagrin.

"*Guten Abend*—oops, sorry Gaby." Einstein nearly stepped on me just like that night earlier in the summer.

"No problem, Herr Professor."

"What's happening up there, Otto?"

"Albeiro—nice view tonight. You can see both stars. Have a look. . . . Hey, why are you wearing your handkerchief? Afraid of getting starburned?" Albeiro was the beautiful double star in the constellation of Cygnus the swan.

I looked over at Einstein. He was indeed wearing the little knotted square of cloth on his head.

"Oh, I banged my head trying to fix a pipe under the sink and it bled. No plasters, so I just put this on."

"Gaby, run in and get Herr Professor Einstein a plaster."

"Sure, Papa."

Two minutes later I came back with the first-aid plaster. I peeled off the adhesive tabs as Einstein removed the handkerchief and bent his head down. Rosa stood next to me.

"Two fine nurses," Einstein said. Rosa and I giggled. "When does your school start, girls?"

"In about a week," Rosa said. Mrs. Ebers had called up after we had been at Caputh a few days and asked if Rosa could stay longer because her grandmother was still sick. Mama said of course, and naturally we were thrilled.

"Are you looking forward to it?"

"Oh yes," we both replied at once.

Einstein's hairline receded drastically, so there was not much hair to contend with. The cut was on the left side. I pressed the plaster onto his scalp. I suppose I should have thought more of this moment. My fingertips were centimeters away from the most brilliant brain in history. But all I remember thinking is that his head was really beautiful.

chapter 20

Folly, thou conquerest, and I must yield!
Against stupidity the very gods
Themselves contend in vain. Exalted reason,
Resplendent daughter of the head divine,
Wise foundress of the system of the world,
Guide of the stars, who art thou then, if thou,
Bound to the tail of folly's uncurbed steed,
Must, vainly shrieking with the drunken crowd,
Eyes open, plunge down headlong in the abyss.
Accurs'd, who striveth after noble ends,
And with deliberate wisdom forms his plans!
To the fool-king belongs the world—

—Friedrich von Schiller,
The Maid of Orleans
translated by Anna Swanwick

Summer never ended abruptly as I always thought
it should when the first day of school arrived. It
was hot and humid. We sat in our first class sweaty,
and Uta Grasse had just gone to raise the window when the
classroom door creaked.

First there was the scent—roses and narcissus—as the
door opened. A long pale hand held the doorknob and

there was a delay of perhaps fifteen seconds until Fräulein Hofstadt swirled into the classroom. She did not so much walk toward her desk as glide in one sinuous movement. We were all, every last one of us, transfixed.

Rosa and I were sitting side by side in a double desk. She nudged me.

"Shoulders!" She mouthed the word. Fräulein Hofstadt was everything we had anticipated. The chic suit, the beautifully styled hair parted on the side with soft finger waves, her makeup so carefully applied. It was so lovely to see a teacher dress up for her class. Most of our women teachers wore drab colors, never went to a hairdresser, and absolutely never wore makeup.

Not only was Fräulein Hofstadt lovely to look at but she had brought cookies for the first day of class. She said that it was a custom in the village she came from. Somehow I could never imagine Fräulein Hofstadt coming from a village. She was so cosmopolitan, so sophisticated.

"Good morning, students. We are going to have a wonderful term!" She walked up to the blackboard and took a piece of chalk. "Indeed we are going to have an extraordinary term." She paused and wrote the word *außerordentlich*, "extraordinary," in large letters. Fräulein Hofstadt had handwriting to match her elegance. Within days Rosa and I were both imitating it, adding curlicues and all manner of ornamentation to our script. But it didn't end there. I also tried to no avail to finger-wave my hair. It remained limp and straight as ever.

A small competition evolved between Rosa and me over the *außerordentlichs*, who could collect the most. Occasionally Fräulein Hofstadt simply shortened it to *außer*, and in some ways these little snippets pruned from the bigger word were the most dear.

During those first weeks of school we began to speculate endlessly on Fräulein Hofstadt's love life. And when she revealed one day that she had studied ballet, Rosa and I both felt that she would have been the perfect choice for the role of the ballerina in the movie of *Grand Hotel*. We rushed to tell her she should have played the part.

"Did you know that they have made a movie of *People in a Hotel*?" Rosa said excitedly. Fräulein Hofstadt looked a bit blank.

"*People in a Hotel*?" she asked.

"Yes, by Vicki Baum."

"Oh, oh yes . . ." she said, her voice slightly breathy. "I have very little time for popular fiction."

"Gaby has read the book four times just this past summer!" Rosa said.

"Have you now?"

I nodded and looked into my soup bowl. I felt a slight wilting sensation deep inside. Was this the first chink in my bright armor of *außerordentlich*? Was this another item for my Diary of Shame—having read *People at a Hotel* four times? *No! Never!* I quickly banished such thoughts and I resumed my worship at the altar of Fräulein Hofstadt.

Ulla had been studying quite hard lately, and she was constantly practicing the violin. Her enthusiasm for going to the conservatory had been rekindled. I am not sure why this happened. Perhaps she was seeing that there might be more to life than Karl or maybe it was that the date of the audition was fast approaching. It was impossible for her to be a conscientious student and work at the same time, so she had quit her job at the Chameleon and begun to practice in earnest for the audition in late November. Karl still came every Friday and Saturday night to take her out. He was actually very nice, and I tried really hard to obliterate that memory of him in the beer garden in Caputh. Maybe I had been wrong about his enthusiasm for the song, I thought.

We had been back in school for almost two months. It was a Monday night, and Ulla and I were both in our rooms, studying. I had whizzed through my math homework and now turned to literature, which was much more challenging this year because Fräulein Hofstadt, as everyone said, taught us on almost a university level. She had assigned several pages of reading, and now I opened the selected poems of Goethe and turned to page sixty, where there was his famous "Mignon" poem. I began reading the first line: "*Kennst du das Land, wo die Zitronen blühn.*" I remembered that night at the Chameleon and once more was struck how truly subversive Max Weltmann had been. I had not yet confessed to Ulla that I had snuck into the Chameleon that night. But I was now bursting to tell her.

I raced into her bedroom. She looked up from the book she was reading.

"What is it? I don't know if I have time to help you now with your homework."

"I don't need help with my homework. I have to tell you something." I plopped down on her bed.

"What?"

"I, well, Rosa and I sneaked into the Chameleon last summer and we saw you and . . . and Max Weltmann . . . and . . . and this poem. . . ."

"You what?"

The story spilled out. Ulla was suitably amazed. "You would never breathe a word to Mama and Papa, would you—about the costume I had to wear and all?"

"No, of course not. You weren't naked like the girls on the stage . . . but Ulla . . . Ulla, I'm proud of you."

"What?"

"That place. Max Weltmann . . . it's subversive."

A shadow seemed to pass across her bright blue eyes turning them almost gray. "I know, I know."

"I think it's very daring of you."

"You do?" She laid her hand softly on top of mine.

"Yes, I do." She looked as if she might cry. "Ulla, really, believe me. I am so proud of you."

"You are?"

"Yes, Ulla, really."

She shook her head quickly and her eyes turned bright again. "So what are you reading for Fräulein Hofstadt? Goethe?"

"Yes, lots of Goethe and other stuff."

"Schiller?"

"Not much. I was hoping we'd do the play that you did. The Joan of Arc one. But I don't think we're going to."

"Bring me the course outline. It will be fun seeing what you're reading."

I went and got the outline.

"Hmmm," Ulla said. "Shakespeare . . . *Hamlet*. That's the play you'll be doing, I guess."

"Yes. Fräulein Hofstadt says she really feels that Hamlet is a perfect hero for these times. He went to Wittenberg University."

"What does Wittenberg have to do with being a hero?"

I shrugged. "How should I know? I think she likes it that it was a German university."

"As opposed to an English one or a Danish one?" Ulla murmured as she studied the course outline.

"She's so nice. And I think I'm doing well."

"Yes, she's the only teacher who seems like she has a life outside of school."

"Does she have a boyfriend?"

"I don't know if she has a boyfriend now, but there was a rumor that she did have a fiancé who was killed in the Great War—at Ypres."

"Oh, how awful. The battle where they used chlorine gas."

There were many stories about the Kaiser Wilhelm Society, but one of the saddest was that of Fritz Haber and the chlorine gas. Haber, director of the Chemistry Institute, was a colleague of Papa's and had the dubious distinction of being the inventor of poisonous chlorine gas near the beginning of the Great War. He was of Jewish descent and as a reward for his war efforts he was made a captain in the German army. Papa was telling the story once to a visiting English scientist who came to our house for dinner. He said that Emil Fischer, one of the founders of the Kaiser Wilhelm Society, was so irritated with Haber that upon learning of his commission he "wished him failure from the bottom of his patriotic heart." I think Papa did too, because the chlorine gas was one of the most horrendous weapons of the war. It burned out the lungs of the men. My mother said that Haber's wife committed suicide because she was so ashamed of her husband's invention.

"That is so sad about Fräulein Hofstadt's fiancé. No

wonder she has never married. I suppose she still might, although she's pretty old—maybe thirty-five."

"Yes, it is sad," Ulla agreed.

"But anyhow, Ulla, I think maybe during Christmas holiday when you have more time you should go back and work at the Chameleon. I mean, not as a naked girl. Just, you know, as the bookkeeper and the cigarette girl."

"I don't think so." There was a weariness in her voice.

"Why not?"

"Oh, it's complicated."

"Mama and Papa?"

"No, not really. Although I doubt they would approve of the nude Brandenburg Gate tableau."

"But Hessie has already told them that the place was all right. They don't know about the gate thing and—" The tune of the cabaret song came back to me. "It's not Karl, is it? He's not the reason, is he?"

Ulla's entire demeanor changed. Her eyes hardened. "No!" she barked. "Let's just drop it, please."

I was taken aback by her sharp tone. It was not like Ulla.

She looked down again at the course outline. "Too bad that you won't get to do *The Maid of Orleans*. But I guess it's to be *Hamlet*. You would have made a good Joan of Arc. Remember the year my class gave it? My friend Anna was Joan." Ulla tapped the outline with her finger. She got a very faraway look in her eyes that was almost wistful. I wondered if she was missing that time in her life. I realized that Ulla now didn't seem as different to me as she had last summer when she and Karl had come to Caputh. She had lost a bit of that languorous quality, some of her ease, and maybe some of her confidence. Maybe she was just nervous about her audition for the conservatory, but that was still about two months away.

However, yet another election was just one month off, and everyone was nervous about that. Would Hitler gain more seats? Could he possibly lose seats, and if he did, would that be the end of him and his party?

chapter 21

The only thing that interferes with my
learning is my education.

—Albert Einstein

On the morning of November seventh when I came to the breakfast table Mama and Papa were almost jubilant. "Look at this!" Papa held up to the *Vossiche Zeitung* with a headline NAZIS LOSE 34 SEATS!

When Hertha came in with the eggs, I tried to judge her demeanor. I had remembered that shadow of a smile when she had listened behind the kitchen door to Hitler on the radio in Caputh. Would she betray any emotion now? No— her face was expressionless.

There was a picture in the paper of Joseph Goebbels, Hitler's right-hand man, looking quite dour. This was the first time in a long time that the strength of the Nazi Party, the great flood, seemed to begin to ebb. Papa cocked his head and looked thoughtful.

"I just hope . . ."

"What is it, Otto? Please, pass the cream, Ulla," Mama said.

"Well, I just hope that this defeat doesn't cause a backlash—like in twenty-nine."

"Do you mean the stock market crash?" I asked.

Mama waved her hand dismissively. "Otto, you cannot compare this to nineteen twenty-nine."

"*Hrrerf!*" Papa made a growlish sound deep in his throat. "In nineteen twenty-nine, we were just beginning to recover from the poverty of the Great War and here we were getting poor again. Millions were thrown out of work. People were looking for scapegoats. Jews were a handy target—books by Jews, ideas that were not Aryan. It was a backlash and it certainly gave Hitler an opportunity. The right-wing National Socialist students at the university began a campaign to 'cleanse' the university." He growled again.

"'Cleanse'?" I asked. "The stone front of the main building was just scrubbed last year. It gleams now, it's so bright."

Ulla dipped her head down and stared straight into her coffee.

"Not that kind of cleansing," Papa replied. "A purge of offensive books. They confiscated several before it was stopped, somehow. Goebbels was behind it, of course. He is a master at this kind of thing. He knew how to exploit the despair and manipulate the student union. If Hitler didn't have Goebbels, he'd be lost."

I stood up and went around the table to look at the picture in the paper of the man who was often called the dwarf.

"Why do they always call him a doctor in the paper?"

"He has a doctorate in literature," Mama said, "unbelievable as it might seem." It did seem not just unbelievable but almost fantastical to me. Had Goebbels read Goethe? Written analyses of the imagery of Goethe? Studied Shakespeare and reflected on the tragic flaws in characters, or in exams been asked to compare the meter of Heine to the iambic pentameter of Shakespeare? And now this man worked for Hitler.

"What does he actually do for Hitler?" I asked.

"He is officially the *Gauleiter*, the regional party leader. But he does much more than a normal party leader," Papa said.

"What?" I asked.

"Well, for one thing he made the 'Horst Wessel Song' the anthem of the Nazi Party. His most important job is that he directs propaganda—that is where his real talents lie. He loves a fight. And now the dwarf has got one." Papa tapped the paper with his fingers.

"How come people often call him a dwarf?" I asked looking at the newspaper. "He doesn't look especially short. It's just an insult, right?" *Giftzwerg*, poisonous dwarf, was a common slanderous term.

"Yes, just an insult. He's not really a dwarf. He has a

clubbed foot that perhaps makes him scuttle along a bit. But dwarf or not, he's one to watch. If Hitler didn't have him, things would be a lot better. But Hitler would probably find another *Giftzwerg!*"

"Don't be so pessimistic, Otto. It won't be like twenty-nine," Mama said.

Papa ducked his head and raised his shoulders slightly. It was a faintly apologetic gesture that I had seen him do countless times. "I'm not pessimistic. I mean, look, it could be worse. Thank God he lost those thirty-four seats. I just worry about Goebbels." Papa still seemed far from optimistic to me.

Two days later I witnessed a scene between my father and an unfamiliar visitor that made me think Papa's pessimism had been justified. It was in the evening. I had just come from Ulla's room where she had helped me with a math problem, and I was heading toward the kitchen for a snack.

"I can't believe that you have come here, into my own home, and brought this . . . this foulness!"

Papa was speaking to someone in the foyer of our apartment. I froze when I heard these scalding words. "Are you actually suggesting that I . . ." Papa's voice dropped. I could not hear the end of the sentence. I crept down the hall just a bit to see if I could catch a glimpse of whoever this was. I pressed myself against the wall and inched forward. Luckily Papa's back was to me, but a tall figure stood facing him with his hand raised in a scolding gesture. His hair was dark and he wore a Kaiser Wilhelm beard although his mustache was not as long and flowing as the kaiser's.

Papa raised his voice again. "Look, that idiot of yours lost two million votes and thirty-four seats in the Reichstag two days ago and now you come to me and you really expect me . . ." Again Papa's voice dropped and I could not hear him. Then I saw him move toward the front door and hold it open. "*Gute Nacht*, Herr Professor Lenard. Go back to Heidelberg."

Lenard! I had heard Mama and Papa speak of him. He was another physicist, the man who had practically invented the term "Jewish physics." That was really all I knew about him, except for the fact that he hated Einstein and had referred to his theory of relativity as the "Jewish fraud." I wondered what he could have possibly said to Papa that made him so mad. It was as if his anger seeped into the very air of the apartment. I forgot about getting a snack.

Not five minutes later I heard Papa actually laughing. He was in his study and evidently on the telephone. I had been on my way to ask him about the man Lenard.

"What, Albert? No! Read that to me again."

I slipped into his study, and he motioned for me to sit down. "Yes . . . yes . . ." He nodded, his face wreathed in smiles. "Yes . . . yes, you're right. I won't give Lenard another thought. *Gut! Gute Nacht*." He hung up the telephone and rocked back in his chair, smiling as if at some private joke.

"Papa, what's so funny?" I asked.

"Einstein. A group of patriotic American women don't want him to come to CalTech in Pasadena for his December trip."

"Why not?"

"They find him dangerous." Papa giggled as he removed his spectacles and wiped them. My own glasses were sliding down my nose. I pushed them up. It was amazing how much better I could see with them. "Imagine anyone thinking Albert dangerous?"

"Dangerous—Einstein dangerous?" Mama shook her head in wonder as she walked past Papa's study on the way to her music room.

"He's a pacifist, isn't he, Papa?" I asked.

"Most assuredly," Papa replied.

"Then he should be anything but dangerous," I said.

"They apparently don't think so, but that won't stop him from going."

"And what about this man who visited you tonight? Lenard?"

Papa's eyes darkened. "Gaby, were you eavesdropping?"

"No, Papa. I was just coming down the hallway to go to the kitchen for a snack and I heard you. You were talking pretty loud, you know."

"*Hrrerf.*" This was the way Papa growled when he did not like something.

"Well, who is he?" I persisted.

"An idiot."

"So is Hitler. I heard you say that."

"*Aachh!*" A different growl from his repertoire of gruff animal noises. Slightly more intense, it denoted not mere dislike but disgust. He waved his hand in front of his face the way he did when he was trying to clear away smoke from his pipe, but he wasn't smoking his pipe. "You shouldn't be troubling yourself with this kind of thing. You are too young."

"Papa, I am not too young! In five years I shall be going to the university. I want to know about this man. This Lenard. It's 'Jewish physics,' isn't it?"

"So it is." He sighed, and his shoulders sagged. He now reached for his pipe and the pen knife he kept on hand for digging out the old tobacco. He became completely absorbed in tending to his pipe, jabbing the point of the knife in. It was a challenging occupation for Papa, for the hand on his weakened bow arm could not be of much help. "Philipp Lenard is a disgrace to science and culture. He epitomizes why Nazi rule and what we call German culture—the culture that produced Goethe, Heine, Bach, and Beethoven— cannot exist at the same time as men who are fundamentally dogs. "

"But Lenard is a scientist?"

"He won the Nobel Prize in nineteen-oh-five."

"He did?"

"Three years ago," my father continued, "he was part of a group that authored a book called *One Hundred Authors Against Einstein* that condemned Einstein's physics as 'fantasy,' 'deceit,' and 'fraud.' There had been talk of Jewish physics before, but no one paid much attention. That book put it on the map."

"What did he want from you, Papa?"

"Oh, for me to sign some stupid manifesto."

"What kind of manifesto?"

"Something against Jewish scientists. He's trying to get them all kicked out of the Institute and the Prussian Academy."

"This was what you were worried about when you said Goebbels would come back and fight, right?"

"Yes, I suppose so. Goebbels will of course use people like Lenard for propaganda. But just remember, the Nazis lost thirty-four seats in the Reichstag."

"Is Professor Einstein worried?" I asked.

"We were just discussing a series of meetings for next spring at the Institute and his travel schedule, for he's going to CalTech in December no matter what these ladies say. And he plans to be back in time for the meetings." Papa smiled. "So I suppose he's not too concerned. But the good news is this." He reached for a paper.

"What?"

"Your school report. It's so good! For the first time your literature marks are as high as your mathematics. And I

know Fräulein Hofstadt teaches literature on a very sophisticated level."

"Oh, really?" I had forgotten that reports were to be sent
out to our families this week. I brightened considerably.
This *was* the first time my literature marks were as high as
my math ones. Although I loved to read, in the past I made
careless errors in my compositions for literature class.

"Yes, Fräulein Hofstadt cannot say enough nice things
about you. Listen to this: 'Gabriella is an inspiration to any
teacher. Not simply a hard worker, diligent, and precise,
she has an extraordinary grasp of the subtlest nuances in
literature. Her analyses of the poetry and rhetorical trea-
tises we have been reading indicate a sophistication beyond
her years. Many of her papers really are what I would call
university level. She is a pleasure to have in the classroom.
Truly an extraordinary young woman!'" Papa looked up.
"Can't beat that, can you, Gaby?"

"Well, she makes it easy to love literature. She's an inspir-
ing teacher."

"Mama and I are very proud of you."

"Thanks, Papa." I caught a certain wistfulness in his eyes,
almost like a mist.

"And Gaby, don't worry about all of this. I think times
are getting better; maybe by spring everything will be back
to normal. And that reminds me, will you help Mama plant
the new tulips? The bulbs just arrived. She always orders
too many. Then she has a stiff back for three days."

"Sure, Papa."

"And remember, things are getting better, I really think so. By spring there will be no more Hitler, just lovely tulips."

He wanted me to believe this so much. So much! I wondered if he would lie to me, or maybe he was lying to himself.

chapter 22

Whoever undertakes to set himself up as
a judge of Truth and Knowledge is ship-
wrecked by the laughter of the gods.

—Albert Einstein

A few days later the telephone rang as we were
eating breakfast. Once Hertha finished serving
me, she walked hurriedly back to the kitchen to
answer it. When she returned, she said, "It's Frau Blumenthal, madame."

"Oh, Baba! I was supposed to call her about the theater
tonight. Are you going, Otto?"

"No, I can't. I'm behind on a lecture I have to prepare. "

Mama got up to take the call and returned a few minutes later. She turned to me and Ulla. "So now since Papa
can't go, I have an extra ticket for this evening. Do either of
you want to go to the National Theatre tonight?"

"I have a date with Karl," Ulla said. She had hardly
touched any of the food on her plate.

"Can I have your bacon, Ulla?" I asked.

"Sure."

I began to reach for it.

"Not that way! We are not barbarians here," Mama scolded. It drove Mama crazy when we would pick food off of each other's plates. She insisted on an entire choreography in the transference of food in this situation. Said bacon would be forked by the giver, Ulla, onto a butter plate that would be passed to me. I would then take the bacon off that plate with my fork and put it on to my plate. It seemed like about three times as many steps as were necessary. It would be so much easier to just pluck the bacon off of Ulla's plate with my fingers.

"So do you want to go with me, Gaby?" Mama asked when the bacon operations had been successfully completed.

"What's the play?" I asked.

"*Gabriel Schilling's Flight.*"

"Never heard of it. What's it about?"

"It is a rather old-fashioned play about a so-so artist who's trying to escape his wife and his mistress and winds up drowning himself."

"*Aachh*, sounds like such fun!" I said.

Papa laughed.

"We'll be sitting with Hessie and Baba, too." Now that did sound like fun, and I could wear one of the dresses I bought with Baba last summer.

"All right, I'll go."

"Good. It's silly to waste a perfectly good ticket."

*   *   *

Karl was there that evening when I came out of my room dressed in my gray dress. Mama had lent me a pearl pin, which made it a bit fancier.

"You look lovely, Gaby!" Karl said. "That color becomes you. You look quite grown-up, in fact!"

It had been my observation that whenever someone commented on how "grown-up" I looked, it actually meant that I still looked rather like a child. But it's not that I didn't take part of his compliment seriously. I think Karl did really believe that I looked nice in my dress and that the color did became me. I was working very hard to try to forget that afternoon in the beer garden. Karl had never been anything but kind to me. Mama and Papa were always saying how courteous they found him, and they actually attributed Ulla's renewed academic vigor to Karl, whom they learned did quite well in his studies of mechanical engineering. "A serious student," Papa said often in reference to him.

Uncle Hessie picked us up in his Mercedes—the big one. An evening at the National Theatre was indeed a dazzling affair. It was very different from going to the Palast Theater, which was rather dingy in comparison and hardly a palace at all. The lobby of the National Theatre glittered with a thousand twinkly lights from sparkling chandeliers. There was a grand central staircase with plush red carpeting and gilt ornamentation everywhere.

Much to my surprise, Professor Einstein and his wife

were in Hessie's box with Mama and Baba and me, along with the British ambassador, Sir Horace Rumbold. I knew that Einstein was a music lover but I hadn't realized that he enjoyed theater. The British ambassador was talking with Einstein, asking him about his impending trip to Pasadena. And just as Papa had told me, Einstein said something about returning to Berlin in the spring to attend some meetings. My English had greatly improved since studying with Fräulein Mayer this term in school. She had a much better accent then my former teacher and I could understand much of what Einstein and Sir Horace Rumbold were saying. I heard Rumbold say that he felt that although it was a relief Hitler had lost the thirty-odd seats in the last election, he still felt that the greatest danger was the private armies—the SA and SS. "Just another way around Versailles," Rumbold said. I heard this, but my eyes were fastened on the crowd swirling below and in the boxes near us.

The Quotation Empress was there with her stepson, Prince Auwi. "They put on a show of affection," Baba whispered to Mama behind her program, which she was using like a fan. "But they loathe each other." Both the empress and the prince wore the ceremonial sashes, hers across a vibrant pink dress, which I saw that Baba noted as a Schiaparelli with a question mark in the little notebook she always carried when she covered such occasions for the newspaper. I leaned over and asked if Schiaparelli was French.

"Italian by birth, but she lives in Paris. You know Hitler is now quite enchanted with Italy. Don't put it past you-know who"—she nodded toward the Empress—"to try and curry favor with him by any means. So I think she has decided to wear this new young Italian woman's design. Too bad she spoils it with that stupid ceremonial sash." The empress's sash and her stepson's were royal blue, beribboned and bejeweled with at least a half kilo of symbols and crests, just to let everyone know who exactly they were, and to remind them that once there had been a monarchy. It seemed to me that the empress wanted to have her cake (the monarchy) and eat it too (Hitler and the Nazi Party).

"Look, Goebbels!" Baba whispered. "Can you see what his wife is wearing, Elske?"

"Not Schiaparelli," Mama replied.

"Where? Where ?" I asked, poking Baba's arm. I was so afraid I was going to miss something.

"Over there in the mezzanine. He hasn't taken his seat yet."

I saw him immediately. Joseph Goebbels, the man Papa said was the real power behind Hitler. I could tell from where I sat that he was quite odd-looking. He was standing up and shaking hands with several people who were greeting him enthusiastically. The first thing I noticed about him was not his size or stature, but how he used his hands when he was speaking. He was slashing the air almost violently, and yet he was smiling all the while. His smile cut across his narrow, dark face like the blade of a knife.

"Look, see the Countess von Oberland!" This was another socialite whose name I had read in Baba's column. Baba pointed discreetly with her program. "She has her arm around Magda Goebbels's waist. It is nauseating how people try to ingratiate themselves with her to get close to him."

"She's very pretty, Frau Goebbels, isn't she?" I said.

"Yes indeed. She was married to a rich man named Günther Quandt. Shortly after they divorced, she met Goebbels. He is a ferocious womanizer. You see, you do not have to be movie-star handsome to get a woman if you have political power, or if you are close to it. There are already rumors of him with a half dozen other women.

"Watch him now," Baba whispered. "He's going to take his seat." He was hobbling down the aisle to his row in the mezzanine, all the while waving his arms wildly in greetings to people. Now and then I could see his hand flatten and slant upward in a Heil Hitler salute. His wife was as lovely and delicate as he was grotesque. She walked in mincing little steps behind him. It was like Mephistopheles and a fairy princess.

Then just before the house lights dimmed, as I followed the path of the Goebbelses to their seats, I caught a glimpse of a familiar face.

"Mama, it's Fräulein Hofstadt!"

"Where, dear?"

"Down there, mezzanine level in the row right behind

the Goebbelses." I could almost detect the scent of roses and narcissus.

But then the theater went completely dark and the curtain came up on the first act of what had to be the most boring play ever written. During intermission I was determined to seek out Fräulein Hofstadt. Mama came with me.

"Gaby!" my teacher cried out. And as always, never rushing, she effortlessly glided toward me. She looked breathtaking in a pale, rose-colored velvet gown embroidered with beaded crystals. She wore long, silvery opera gloves. Velvet became her. If one could have a signature fabric, this was Fräulein Hofstadt's. Velvet epitomized her sleek, soft beauty. Every head turned to look at her, and I felt quite special that she was making a fuss over me.

"And of course Frau Schramm, the mother of this extraordinary young lady, and how fine she looks. My goodness, I love your dress, Gaby." I had loved it too until that moment when, standing next to Fräulein Hofstadt, I felt as dull as a pigeon. I was very happy to see that she was with an elderly man whom she introduced as her uncle. He was not especially attractive. His collar was a bit frayed. He was not "well barbered," as my mother would say. I spotted hair growing out of his ears, and his beard was ill kempt. I would have been crushed if she had been with a handsome man of her own age. It would have seemed so unfaithful to the memory of her soldier boyfriend. I had told Rosa what Ulla had told me about the rumored fiancé, and we were both convinced that she was still mourning him and would for the rest of her life. Baba came up to us and we introduced her. I noticed Baba's nose twitch as she took in the scent of roses and narcissus. I was sure it was some new stylish perfume, but Baba didn't seem to like it.

Fräulein Hofstadt seemed rather impressed that the celebrated social columnist was our friend. This gave me a little thrill of excitement. The lights began to blink signaling us to return to our seats. Fräulein Hofstadt gave my hand a little squeeze. "See you in class." I couldn't wait to tell Rosa about all this.

You won't believe the story I have to tell, I wrote on a piece of paper. *Meet me in the corner of the schoolyard by the linden tree at second break.* I passed her the note during Latin.

Rosa had missed the first half of the school day. She had had to stay with her grandmother, who had been feeling dizzy that morning due to her heart problems, until her mother could come back from an important morning meeting at the university. I was practically having a heart attack myself, bursting with the events of the previous evening at the theater. I kept waiting and waiting. But she only showed up toward the end of the school day.

Rosa's eyes widened as she read the note. She began to scribble something on it but then stopped as our Latin teacher, Fräulein Gompers, ambled down the aisle toward her.

"Now, I want you all to check your translation of that Cicero passage. It's a very short passage. Then pass it to your neighbor and you will check each other's work." Fräulein Gompers liked us to learn from one another. She believed in what she called collaborative learning. "See if perhaps your neighbor had a better or less graceful way of translating a word or a sentence. You be the judge."

Rosa and I looked at each other. Just before she passed me her Cicero paragraph she wrote in pencil in the margin, *Quid est haec fabula? Dic!*

I read the margin note, which of course had nothing to do with Cicero but asked in Latin, "What is this story? Do tell!"

"How clever!" I whispered. She was a much better Latin student than I was, and there was no way I could even give the slightest hint in Latin as to the details of the story. All I could write back was *Expecta secessum.* "Wait until break." Finally break came.

"I thought you'd never get here!" I was practically dancing with excitement.

"Well, what is it?"

"I saw Fräulein Hofstadt last night at the National Theatre. She was beautiful, gorgeous. A vision."

"Was she with a man?" Rosa asked.

"An old man!"

"Old man—that's so sad."

"No, not a boyfriend, she introduced him as her uncle."

"Oh, thank heavens. I hate to think of her fiancé's bones rotting away in a battlefield and her, well you know, with another man."

"Yes, I'm sure she'll grieve forever."

"Did you talk to her?"

"Of course. That's the best part. Baba was with us and Fräulein Hofstadt was so impressed that we knew Baba. I could see that she hoped that Baba might mention her in her social column."

"Will she?"

"I'm not sure. I got a feeling somehow that maybe Baba didn't approve of her in some way."

"Really? How could anyone not approve of Fräulein Hofstadt?"

I shook my head in wonder. "I don't know."

On November seventeeth, the very day after I told Rosa this story, an odd chain of events seemed to begin, and it was as if we, Berlin, Germany, and soon all of Europe were launched on an inexorable course. The first event in the chain was the resignation of Chancellor Franz von Papen. Then members of his cabinet had to resign, too. That was the way it worked. Baba said it was Schleicher, whom she also called "the king-maker," who "unmade" Papen. He was a crafty behind-the-scenes political operator, but Baba liked him well enough. She was very close with Scheicher's wife. So she got a lot of information. The day Papen resigned, Baba was at our house for dinner. She was full of news and optimism now that the "fool" Papen was out. We were all at the table. Hertha had made sauerbraten. It was so tender you didn't need a knife to cut it. I was scraping off the vegetables and putting them to the side. I didn't like it when food touched. Meat and vegetables should be separate, in my opinion. I could feel Ulla looking at me slightly critically.

"I'm not so sure this is good, Baba," Papa said in answer to Baba's remarks.

"Let me just say this before we get to Papen," Baba said, looking up at Hertha who was passing the platter. "Hertha, this is the best sauerbraten ever! It's so tender. So sweet. No sugar, right?"

"Never sugar, madame. Beet juice, apples. It's the same recipe made by the chef at the Kaiserhof Hotel." It was as if the air in the dining room froze. The Kaiserhof! Hitler's favorite hotel in Berlin. Unofficial Nazi headquarters. Mama coughed nervously. Baba looked as if she might choke on her sauerbraten. I stole at look at Hertha. Her face was as placid as a lake, as expressionless as a potato. When she finished serving, she carried the plate out of the dining room, but the tension lingered.

Baba turned to Papa, and in an effort to smooth over an awkward moment she asked, "So, Otto, to resume our conversation, why is it not so good that Papen resigned?"

Papa patted his mouth lightly with his napkin and then leaned back in his chair. "Papen has resigned. There is a vacuum. Nature, as they say, abhors a vacuum. Watch, the Old Gentleman is weak. He is going to be pulled, sucked into the vacuum, and then the stage will be set for Hitler."

He looked around the table slowly at each one of us. I felt a terrible dread, a taste of darkness rising from deep inside me. For me it was not simply a vacuum. After the vacuum that nature hated was filled, there would be Hitler. And Hitler wasn't a vacuum, he was a black hole, a collapsing star whose gravitational pull is so strong, the force so powerful that not even light can escape. My middle name, remember, is Lucia. I was named for the light of a star. And now it was as if I and everything dear to me were being dragged in.

Papa was right. Two days after Papen resigned, Hindenburg, the president of Germany, had a meeting with Hitler. I did not understand it. Vacuum or not.

"Hitler lost thirty-four seats. There isn't any majority because there are too many parties, but just because he has a few more seats than any other party, how come he gets to meet with the president?"

"Well, I think the other party leaders got to meet with Hindenburg, too, probably," Rosa said.

We were talking about this as we walked home from school on Monday following the election. We had reached the northwest corner of the schoolyard when I noticed a sleek dark limousine parked down an alley off the main street. From this point on, the limo would become inter-twined in the links of the chain.

"Look! It's Fräulein Hofstadt!" I said. She was coming around from the other end of the alley, her head bent down. I started to raise my hand to wave and call out. But Rosa grabbed it.

"Shhh! Let's watch." The car door mysteriously opened from the inside and an arm reached out. Fräulein Hofstadt took the proffered hand and stepped into the limousine. Rosa and I watched in silence as the limousine pulled away, then we turned to each other and didn't say anything for several seconds. I knew immediately that Rosa had been right to pull my hand down and shush me. We had wit-nessed something but were not quite sure what. Teachers did not get picked up in limousines. Not only that, but Fräulein Hofstadt was wearing a rather lovely hat with a deep brim that dipped down over one eye. She was always very fashionable, but she never would wear such a hat in school. Had she carried it in a hat box? If so, where was the hat box now? There were an awful lot of unanswered questions.

Finally Rosa spoke. "You said she was with a very old man at the theater."

"Yes, her uncle." I paused. "At least, she introduced him as her uncle. But I don't think he was the kind to have owned a car like this, a limousine," I said, recalling the hair sprouting from his ears.

"What made you think that?"

"He was just not fancy. Can you imagine Herr Doktor Berg having a limousine?"

"No!" Rosa said firmly.

It was funny I should mention him. I had not thought of Herr Doktor Berg for some time. I never saw him now that we had moved into the other building. I had almost forgotten about my two confiscated books. Hessie had found me another copy of *The Call of the Wild*, but I sensed that the translation wasn't as good.

Snowflakes had begun to fall. "I'm cold," Rosa said. "No use standing here wondering about Fräulein Hofstadt. Her life is obviously more exciting than ours."

"More *extraordinary*," I said, and we both laughed.

A few days after we saw Fräulein Hofstadt getting into the limo, I came home from school and Papa was already home. The weather had turned quite cold. There was a fire lit in the fireplace and he and Hessie were having a *Schnaps*. I heard them talking as I walked in.

"But so far Hindenburg seems to be holding off, thank God."

"Holding off what?" I asked as I came in and dropped my books on a chair.

"Gaby, you know Mama doesn't like you simply dumping your books on the furniture."

I picked them up again. "All right, but what's Hindenburg holding off on?" That fear I had felt before at the dinner table when Papa had described how Hindenburg would eventually be sucked into a vacuum created by Papen's resignation returned. Once again I felt that dark dread and imagined myself like a collapsing star.

Hessie answered. "He has refused to appoint Hitler chancellor."

"That's good, isn't it?" I asked.

"Yes," Papa said. "So far. Let's see how long his resolve will last."

"Maybe until Christmas," Hessie said

"I honestly doubt it," Papa replied

"Want to bet?" Hessie said with a twinkle in his eye.

"I shouldn't bet against a rich man."

"A dinner at the Drachenhaus?"

"It's a deal." They shook hands on it.

"Can I go, too?" I asked. The Drachenhaus was an unusual Oriental-style restaurant a bit outside of Berlin. It was like stepping back into another century on another continent. I loved it.

"Don't be ridiculous!" Papa laughed.

"What's so ridiculous?" I asked.

"I'll tell you what, Gaby," Hessie said, "if I lose and the dinner is on me, you can come."

"Honestly, Hessie, you spoil her."

"Why not?" he replied merrily. At that moment Ulla arrived.

"Ulla!" Hessie exclaimed. "How did the audition go?"

Ulla smiled and held up her hands with fingers crossed. "I hope well. One never knows."

"Well, if you get into conservatory, I suggest a celebration at the Drachenhaus for you!"

"Oh, that would be lovely," Ulla said.

"And of course your beau is invited. Karl? Is that his name?"

"Yes, Karl." She nodded and smiled, but her smile seemed strained. Indeed the summer languor had vanished, and she seemed tight as a drumhead.

On December third, I was dining at the Drachenhaus with Papa and Hessie! The day before, Kurt von Schleicher was appointed chancellor and not Hitler, to everyone's profound relief. Hessie and Papa were drinking champagne.

"A reasonable man, von Schleicher." Papa paused, then added somewhat hesitantly, "At least, I think he is. A man of the old values." By old values Papa meant Prussian values, like loyalty, discipline, and responsibility.

Uncle Hessie nodded. "Baba, of course, is very close with his wife, Elisabeth. I've never been so happy to lose a bet, given the alternatives."

I was feeling very grown-up, and thankfully no one had

told me I looked that way, for it would have wrecked the feeling completely. Hessie was not only paying for our dinner, but he had sent me a pretty dress for the occasion as an early Christmas present. It was dark green velvet and had long sleeves with a lighter green satin cuffs and pearl buttons down the front.

"Can I have a taste of champagne to celebrate Schleicher and the old Prussian values?" I asked.

"Don't be ridiculous, Gaby!" Papa said.

This was always Hessie's cue to come to my service. "Of course you can, dear. Waiter! Another glass please for the young lady."

The waiter brought the glass, and Uncle Hessie poured a small amount of champagne into it. We then lifted our glasses and clinked them.

"Here's to old Prussian values," Hessie said. "And as King Frederick said, 'As a king, I am the first servant of my state.'" King Frederick had been the King of Prussia in the mid-1700s. Hessie felt he was the very essence of enlightened rule.

The dinner was delightful, but even with the good news of Schleicher instead of Hitler, nothing seemed settled. Over the next few weeks the changing characters in the cabinets, the endless discussions of the Old Gentleman, and the instability of the Reichstag continued. For Rosa and me all of this was merely a backdrop for the limousine that wound through the shifting political landscape like a dark, shiny beetle, and in its gleaming carapace was our darling and beloved teacher. There had been other sightings of the limousine, of the mysterious arm that would reach out and open the door.

Rosa and I knew where Fräulein Hofstadt lived. She had said one day in class that her apartment was off Kufsteiner Strasse in a large building. So we had set up a watch system. The limousine would never pull up in front of her building but usually into one of the smaller alleys to wait for her, a different alley almost every time. We began to imagine that Fräulein Hofstadt was involved in some sort of espionage. She was a spy! It seemed to me like a book that Vicki Baum could have written. We couldn't wait until school let out for the Christmas holidays and we would even have more time to follow her. But then just a few days before vacation she invited us to her apartment for a holiday tea, and this changed everything. It seemed terribly wrong to go to someone's house for tea and at the same time be spying on her. We both felt slimy and agreed that we were completely disgusting girls.

So this became item number seven in my Diary of Shame.

1) SA officer on Kurfürstendamm
2) Beer garden in Caputh when boy sings" The Watch on the Rhine"—K's eyes

3) U doing it with K
4) K's spitting in our basin; K's toothbrush
5) "Heil Hitler" in the alley; alley dream. Paint squad boy
6) Baby Hitler naked on mother's fat shoulder
7) Accepting invitation to Christmas tea with Fräulein Hofstadt after spying on her

chapter 23

If people bring so much courage to
this world the world has to kill them
to break them, so of course it kills
them. The world breaks every one and
afterward many are strong at the broken places. But those that will not
break it kills. It kills the very good
and the very gentle and the very brave
impartially. If you are none of these
you can be sure it will kill you too
but there will be no special hurry.

—Ernest Hemingway, A Farewell to Arms

There were only four of us invited to Fräulein
Hofstadt's: Helga, an upper-class girl who was a
Vertrauens-Schülerin, or trusted student, and a member of the student council; Hannah, the head of the student
council; and Rosa and me. We were the only girls in our
year who were invited. Fräulein Hofstadt's apartment was
elegant in a quiet way. There was nothing ornate, the furniture was of simple lines. I think Mama would have said
it was sophisticated. The walls were the color of sand, and
the couch and easy chairs were covered in some material
that reminded me exactly of café au lait. Fräulein Hofstadt

was dressed in cream-colored cashmere pants and a sweater that honestly were nearly identical to an outfit Joan Crawford had worn in a picture I had seen in a fashion magazine.

She had the table beautifully set and a fire lit in the pretty porcelain stove. There was a tiered platter with an assortment of tiny little cakes decorated with Christmas frosting designs and a silver pot of tea. At each of our places was a gift. When we opened them, we each found a glass pendant with a wildflower pressed inside it.

"Every one is different," she said. "But they are all flowers from my home village in the mountains of Tyrol."

"Did you ski a lot?" Helga asked as she reached for a tiny cake.

"Oh, most certainly." Fräulein Hofstadt looked down into her plate and a blush crept across her cheeks. "As a matter of fact, would you believe that I once had a part in a movie?"

"What!" We all gasped, our mouths half stuffed with cakes.

"Oh yes, I mean, just as an extra," Fräulein Hofstadt explained. I marveled at how neatly she ate. No crumbs on her mouth. I already had crumbs in my lap and a few scattered to one side of my plate. I felt like a complete slob.

"What movie?" Helga asked.

"The Holy Mountain."

"With Leni Riefenstahl?" Hannah's eyes opened wide.

It was all too unbelievable.

"Yes, indeed. That was her first film, I think."

"Did you meet her?" Hannah asked. "My aunt, Lotte

Gruen—you know, the wife of the industrialist Hans Gruen—met her once." Rosa was sitting next to me and I nudged her foot with mine under the table. That was so like Hannah. She came from a very wealthy, important Berlin family and was not modest about it. She was always name-dropping.

"Yes, of course, but she was the star. I was only an extra. A speck on the mountain, really. I just had to ski down a slope of virgin snow. You see, I am not an actress but I can ski. They needed someone who could make nice, clean tracks in the snow. It's supposed to be Leni in the film skiing, but to tell you the truth I skied so much better. They couldn't count on her to make those tracks. So the director, Arnold—"

"Arnold Fanck?" Rosa gasped.

"Yes, of course. Arnold Fanck." Rosa and I exchanged looks. Arnold Fanck was one of the most famous movie directors ever. And Fräulein Hofstadt had just called him "Arnold" as if they were old pals! "So Arnold said, 'Now, Trinka'—my nickname, you know. My real name is Katrina. He says, 'Trinka, when you see me drop the flag, you start skiing down the slope. At the halfway point, you carve a great big sweeping turn and stop right where the marker is. Then we'll get Leni up there, and I'll cut to her.'"

We were all so excited that we vowed to go to the movie the next time it played in Berlin. And best of all Fräulein Hofstadt said she would come with us.

"We'll make it another party!" she said.

•   •   •

The Christmas tea party was lovely, and on our way out I noticed a picture of a very handsome young man in a uniform on a bookshelf. Fräulein Hofstadt saw me looking at it and she went over and got the picture down.

"Ah yes, a very dear person in my life." She blinked, and I could see a tear sparkling on her eyelashes. That was all she said as she put the picture back on the shelf.

It was cold when we stepped outside, and Rosa and I both resisted looking down the alley for the gleaming black limousine.

"I wonder," Rosa said, "if maybe she had a romance with Arnold Fanck."

"Are you crazy?" I stopped stock still as the snow swirled down around us.

"Well, she called him 'Arnold.'"

"That's no reason to think they had a love affair. Didn't you see how she looked when she showed us that picture? That was *him*. That was her fiancé. She is faithful to his memory. She will never, ever stop loving him. I know it." I paused, then said in a dreamy voice, "And her name is Katrina."

"What does that have to do with anything?" Rosa asked.

"Katrina is the same as Catherine, like Catherine Barkley."

"Who is Catherine Barkley?"

"Oh, Rosa, she's the main character in the best book I have ever read. *A Farewell to Arms* by Ernest Hemingway. It is so romantic. I'll read some of it to you tonight." Rosa and

I were headed back to my apartment. Mama had said she could sleep over.

So when we got home and tucked into the twin beds in my bedroom, which now seemed too pink and fussy after the sophistication of Fräulein Hofstadt's apartment, I started by reading a love scene from *A Farewell to Arms*. It was the scene where Catherine unpins her hair. I was sure that Hemingway wrote all these details because he must have had just such a love affair. So while the snow fell outside the window of my bedroom, collecting like miniature ski slopes in the corners of the windowpanes, I read.

> "'I loved to take her hair down and she sat on the bed and kept very still, except suddenly she would dip down to kiss me while I was doing it, and I would take out the pins . . . and it would all come down and she would drop her head and we would both be inside of it, and it was the feeling of inside a tent or behind a falls.'"

Rosa sighed. "That is so beautiful. He must have really taken some girl's hair down and then . . . and then, you know, they did it."

Yeah, I thought. *Like Ulla and Karl doing it.* I touched my own short-cropped hair. *Maybe I should think about growing it again.*

chapter 24

The things that happened could only
have happened during a fiesta. Everything became quite unreal finally and
it seemed as though nothing could have
any consequences. It seemed out of
place to think of consequences during
the fiesta.
—Ernest Hemingway, The Sun Also Rises

Even though Baba was Jewish, she always celebrated Christmas with us. She would come
midafternoon on the day of Christmas Eve to help
Mama and Hertha decorate the tree "in secret." In secret
simply meant away from the eyes of children. That was the
German custom. The decorated tree was to be a surprise,
unveiled before the traditional Christmas Eve dinner. Baba
had called to say that she would be a bit late and that Mama
and Hertha should start without her. I took the call and
then went to find Mama to give her the message. I heard
her voice coming from Papa's study. Papa had come home
from his office early since it was a holiday.

"He'll come back, won't he?" I heard Mama say. "He has
papers here, doesn't he?"

"Yes, important ones."

I stopped outside the study door to listen. At first I wasn't sure who they talking about. But the next words clarified everything.

"But when I went with them to Caputh just before they left, you know, so they could close it up, when we walked out the door he turned to Elsa and said, 'Take a good look. You will never see it again.'"

It all made sense. More than two weeks earlier, Papa had gone with Einstein to help him lock up the house and look at a water pipe Einstein was concerned about shortly before he and his wife left for America. He was much more concerned about the plumbing than the angry American women who had protested his anticipated visit.

"Really?" I heard Mama gasp. There was silence, then my mother's voice again. "But the Prussian Academy, the spring conference." There was another long pause. "Otto, you said there had been some rumors back then. And now, has he resigned?"

At this point I tromped my feet lightly on the carpet as if I were just arriving outside the study door and called out, "Mama! Baba called and said she is going to be a little late and you and Hertha should start decorating the tree."

Mama came out of the study, her face creased with worry. She was wringing a handkerchief. This was a habit of hers that resulted in a lot of shredded handkerchiefs. She even refused to buy any fancy handkerchiefs, particularly those with lace trim, because she knew they wouldn't last. I don't know whether it was the light or just the lines etched in Mama's brow, but I suddenly noticed that she looked old. Maybe it was the way she was standing, but it gave me a terrible fright.

"Mama!" I said sharply. "Stand up straight. You look like a little old lady." I was taken aback by my own words. I never spoke to Mama this way. But she just blinked and stood up taller.

Maybe I was the one who had suddenly grown older. I didn't know. But I was frightened for some reason. All I could think of was that this was not the way I should have been feeling on Christmas Eve. Had I outgrown Christmas?

"Go write your *Briefe ans Christkindl*."

"Yes, Mama, of course."

"And tell Ulla to start hers as well. By the time you finish, we'll have the tree almost done."

How much did she think I had to write to Father Christmas? It was the custom to place a letter to Christkindl on one's the window sill on the first Sunday of Advent, but we always did this on Christmas Eve. It was called a *Briefe ans Christkindl*. They would, of course, blow away after a short time. Nonetheless we wrote them in fancy ink and decorated them with colored sugar glued to the paper. When we were younger, Ulla and I always went to great lengths to make them pretty. But as we grew older we took less time with them. Now I felt it was just a bit of a childish old tradition. I went to Ulla's room and gave her some of the colored-sugar packets Mama had prepared.

"We're supposed to write our windowsill letters." I suddenly noticed that her eyes were red as if she had been crying.

"What's wrong with you?"

"Nothing."

"Did you have a fight with Karl?"

"No! What makes you think that?"

"It looks like you've been crying."

"I don't cry when I have fights with Karl," she said fiercely. I found this such an odd response that I couldn't say anything except, "Here's the colored sugar."

I went to my room and didn't really know what to write. Everything just seemed off in our house. But I spread some glue around the edges of the paper and aimlessly sprinkled some silver sugar grains on, then a few pink ones over that. I dipped my pen in the gold ink that I kept for special occasions and began to write.

"Dear Christkindl . . ." I stopped. I didn't know what to say. Yes, there were things I wanted. Mama already knew about them. A cardigan sweater and matching sleeveless one to wear under it, which I had seen in the window at Wertheim. But then I thought of the SA guards there and my desire for it just faded. The Jack London book, but I couldn't even remember the translator's name. As I said, nothing seemed quite right. What did I really want? New telltales for *Ratty*? I suddenly remembered that sunstruck day early in summer messing about in boats. Me at the tiller of *Ratty*, Hessie as my crew, and Professor Einstein and Papa in *Tümmler*, both of them so involved in imagining a universe that they paid no heed to the wind that had begun to stir on the lake.

"Auf wiedersehen!" Uncle Hessie had called, tipping his hat as we sailed past them. But now it was *leb wohl*, not *auf wiedersehen*. For this was truly good-bye. Einstein had told his wife to take a good look when they left their house in Caputh. For in fact, it was good-bye to all that. I just knew it.

So that was all I wrote in my windowsill letter. *Dear Christkindl, Leb wohl. Your friend, Gaby.*

"All right, all right!" Mama came walking down the hall. "You can come out now. Tree's up. Baba's here." Mama looked much better. She had freshened her makeup and changed into a pretty long skirt and silk blouse. I was wearing the dark green velvet dress that Hessie had given me.

"Oh, Gaby, you look so nice!" Ulla said. She herself looked fine now and seemed to have recovered from whatever was bothering her.

"Do you have Mama's and Baba's gifts?" I whispered.

"Yes, they didn't have the scarf in the blue, I got it in a very nice pale green. And I got the handkerchief set for Baba. Do you have Papa's photo album?" She asked.

"Yes, and I got it monogrammed with his initials. They didn't charge me extra because he is such a good customer at that shop."

Mama had begun playing the song "O Tannenbaum" on the piano. Our celebration always took place in the music room because music was a big part of our Christmas.

"Oooh, Mama!" we exclaimed as we always did on Christmas Eve when we walked into the music room and saw the tree glowing with lights and the Venetian glass icicles that Mama and Papa had bought on their honeymoon to Italy. There were also wonderful marzipan ornaments that Mama and Hertha molded from almond paste and painted over the years. Our first task was to find the new ones.

"*Ratty!*" I squealed as I saw a replica of my little sailboat bobbling on the end of a branch. Mama always tried to do something very personal for each of us. "Look! Look, Ulla, even with the sails! What's yours?" I asked.

"Well, I haven't found it yet."

"Go a little to the left, *Schatzi*," Mama directed Ulla.

I saw Ulla's hand reach out toward a little two-inch-long violin.

Papa came over holding Ulla's old violin case, but a big blue ribbon was tied around it.

"No . . ." Ulla seemed to breathe the single word more than actually say it. She sat down on the piano bench, untied the ribbon, and opened the case. Inside lay a brand-new darkly gleaming violin.

Ulla lifted her eyes. There were like twin blue lakes trembling with tears.

"You got in," Mama said.

"Vienna! I got in?"

"So soon!" I exclaimed. The audition had only been a few weeks before.

"They must have really like Ulla's performance. Look, it's not a Stradivarius," Papa said. "But you need a decent instrument." Suddenly tears were streaming down Ulla's face. She jumped up and ran from the room.

"What's wrong with her?" Papa said. "She got in. Why is she crying?" Baba gave me a nervous glance.

"She'll be all right," Mama said. "She's just so shocked. You know she was very anxious and now . . . and now . . ." Mama's voice began to dwindle. She looked old and worried again.

"I'm fine! I'm fine!" Ulla came back into the music room blowing her nose heartily. "I don't know I just . . . I was just overcome, that's all. I'm so excited. I just didn't know how I really did at the audition."

"Well let me pour us something to drink and let's toast your career," Papa said.

"It's not a career yet, Papa." Ulla laughed.

"Try out the violin. Play us something."

Ulla picked up the violin and plucked each of the four strings. Mama went to the piano and played a chord, to help her tune. This went on for perhaps a minute or so and finally Ulla looked at Mama, nodded, and began to play "Greensleeves."

She played this old English ballad so beautifully. Clear, limpid notes sparkled in the air. In those first measures it was as if when she drew the bow across the strings she were releasing the music into the sky, each sound illuminating the night. And there was such purity, such tenderness. Mama played the harmony, and she nodded at Baba to sing, for Baba had a lovely voice.

It is odd how quickly feelings and perceptions can change. Like shadows that stretch longer in the dwindling hours of the day, the one of Hitler had cast us into a long, steadily darkening afternoon. But every once in a while there would come a perfect moment, like a gleam of sunlight that gilded our lives. Right now was one of those moments as Mama and Ulla played "Greensleeves" and Baba sang. I thought again of that moment on the lake with Uncle Hessie, Papa, and Einstein. If only these two moments could last forever.

chapter 25

We did not return to school until the middle of January. Fräulein Hofstadt swirled into class looking as if she had just come off the set of *The Holy Mountain* or one of the other fabulous mountain movies. These films always featured the great outdoor landscapes of Germany or Austria with beautiful, vigorous blond actors and actresses skiing or climbing up peaks.

She was tanned, her hair a few shades lighter, and she seemed brimming with enthusiasm and anticipation for the "extraordinary" second term of school. We would be reading *Hamlet*, and in fact that was to be our spring play. In a few weeks, casting for the roles would begin. It seemed to me like an odd play to be putting on in an all-girls' school.

But logic seemed to have little to do with it. When Anneliese Freiborne questioned how any girl could ever play Hamlet, and of course all the other male parts, Fräulein Hofstadt seemed taken aback. She launched into a spirited lecture on how Hamlet was the quintessential German warrior, which of course had nothing to do with the issue of girls playing male parts.

I raised my hand. "But Fräulein Hofstadt, I don't understand. I thought Hamlet was supposed to be melancholy and indecisive."

"That is the old interpretation. We must look between the lines when we read *Hamlet* and understand the play in a new way."

I found that *Hamlet* would be the least of my problems.

After school that day Rosa and I passed a newsstand and saw a two-inch-high headline. HITLER'S PARTY WINS BIG IN LIPPE!

That the Nazis had won a parliamentary election in Lippe, a small state in central Germany, far from Hitler's native Austria to the south, was alarming to say the least. But Rosa quickly noted which paper we were looking at. "Look it's the *Völkischer Beobachter*." The People's Observer was the official paper of the Nazi Party. Not one of the other papers on the newsstand appeared to have any mention of this "Big Win."

Rosa and I parted ways at the corner, for she had a doctor's appointment and I continued back home. When

I approached our building, Herr Hölle practically danced through the door to greet me, holding a copy of the *Völkischer Beobachter* in his hands. I stopped and looked at him hard. I wanted to say something, but I was frightened and the words became tangled in my brain. So I just shook my head, looked down, and stomped through the door. He began whistling the "Horst Wessel Song" as I passed, and the only thing I dared do was clamp my hands over my ears. He laughed at me. So I could now add item number eight to my Diary of Shame.

1) SA officer on Kurfürstendamm
2) Beer garden in Caputh when boy sings "The Watch on the Rhine"—K's eyes
3) U doing it with K
4) K's spitting in our basin; K's toothbrush
5) "Heil Hitler" in the alley; alley dream. Paint squad boy
6) Baby Hitler naked on mother's fat shoulder
7) Accepting invitation to Christmas tea with Fräulein Hofstadt after spying on her
8) Didn't have the courage to call Herr Hölle a complete shithead.

And then I wrote this in my diary: *I am completely gutless. Why couldn't I say something? I wanted to say he was lower than low, that his stupidity was mind boggling; that if Hitler won, the rest of the world would think of us as scum. Why did the words become all mixed-up for me? Am I such a perfect German child that I dare not say anything to my elders even when I know they are morally wrong, monstrously immoral? I am pathetic.*

The news about the Nazis' big win in Lippe did make it to the radio. I heard it blaring from Papa's study as I came into the apartment. Hertha was lingering outside the study with her dusting cloth, taking a very long time to polish the hallway credenza with its old pieces of family silver. A very slight smile played across her usually impassive face. I walked by her and entered the study. My parents looked tense, but as soon as I came in they affected an almost overly casual manner.

"Lippe," I said. "That's bad, isn't it?"

"Nonsense!" my father said dismissively.

"It means nothing," Mama said. "Nothing at all. It's a tiny state. The total vote was ninety thousand and Hitler only got thirty-nine thousand of that."

A half hour later we were having tea in the music room when the telephone rang. Hertha came in to say that Frau Blumenthal was calling. Mama went to speak to her. When she returned, she looked slightly worried.

"Baba says that for some reason this win in Lippe, though not much, impressed some of the men behind the Old Gentleman."

"Chancellor Schleicher?" Papa asked. "Did it impress him?"

"She didn't say." Mama cocked her head. "You know, that is odd, she didn't mention him. And now that I think about it, she seemed . . ." Mama hesitated. "She seemed rather guarded on the phone."

"Baba needs to be a little more guarded. I worry about her," Papa replied.

"You mean because she's Jewish?" I asked. Papa looked at me. There was that gray, sad mist in his eyes that I had never seen until this past year.

"Yes, because she's Jewish," he answered.

"But Papa, I thought you said Lippe didn't count for much."

"It doesn't." He paused. "But these are just not good times."

"Don't worry her, Otto," Mama said.

This angered me. "Mama, don't talk like that. First of all, I am here in the room. You don't have to say 'her' when I'm right here. Secondly, I'm not a baby."

"Don't speak to your mother that way, Gabriella."

I closed my eyes. So would this be item number nine? I have the guts to speak to my mother rudely but not Herr Hölle? I went to my room to study before dinner.

It had begun to drizzle and then a wind from the west side of the city came, which always seemed to swirl up old leaves from the courtyard garden below, and now rain-splattered leaves were flattened against my window. I noticed, however, some smeary colors against the pane that were hardly from nature. I went over to the window to examine what was stuck there more carefully. An envelope! My windowsill letter to Christkindl? After almost three weeks?

But it was not my letter. It was Ulla's. The sugar and the colored inks had smeared until it was barely legible. The only word I could make out was *freund*, friend. And then it looked as if she had written the words "help me," but I couldn't really tell. There were many other illegible words on the paper. I wasn't sure quite what to do with it. One was not really supposed to read another's windowsill letter. It was private, for Christkindl. But I didn't think I should return it to Ulla, either. So I tore it up into very small bits, and put it in my trash bin.

A week later we were sitting at our dining table with Uncle Hessie and Baba for dinner when the telephone rang. Hertha came into the dining room looking quite agitated.

"I am sorry to interrupt, but it is a call for Frau Blumenthal." The color rose in Hertha's face and her eyes sparkled fiercely. "It is the chancellor's wife, Frau Schleicher, calling and she says it is urgent."

"What?" Baba looked as stunned as the rest of us. She got up automatically and followed Hertha to the kitchen. Elisabeth von Schleicher was an old friend of Baba's but that she should call her here at our house seemed strange.

Two minutes later Baba returned. She seemed to be in some sort of a trance. She stopped at Papa's chair and looked down at him. Her lips trembling. "Otto, you were right."

"Right about what, Baba?"

"The Old Gentleman—he is so weak. He is getting sucked in. Hindenburg's son, Oskar, went with Hitler to von Ribbentrop's for a meeting."

"What?" Papa said.

"This can't be good!" Uncle Hessie said, starting to rise from the table.

I thought I had heard this name before—von Ribbentrop. He was a Nazi. He was perhaps like the steel millionaire Fritz Thyssen whom the newspapers sometimes called Hitler's banker. Perhaps von Ribbentrop was another source of money for Hitler, I wasn't sure.

Mama put her hand out and touched Hessie's arm gently. "Sit down. What can you do?" Suddenly I noticed the color had drained from Ulla's face. Beneath her eyes was a greenish tinge. She jumped up from the table. "I feel sick," she said as she ran out of the dining room.

Mama turned to me. "Gaby, go check on Ulla."

There wasn't much to check on. Ulla was on her knees throwing up into the toilet. She waved me out with one arm. "Out! Out! I'll be fine. Just something I ate at lunch."

"You sure?"

"Yes, I'll be fine," she said. I shrugged and walked away.

When I returned to the table, Mama asked me how Ulla was.

"Fine, just something she ate earlier today." I looked around. "Who's this von Ribbentrop man?"

Baba sneered. "A wine merchant who married money and paid for his title. Thus the 'von.' His wife makes Lady Macbeth seem like a pussycat. Horrid woman. But he's always been there behind the scenes for Hitler, ready with the money. He paves the way for him."

"Yes, right to the coffers of the biggest industrialists in Germany," Hessie added.

"But what can Ribbentrop do for him now?"

"Why would Hindenburg? . . ." Papa and Mama were both talking at once.

"It's the Osthilfe scandal," Hessie said.

"It's bribery!" Papa fumed.

"Wait! Wait!" I held up my hands almost shouting. I was completely frustrated. I had no idea what this scandal was, but I sensed it was important.

"What's in God's name is the problem, Gaby?" Papa exclaimed. "We don't shout at the dinner table."

"Yes, we do!" I said heatedly. "I don't understand a thing you are talking about except that it's all bad. You think someone is paying so Hitler can be chancellor? Is that it?" No one answered.

"I know the Nazis have a lot of seats, but they don't have a majority because no one does. So I don't understand. It's a democracy, isn't it? But now it's like they are changing the rules. You can't change the rules in the middle of a game. It isn't fair."

Everyone looked down into their plates of uneaten food. No one answered.

"Is it?"

I felt something collapsing in me. No, not just in me. I looked around the table at everyone's faces. It was that sensation again, not of a vacuum, but of the black hole of a dying star with a gravitational pull so strong nothing would escape. Not even light.

chapter 26

Mr. Walters fell to "showing off,"
with all sorts of official bustlings
and activities. . . . The librarian "showed off"—running hither
and thither with his arms full of
books. . . . The young lady teachers
"showed off." . . . The young gentlemen teachers "showed off". . . . The
little girls "showed off" in various
ways, and the little boys "showed
off" with such diligence that the
air was thick with paper wads and
the murmur of scufflings. And above
it all the great man sat and beamed
a majestic judicial smile upon all
the house, and warmed himself in the
sun of his own grandeur—for he was
"showing off," too.

—Mark Twain,
The Adventures of Tom Sawyer

So this was how the chain worked. These were the
links. First there was the black limousine with the
hand mysteriously opening the door and Fräulein
Hofstadt getting in. Next, Papen's resignation as chancellor
in early December. Then Schleicher becoming chancellor.
Einstein leaving Germany for good. Papa's prediction that

the Old Gentleman would be sucked in. Then on January twenty-eighth, after fifty-seven days as chancellor, von Schleicher resigned and yes, it happened—January thirtieth, the Old Gentleman finally gave in and asked Hitler to form a new government. At this point, the Austrian corporal, a corporal no more, became chancellor. And thus began the first link in a new segment of the chain. The segment that would become the Third Reich, the name for the totalitarian dictatorship under Hitler that was supposed to last for one thousand years.

It was Tuesday, January thirty-first, the first day of school after Hitler became chancellor. Rosa and I walked into the classroom and sat at our desks as usual. Fräulein Hofstadt jumped up. No, it would be more accurate to say that she exploded from her chair and raised her right arm at an angle from her chest, the palm of her hand down. "Heil Hitler!" she shrieked. And guess what? I jumped up with the rest of the class and raised my arm as well. *This* was item number nine in my Diary of Shame.

1) SA officer on Kurfürstendamm
2) Beer garden in Caputh when boy sings "The Watch on Rhine"—K's eyes
3) U doing it with K
4) K's spitting in our basin; K's toothbrush
5) "Heil Hitler" in the alley; alley dream. Paint squad boy

6) Baby Hitler naked on mother's fat shoulder
7) Accepting invitation to Christmas tea with Fräulein Hofstadt after spying on her
8) Didn't have the courage to call Herr Hölle a complete shithead
9) Saluted Hitler

And this is what I wrote: *"I am no better than Herr Hölle."*

I didn't tell Mama and Papa about what happened in school. They were too upset about what was happening at the university. My little world of school was minor in comparison. I was tempted to tell Ulla, but she seemed very distracted and worried about something. I did hear her arguing with Karl on the telephone, and she certainly was not crying. She actually called him a *Dummkopf*. But then the next minute her voice turned sweet and she was apologizing and saying she hadn't really meant it.

The following day, February first, Fräulein Hofstadt called a special meeting of what she called "my girls" after school. I was nervous. Ever since she had shouted out "Heil Hitler," I was uncertain how I felt about Fräulein Hofstadt. She was not the only teacher who had done this, but one of the few. Maybe it was required now, and not every teacher got the word or something. It was unsettling, nevertheless.

The special meeting included Rosa and me and Helga and Hannah—the four of us who had attended the Christmas tea party. I thought a first that it was going to have something to do with the play *Hamlet*, although seeing as Helga and Hannah were not in the same class as Rosa and me, I wasn't sure why I would have thought this. As I walked into Fräulein Hofstadt's apartment, I felt my stomach tighten when I saw that on her collar she was now wearing a glittering jeweled swastika.

"Fräulein," said Fräulein Hofstadt, "I have something very exciting to share with you." She paused and looked at each one of us. There was a little plate of cookies and teacups already set out. She began pouring the tea and talking at the same time. Her movements were so smooth, so graceful. I could never pour tea into tiny cups and talk at the same time. I would have spilled it at best or scalded someone at worst. "Since our Führer has become chancellor, I have been given permission to form a BDM and I want you, my girls, to each become a candidate for *Jungmädelschaftsführerin*. A leader."

We looked at each other in amazement. The BDM was the girls' division of the Hitler Youth group. It stood for *Bund Deutscher Mädel*. Fräulein Hofstadt began to hand out pamphlets to each of us with a picture of a girl on the cover. My hand shook as she handed me the pamphlet. I dared not look at Rosa.

"Gaby, doesn't she look just like you before you cut your braids?" Helga said, remembering me from the other school building when we were both there. The girl on the cover of the pamphlet had long blond braids, and she was standing on a mountainside with a tiny alpine village in the background. Looming over everything was a dark iron statue of an eagle. The eagle looked left, which meant that it was the symbol of the Nazi Party. When the eagle looked right it was considered the symbol of Germany.

"I don't think she looks anything like me," I said adamantly. But in truth, at first glance she did. She was an Aryan paragon of the Third Reich. I could not stand to be anyone's ideal. To be an ideal was to be less than human.

"If you join the BDM, you will be eligible to go to summer camp. Take a look at the booklets. There will be all sorts of sports, because the Führer believes in developing young women's strength through joy. There is a membership fee and a cost for the BDM uniform, but it's very small."

On the very first page, written in a flourishing script printed just beneath a swastika, were these words: *The role of girls in the Third Reich is a sacred one. It is above all their duty to become strong and healthy and to produce healthy children. . . .*

I read this and flipped quickly through the book. There were photographs of girls who looked to be about my age swimming, hiking, playing outdoor games.

"But I don't understand," I said, flipping back to the first page. "What is this about having babies? Are we supposed to go to the summer camp to get babies?"

There was an eruption of giggles. Even Fräulein Hofstadt laughed. "No, not right away. But you must develop your body, your constitution, to have children. That will be your gift to the Reich." I felt a cold sweat begin to creep over me. There was something indecent about people, Fräulein

Hofstadt, whoever wrote this book, anyone, telling me about having babies. This wasn't the facts of life, a birds-and-bees talk that a girl has with her mother. This was the government, the Third Reich. I felt Rosa shift in her chair.

"Yes, Rosa, do you have a question?" Fräulein Hofstadt asked.

"Why isn't Ellie Schuman here?" Rosa asked. "She's president of student council."

Fräulein Hofstadt cocked her head and smiled sweetly at Rosa. "But Rosa dear, she's Jewish."

"Oh," was all that Rosa said.

I can't do this! I thought. *What will Mama and Papa say? I have to tell her no.* Yesterday had been bad enough when I jumped up like a jack-in-the-box in response to Fräulein's Hofstadt's "Heil Hitler," but did Fräulein Hofstadt have to be the organizer of a Hitler Youth Group in our school? It just didn't seem to fit with a teacher who loved literature as she did. Marching about? Strength Through Joy and not joy through language and poetry?

I was staring at my hand, which rested on the desk. "Gaby! Gaby!" called Fräulein Hofstadt. Rosa gave me a nudge. "Gaby, *Herzchen*, have you gone deaf? I am asking you a question. Will you and Rosa be leaders?"

"Uh . . ." I looked at Rosa. I had been so distracted that I had no idea how she had answered this question. "I would have to ask my parents."

"Yes, yes of course," Fräulein Hofstadt replied tersely. She seemed slightly irritated but continued. "Rosa said that her mother might not be able to afford the fee, but I can assure you, Rosa, that this is not a problem. There is a relief fund for those who are financially burdened. I am sure that is not the case with you, Gaby."

"I don't know. It might be."

Now Fräulein Hofstadt looked really annoyed. "Well." She sniffed. "Believe me, there are others willing to take your place. This is a great honor. I would not pass it up if I were you."

You're not me! I wanted to scream. But did I say it? Did I mutter even a syllable? No. I just got up and left the room.

"I can't believe it!" Rosa said as we walked home from school.

"I hate her. I hate her!" I kept repeating. But in truth it was not really hatred I was feeling, it was heartbreak. How had I believed in Fräulein Hofstadt so completely, how had I worshiped her? She had become like a religion to me, a religion of style and grace. She was not like a movie star up there with a gorgeous, flawless face that, magnified by the camera lens, stretched from one side of the screen to another but was still remote and unreachable. She was my teacher. She was close up. She graded my papers, invited me for tea. She was real.

"What are you going to tell your parents?" Rosa asked.

"I don't know. Maybe nothing." But I knew that I would have to tell them something. I just wasn't sure how or what.

• • •

It turned out to be easier than I thought.

When I came home, Baba was there. She and Mama were having tea. "I'll tell you, Elske, the swastika is becoming a decorative accessory. I saw a dog being walked with a swastika-ornamented collar."

"Speaking of bitches . . ." I said.

"*What?*" Mama shrieked. Baba's teacup clattered in its saucer as she set it down.

I squared my shoulders, squeezed my eyes shut, and began speaking as rapidly as possible. I wanted to get it out—all of it, quickly. "Fräulein Hofstadt wore a jeweled swastika pin today and we have to say Heil Hitler before almost every class and she has asked me to be one of the leaders of the BDM." I opened my eyes.

"What? What are you saying? She's a Nazi?" Mama asked.

"Yes." Something flared in me, a pent-up anger. Did I have to spell it out for Mama? Why else would one wear a jeweled swastika?

"DMB? What?" she whispered.

Why was she being so dense? "BDM, Elske, the *Bund Deutscher Mädel*, the Girls' Service League," Baba said.

"The Hitler Youth." Mama's mouth seemed to struggle around the shape of the words. My anger died. I felt sorry for Mama. She was confused. I was confused. I leaned forward and touched her hand gently.

"Yes, Mama, she wants me to be a leader of the Hitler Youth."

Mama stood up. She was shaking. "I have to call your father at his office immediately."

Tears made the whole room swimmy. I felt something inside me collapsing, turning dark, pulling me toward that precipice of blackness.

The note that I brought to school the next morning was polite but to the point.

Dear Fräulein Hofstadt,

Our daughter Gabriella shall not be participating in the BDM activities. We feel that although Hitler is now the chancellor, participating in his youth group is not part of the education we have envisioned for our daughter, as stated in the Gymnasium Kaiser Frederick Wilhem's educational philosophy, which proposed to encourage "intellectual curiosity" and "independent thinking."

Sincerely yours,
Mrs. Otto Schramm

Professor Otto Schramm
Chairman of the Department of Photoastronomy
University of Berlin

Rosa's mother wrote a similar letter.

We presented our notes to Fräulein Hofstadt before class. She read first the one from my parents and then the one from Rosa's. She set them down and looked at us coldly. Then a brief smile cracked her face. "This is a shame. I think your parents will see the error of their ways. But there are many others who will be very happy to take your place." She drew out a small book and wrote something down in it. This was not the last time that we would see Fräulein Hofstadt write in this book. She now kept it with her at all times, or so it seemed.

Within that first month after Hitler became chancellor there were several changes at the Gymnasium Kaiser Frederick Wilhelm. Some were immediately noticeable. Soon after Hitler's appointment, a truck with SA men had driven up and unloaded several large boxes. By the next morning a photograph of Adolf Hitler had been hung in every classroom as well as the assembly hall and the library. The portraits were always flanked by a German flag on one side and on the other side a Nazi flag. Under the new rules of the Third Reich, we were to face the flag during our morning Heil Hitlers, which were required at the beginning of every school day.

The days following Rosa's and my refusal were awful. Although Fräulein Hofstadt was not our only teacher, she had emerged since Hitler's triumph as clearly one with the most authority in the school. Because of this our lives were made miserable in subtle ways. Fräulein Hofstadt basically ignored us in class. She rarely called on us to recite and when we raised our hands to answer a question, she would call on us only when no other hands were raised. Once, rather than call on me, she simply grimaced and gave the answer herself.

I felt it was as if we, Rosa and I and Fräulein Hofstadt, were circling one another like wary animals. We were not the only girls whose parents did not want them to join the BDM. She did not treat them any better.

But Fräulein Hofstadt had been right. There were others only too happy to take our place in the BDM.

Girls started vying for Fräulein Hofstadt's attention. They began showing off, waving their hands madly in class, doing work for extra credit, wearing swastika barrettes. Even other teachers seemed to be trying to impress Fräulein Hofstadt. She had created her own small solar system within our school, with herself as a dazzling sun that was the center of everyone's orbit, save for a very few.

Fräulein Hofstadt's behavior toward the Jewish girls was not so subtle. On the first day after Hitler became chancellor, desks were rearranged so that the Jewish girls sat apart. She never called on them or looked at them. If there was a shortage of books or handout sheets, they simply didn't get any, but were still expected to do the homework. And although her conduct toward the Jewish students now seemed pronounced, I realized that Fräulein Hofstadt had never really been particularly warm or welcoming to them. Miri Goldfein, who was probably the smartest girl in our class, never got high marks from Fräulein Hofstadt, and she did more extra credit work than any other student. Because of her only middling grade in Fräulein Hofstadt's class Miri missed being the top student in our grade.

On some level I must have realized this, but why had I never thought about it before? Why had I so conveniently ignored it in my enthrallment with Fräulein Hofstadt? Had I been mesmerized, transfixed, bedazzled by this glittering goddess? Rosa and I were bewildered by the change in Fräulein Hofstadt and by our own blindness. Why had we not seen through the gloss to the tarnished darkness?

One day after school I sprinted across the one hundred meters to the neighborhood library looking for a book of commentary on Virgil's orations for Latin class, I caught the familiar scent of roses and narcissus, then I heard Fräulein Hofstadt's voice. She was at the desk, addressing Frau Grumbach, the librarian. Over Frau Grumbach's desk just under the newly hung Hitler portrait there was a poster of the girl from the BDM booklet, the one with the braids and the iron eagle. Posters like this one, along with the flags and portraits of the Führer, now proliferated throughout public spaces.

"Frau Grumbach, I received your note. I am afraid this is unacceptable. You are aware that just two and a half weeks ago the Decree for the Protection of the German People was passed. A Ministry of Public Propaganda and Enlightenment is now forming, and it will be producing a list of all books which are to be banned from the library. We need a list of the students and other people of the community who use this library and who have checked out the kind of books that will be banned."

I was in the shadow of two rows of shelves. I pulled out a fat book of Latin commentaries, which gave me a perfect slot to view this conversation yet not be seen. Fräulein Hofstadt, in her elegantly tailored suit with its generous shoulder padding, towered over the tiny librarian, who stood on the opposite side of the checkout desk.

"First of all, Fräulein, the decree you cite is only a temporary emergency decree as declared by the Reichstag," said Frau Grumbach. "It does not call for the confiscation of literature, and it has not as yet created a list of banned books. It would be impossible for me to know which books you are referring to as being dangerous."

"Well, I have a preliminary list right here with me."

"'Preliminary'?" Frau Grumbach shook her head wearily. "It is not official, Fräulein. If it is not official, I cannot accept it. And I have no idea how you would come to have such a list."

"Are you questioning my authority?"

"Well," Frau Grumbach said, and with a slight twist of her mouth, she flashed a sardonic smile, "I suppose I am.

But it doesn't matter, because I don't have time for your supposed list, or time for making up a list of our library patrons for your perusal. If you think it is so important, you do it."

"Me? I'm not a librarian. You're the librarian."

"Precisely, Fräulein Hofstadt." She adjusted the dark rimmed pince-nez spectacles that she always wore. "It is not the job of a librarian to spy on readers and their selections. I am a civic employee and you are an employee of the Frederick Wilhelm Gymnasium. You are seriously overstepping boundaries. I do not come into your school and tell you how to do your job, and you should not tell me how to do mine."

Fräulein Hofstadt took out the little book she always carried and wrote something in it . "You will see whose job it is then!" she snapped, and walked out of the library, her immense shoulders twitching in what now seemed to me to be a ridiculous show of indignation.

The following morning at break I went to the library to get another book I needed. There was a woman I did not know sitting at the checkout desk.

"Excuse me, where is Frau Grumbach?"

"She's left."

"Left?"

"Yes, she will no longer be working here."

"Where has she gone? To another library?"

"I have no idea. But can I help you find something?"

"No, thank you." I shook my head. "I can find it."

"Oh, good. I am just getting used to the system, learning it, you know. So you might do better than I would." She smiled, but I was confused. I didn't think each library had a different classification system.

"Did the library you worked in before use a different system?"

"Oh dear, I was never a librarian. I'm a stenographer."

And then I understood. Frau Grumbach had been driven out of her job at the library because of her refusal to comply with Fräulein Hofstadt's list. She was an "undesirable," and this was just the beginning of the removal of "undesirables." Usually this meant Jewish teachers. Jewish students were also starting to leave our school. Miri Goldfein had slipped me a message that she could not work on our biology project because she was "going away for a while."

chapter 27

It was a close place. I took it up [the
letter I'd written to Miss Watson], and
held it in my hand. I was a-trembling,
because I'd got to decide, forever,
betwixt two things, and I knowed it.
I studied a minute, sort of holding my
breath, and then says to myself:
"All right then, I'll go to hell"—
and tore it up.
It was awful thoughts and awful
words, but they was said. And I let
them stay said; and never thought no
more about reforming.

—Mark Twain,
The Adventures of Huckleberry Finn

There were many things that I decided simply not
to tell my parents about. Nor was I tempted to
confide in Ulla, who seemed increasingly distant
these days. I actually was fearful that if my parents began
to complain too much, our family might be singled out
in some way. The librarian, Frau Grumbach, had simply
disappeared when she had refused to comply with Fräulein Hofstadt's orders. There were stories of other people,

friends of friends, who were fired from their jobs or simply disappeared without any explanations.

One of the things I decided not to tell them about was the swastika assignment. During the first month of Hitler's chancellorship, all the students at my school were given an excerpt from the book *Mein Kampf*, in which Hitler wrote about the swastika and how he worked on its design as the symbol of the Nazi Party. We were to study this and to research the history of the symbol of the broken cross. We would be given a test on all of this material. For extra credit we could describe a product or accessory in which the swastika could be incorporated. There would then be a vote on the best design scheme. How democratic!

The BDM members had started wearing their uniforms to school. This engendered much excitement. Passing through the corridors one could hear arguments about the proper way to wear the neckerchief with the leather slide.

"You know," Helga was saying, fingering the brown leather slide through which her neckerchief tails were threaded, "the *Mädelschaftsführerinnen* get to wear the special lanyards." Hannah and Helga and the two other girls who had been picked in Rosa's and my place were training to become *Mädelschaftsführerinnen*, the girl leaders of the BDM.

"My cousin is a *Mädelschaftsführerin*. That's even higher, it means you're the leader of at least four groups. And she gets to wear a green lanyard," Nadia, a plump girl with bright red hair, said.

"Fräulein Hofstadt says . . ." another girl interrupted Nadia.

That was the name that one heard most often in the classroom. She was now the object of worship for almost every girl in the entire school, even those who did not take her literature course. Indeed her renown had spread to the youngest gymnasium students. If they were outside when Fräulein Hofstadt was on schoolyard duty, they would surround her until the older students came out for our break. Then they would sit on the sidelines and watch in envy, dreaming of when they could become *Jungmädel*, young maidens in the BDM. Despite the portraits of Hitler in every room, the Nazi Party flags hanging from every available flagpole or stand, the constant talk of the BDM hierarchy and the colors of lanyards, it was in the schoolyard just after school broke up that the changes were perhaps the most insidious.

It was now February twenty-seventh, a few days after the confrontation between Fräulein Hofstadt and Frau Grumbach in the library. School had just ended and I was standing with Rosa by the linden tree where we so often met. I couldn't help but notice how different the schoolyard appeared now that Hitler was chancellor. In December, one would have seen girls milling about, talking, perhaps a few with jump ropes. But now there was no milling, no randomness to the configuration of students. The activity in the yard itself had redistributed students in a manner I had never seen before.

Scattered around the edges were perhaps half a dozen girls either alone or talking with a friend. Rosa, these six or seven other mostly Jewish girls, and I were the only non-members of the BDM. In the center of the yard were four phalanxes of ten or more girls marching about, singing what was known as "The Banner Song."

Unsere Fahne flattert uns voran.
Unsere Fahne ist die neue Zeit.
Und die Fahne führt uns in die Ewigkeit!
Ja, die Fahne ist mehr als der Tod.

Our banner flutters before us.
Our banner represents the new era.
And our banner leads us to eternity!
Yes, our banner means more to us than death.

On some sort of stick they were flying Fräulein Hofstadt's new red silk scarf with a black swastika on a disc of white. It was cold, and sharp, stinging bits of snow swirled through the air. Rosa and I shivered on the sidelines with perhaps four or five other girls. We all would have been warmer had we been marching. Perhaps even talking would have made us warmer, but we didn't. We had most likely all been given the same advice by our parents: "Be quiet, don't make a fuss, be respectful.'" There were always the implied quotation marks when my parents mentioned the word "respectful" in reference to the Third Reich. The quotation marks were the necessary veneer that covered in truth their contempt.

As I watched the other girls marching I was wondering: if I could hardly endure the next day of school, how in the world could I possibly endure the next thousand years of this Third Reich? Not that I would live a thousand years. But a year? Even that seemed impossible.

Rosa nudged me.

"What's that?" she asked, pulling me from the dismal reveries that swarmed in my brain.

"What's what?" I turned my head in the direction she was looking.

Two SA men were escorting a thin figure across the schoolyard toward us.

"*Mein Gott*, it's Herr Doktor Berg!" I whispered.

The two SA men raised their arms. "Heil Hitler!" Rosa and I immediately raised our arms and responded "Heil Hitler."

"Which one of you is Fräulein Gabriella Schramm?"

My throat constricted. "Me. I am."

"The Jew teacher wishes to speak with you."

"We have allowed this," the other said brightly, as if he had just granted some sort of extreme indulgence.

Herr Doktor Berg stepped forward. He had a package in his hands. "Fräulein Gabriella, I think these belong to you." *My books!* The two books he had confiscated from me more than a year before—Helen Keller's *The Story of My Life* and Jack London's *The Call of the Wild*. I knew it before I even felt their weight as he handed them to me.

"Are you going someplace?" I stammered.

"Yes, I am no longer to teach here."

"So you're going to another school?"

The two SA men snickered and barked, "*Auf geht's!*" Get going.

They spun Doktor Berg around, shoving him ahead. But he turned back and shouted over his shoulder.

"Buck! Buck! I loved that dog! What a dog!"

I was still standing there, clutching the books to my chest and looking in the direction the SA had taken Doktor Berg when the sweet scent of flowers enveloped me on this biting cold day. A voice behind me said, "I'll take that!"

"What?" I turned around. "What are you talking about?" Fräulein Hofstadt was facing me, her eyes glittering like blue glaciers, her head wrapped in a fashionable blue velvet toque.

"I am talking about that package that Herr Berg just gave you. Those officers should not have let a man they are taking away give a package to a student. It must be examined. That was very lax on their part. Now, hand me that package."

Somewhere from inside me, inside my soul perhaps, a flame began to flicker.

"No, Fräulein Hofstadt. These are mine." I clutched the books tighter to my chest.

"I am the teacher, Gabriella. This is a command."

"I do not take commands from you, Fräulein Hofstadt."

"Gabriella, this constitutes extraordinary disobedience."

"And you are a very ordinary person, Fräulein Hofstadt. Coarse, common, ordinary. And you wear entirely too much perfume. You reek!"

chapter 28

Bill opened his mouth to speak, but
changed his mind. Instead, he pointed
towards the wall of darkness that
pressed about them from every side.
There was no suggestion of form in
the utter blackness; only could be
seen a pair of eyes gleaming like live
coals. Henry indicated with his head
a second pair, and a third. A circle
of the gleaming eyes had drawn about
their camp. Now and again a pair of
eyes moved, or disappeared . . .

—Jack London, White Fang

Rosa stood there gaping at me as I turned and ran
out of the schoolyard. I vowed I would never
return to the Kaiser Frederick Wilhelm School. I
ran around the block and stood in the shadow of a chest-
nut tree on the corner, where I watched the SA men push
Herr Doktor Berg into the back end of a van as I pressed the
package to my chest. I knew neither Mama nor Papa would
be home at this hour. This was Mama's day to go to the conservatory for a meeting with other pianists. They swapped

music scores. I couldn't go home. I didn't want to be alone, and I didn't want to face Mr. Hell and be interrogated as to what had happened in school. I needed to talk to someone, some normal adult. I needed to explain all I had been feeling, and the terrible thing that had just happened in the school-yard. Baba would most likely be at home writing her column. She had connections through the newspaper world, being a reporter. She heard things that others didn't hear. Hadn't Frau von Schleicher called her up that evening at our house during dinner to say that Hitler and Hindenburg's son were on their way to the Ribbentrops'? Maybe Baba would even know where they were taking Herr Doktor Berg. Or where Frau Grumbach had gone. And Miri Goldfein!

"What sort of a license plate has only two numbers?" Those were my first words when Baba opened the door.

"Gaby, what are you doing here?"

I started again to ask my question about the license plate, it was the plate I had seen on the back of the limousine Fräu-lein Hofstadt had been riding in, but I burst into tears.

"Come! Come! Let's get you some tea." She folded me into her soft arms. "Now, now, dear, nothing can be that bad."

"Oh, but it is!" I said, pulling my face away from her shoulder. My tears and runny nose had stained her silk blouse. "I'm never—never *ever* going back to school! I don't care what Mama and Papa say."

She led me into the sitting room. The same room, the same sofa where I had sprawled in July reading *The Sun Also Rises*. The schoolyard story tore from me in jagged, sharp-edged chunks that seemed to leave gouges inside me from the very telling. When I had finished, Baba looked at me and did not say anything right away. When she did speak, what she said surprised me.

"About the license plate. I am sure it is Goebbels's."

"Goebbels? You mean *the* Goebbels, Hitler's adviser?" My voice dropped. Joseph Goebbels was now the most important adviser to Hitler. He was the highest ranking in Hitler's innermost circle of counselors, although he had no official position.

"Yes." She paused. "You're old enough to know. And now there is absolutely no reason you shouldn't know. Fräulein Katrina Hofstadt is Goebbels's new mistress. One in a long line. I am sure there will be more to follow. Or perhaps he has three or four right now. He is an infamous womanizer. His affair with your teacher has been going on for a few months. Your mother and father were very upset when they heard about it but they didn't want to disrupt your studies in the middle of the year."

Fräulein Hofstadt's romance with Goebbels made it all clear to me now. It explained her increased power at the school, the whole thing with the BDM, the firing of Jewish teachers, the harassment of Jewish students. It all fit.

"And what about this list of books and the students who were reading them?"

"Ah." Baba crossed one leg over the other, leaned back against the sofa pillow, and gave a sound that was halfway between a chuckle and a snarl. "Well, Herr Professor Goebbels holds an advanced degree in literature. In fact, last night I was at the annual Opera Ball and he was discussing *Hamlet*."

I opened my eyes wide.

"Yes, you don't expect Nazis to be discussing Shakespeare, do you?"

"Well, now I understand why that is the play Fräulein Hofstadt is planning for the spring, and not Schiller's play about Joan of Arc," I said.

"Oh, yes, you see, Goebbels now suspects Schiller for his radicalism, and he even feels that Goethe's works are not as patriotic as they should be. But he is determined to Aryanize Shakespeare. After all, Hamlet was a Dane, and he went to Wittenberg. Last evening Goebbels was expounding on the parallels between Hamlet being deprived of his rightful inheritance and Germany's losses because of the Versailles treaty. Shakespeare, he says, foreshadowed what was to come." She snorted and continued. "So I don't think you need to worry, Gaby, about your parents insisting that you stay in such a school, because obviously you won't be receiving much of an education from Goebbels's mistress."

I shook my head slowly in wonder. "But Baba how are we going survive this?"

Baba bit her lip lightly, "I don't know, *Herzchen*, I don't know."

*   *   *

No one was home when I arrived at our apartment. I went immediately to my bedroom and untied the string on the package Herr Doktor Berg had given me. There were not two books but three. On top was *The Story of My Life*, by Helen Keller. That one he had confiscated the first term of the previous year. Then there was *The Call of the Wild* by Jack London. And the third was one I had never known about, *White Fang*, also by Jack London and the same translator as *The Call of the Wild*. Inside there was a note from Doktor Berg.

Dear Gabriella,

I kept these books longer than I intended.
Indeed I have had in my possession the
Helen Keller book for over a year now, and
Jack London's *Call of the Wild* for six months.
At today's interest rates, if I were to com-
pound them twice annually, I think I would
owe you 28 marks. Instead of money, I
thought perhaps you would enjoy another
Jack London book. I hope you haven't yet
read it. I couldn't resist when I saw it was
translated by the same person. There is an
elegance to his translation that is quite wonderful.

Good luck to you.
Your friend and professor,
Hermann Berg

I stared at the letter for a long time after I read it. My hands trembled as I held the paper. I had always thought of Doktor Berg as so stern, which he was. But I saw something else now. He was not simply a harsh schoolmaster. He was noble, and he was very brave.

Baba was right. Mama and Papa seemed almost relieved when I said that I didn't want to go back to school. When I told them what had happened, they were not shocked. The same thing was happening at the university. Jewish students were leaving in droves. Jewish professors were being cut. The SA was a constant presence. Einstein's office had been rifled, and it was rumored that his apartment, now empty for almost two months since he had gone to America, had been searched as well. An SS officer had appeared in Papa's office that morning demanding to see his files. Papa chuckled sourly.

"I gave him the copies of the Belopolsky formulations of redshift lines for spiral nebulae and of course fifty pages of calculations. I then began a lengthy explanation of the possible mathematical inconsistencies between that and the Doppler-Fizeau effect. Needless to say, he got bored immediately and just took the papers." Papa seemed quite pleased with himself. He then said that he would call my school the next day and tell them that I would not be returning. "We'll find a new school for you next year," Papa told me. "Until then, I'll teach you at home."

"What about Rosa?" I asked.

"Well, that's a decision that Rosa's mother will have to make," Mama said.

I knew that Rosa's mother would not allow her to leave. Rosa's mother was somewhat timid about such things. She had been reluctant when Rosa had said she did not want to join the BDM. She'd never let Rosa leave school.

Papa had promised that he would try to find out where they had taken Doktor Berg. "Another one for my list," he said with a sigh, and from inside his vest pocket he withdrew a piece of yellow paper.

"What list, Papa?" I asked.

"List of people—friends, friends of friends—who have been suddenly taken away by the SA."

That evening after dinner I started reading *White Fang*. I finished it at midnight. I closed the book and turned out the light but, still propped up in bed against my pillows, I stared into the night through the frost-rimed windowpanes. I thought of the two men from the book, Bill and Henry, alone in the Canadian wilderness.

Somehow the book, the words of Jack London, and my thoughts about Doktor Berg began to entwine. I wondered where he was right now. Where had they taken him? What might he be doing this very instant? It was cold out tonight. Was he shivering? He had been wearing just a light suit jacket, no overcoat, no gloves. Had they not even given him time to get those things? I knew so little about him. I had not even known he was Jewish. I wondered if he was married. What would his wife think if he didn't come home after school? I started to cry silently.

The book Doktor Berg gave me was a tale about men, dogs, and wolves. It was supposed to be just a made-up story—a story that took place in the north country of Canada, in a region called the Yukon. In the beginning, two men and their dogs are out in the wilderness being tracked by a pack of starving wolves. One by one their dogs are devoured by the wolves. And at night the wolf pack begins to press in on their campsite, their eyes gleaming. They creep closer and closer on their bellies, just outside the rim of firelight. The she-wolf "slinks" in a lovely "peculiar, sliding, effortless gait," her eyes wistful with hunger but not affection. My own eyes grew heavy. "'It's a she-wolf,' Henry whispered back to Bill, 'an' that accounts for Fatty an' Frog. She's the decoy for the pack. She draws out the dog an' then all the rest pitches in an' eats 'm up.'"

The face of the she-wolf with her red-hued fur bristling with frost loomed in the night. The fur became creamier, blondish, falling in soft waves, finger waves. It was a slow transformation until the wolf head became that of a beautiful woman, a human face of pure malignancy. Fräulein Hofstadt. Two fangs slashed the night.

I woke up with a silent scream tearing through me. I was gasping. But there was another sound coming from the bathroom. A horrible retching noise. I was confused. Had I been dreaming? Yes, it was a terrible dream, a nightmare but I was hearing this other animal-like sound. Then a sob.

I got up and went to the bathroom. The door was open just a crack. Ulla was on her knees.

"Ulla!" I whispered. "Ulla, what's wrong?"

"I'm pregnant."

chapter 29

Each day mankind and the claims of mankind slipped farther from him. Deep in the forest a call was sounding, and as often as he heard this call, mysteriously thrilling and luring, he felt compelled to turn his back upon the fire . . . and to plunge into the forest. . . . But as often as he gained the soft unbroken earth and the green shade, the love for John Thornton drew him back to the fire again.

—Jack London, <u>The Call of the Wild</u>

"What are you going to do?" I asked Ulla.

"I don't know." Ulla drew back from the toilet and flushed it. She remained sitting on the tile floor. I sank to the edge of the tub and looked at her.

"You have to tell Mama and Papa."

"I know."

"Have you told Karl?"

"Sort of."

"What do you mean?"

"Well, you know, I said I had missed my period. But this happened once before and it was nothing, so maybe . . ."

"Will you get married?"

"I guess. Karl really wants to. I mean, in a way, Karl is happy, or at least he was when I thought I might have been pregnant a while back. As I said, I haven't exactly told him this time."

"Why would he be happy?"

"I don't think he really wants me to go to Vienna to the conservatory next September."

"Oh" was all I could say. I was trying to imagine how she could go to Vienna with a little baby. Or maybe I could help take care of the baby after school.

Suddenly we began hearing sirens. The blare grew louder and louder, the long shrill blasts scoring the night.

"What's going on?" Ulla stood up suddenly.

We looked out the bathroom window. There was a red glow in the sky. I heard Mama and Papa coming from their bedroom down the hall. The sirens were becoming louder.

"Clean yourself up," I whispered. "I'll go find out what's happening."

I went out into the hallway and nearly slammed into Papa, who was putting his winter coat on over his pajamas.

"Where are you going?" I asked.

"To the roof," he replied. His face was dark. His hair was rumpled as if he had been running his fingers through it.

"I want to come, too!" I said.

At that moment the phone rang. "Get the phone, Gaby!" Mama shouted. Mama never shouted. But everything seemed suddenly frantic.

I ran for the phone. "Schramm residence."

"The Reichstag's on fire!" the voice gasped. Had I heard right?

"Baba!" I shouted into the phone. "Baba, the Reichstag? Are you sure? What's happening?"

"Just what I said. The Reichstag is on fire."

"Where are you?" I was suddenly worried that maybe she was there at the Reichstag, although why Baba would be at the German parliament past midnight, or at any hour, I didn't know.

"I'm at the Esplanade Ball. I was sitting with the Italian ambassador and Colonel Schaumburg, the Commander of the City of Berlin." She dropped her voice. "Horrible man, but his aide came to the table and announced that the Reichstag was in flames."

"Who is it?" Mama came in her heavy flannel wrapper.

"Baba!" I replied. "She says the Reichstag is burning."

Mama grabbed the phone.

"Is it true?" Mama asked me.

"Of course it's true, Mama." She flapped her hand for me to be quiet as she spoke into the receiver. "Baba, I'm scared. I think you have to get out. It's . . . it's all disorder!"

I looked at my mother. "Disorder" seemed like such an odd word. It was a catastrophe, not just disorder. "Yes, yes." She was nodding into the phone. "No, I know. No, she won't be going back to school. Not now. Not here, at least. Ulla can still go to Vienna in the fall."

Oh God, I thought. *This really is becoming a mess.*

She hung up the phone. "Mama, can I go up on the roof with Papa?"

She shook her head wearily.

"Why not?"

But she gave in a minute later.

We all went up. Ulla, too. All of us bundled into our winter coats, fleece-lined snow boots, ski hats, mittens. We were not the only ones on the roof. Four other families lived in our building and most of them were up there too, even Herr Professor Blumen, on his two canes. And of course Herr Himmel, our stalwart *Hausmeister*. He was bobbing up and down with excitement.

"It's the Communists!" he announced. "The Reds. They're the ones who set the fire."

Papa looked at him sharply.

"Herr Himmel." Papa's voice was low and level. It reminded me of a file with a rasp edge. I hoped he was going to grind this man down. "We would all prefer if you would keep your speculative remarks to yourself. You know nothing of this situation, but if you talk much more we might begin to think you know more than you should and that might prove dangerous for you and your job here. Your job, Herr Himmel, is *Hausmeister*, not political commentator."

I was so proud of Papa, I could have hugged him right

there. But I didn't. I noticed, however, that the other tenants of the building were smiling and nodding in approval.

We could now see the flames quite clearly, even though we were nearly a half mile from the Reichstag. And when the wind changed, we could smell it. Despite the cold, most of us stayed on the roof for almost two hours.

By the next afternoon, speculation was rampant. When I came down with Mama, Herr Himmel was standing by the door, a newspaper prominently in one hand with the headline COMMUNIST SUSPECT ARRESTED. There was a look of sheer vindication on his face. We were setting off to meet Baba at Olbermann's Konditorei, a favorite pastry shop of hers. Now that I was not going to school, I got to join them. I had lied to Mama about Ulla, who once again was vomiting in our bathroom. I just told Mama that that she wasn't feeling well. I dared not even mention throwing up. So I said that she had a sore throat and we should stop at the pharmacy on the way home for some throat lozenges.

"What's she doing outside the pastry shop?" Mama asked as we rounded the corner and spotted Baba standing by a lamppost with a quizzical look on her face. As we approached Baba said nothing, but she hitched her thumb in the direction of the shop. There was a sign in the window of the pastry shop. *Juden werden hier nicht bedient.* Jews not served here.

• • •

History in the making became my full-time curriculum. I read the papers and listened to the radio constantly. Mostly I listened to the one in my father's study. I was no longer comfortable listening in the kitchen while Hertha cooked, not since what happened three days before the Reichstag fire. I had been eating strudel and doing some math problems Papa had set up for me. A broadcast of popular music was interrupted with a breaking news story.

"The police this morning raided Communist headquarters where they are said to have found plans for an uprising."

"Aha!" Hertha exclaimed. A look of triumph glittered in her eyes. She then returned to peeling the carrots for dinner. I watched her as the announcer continued. She nodded in approval as he reported that "The Führer has ordered the immediate confiscation of all printing presses owned by Communist groups."

"Very smart," she whispered. "Very smart indeed. A wise man."

I got up and walked out of the kitchen.

I waited until Mama finished her piano lesson, but as soon as the student had left, I went in to the music room.

"Mama, I have to talk to you about Hertha."

She took a short little breath. I almost had the feeling she was expecting what I said next. "What about Hertha?"

"I think she's a Nazi." Mama didn't say anything right away. She just looked down at her hands and, twisting her wedding band, she finally nodded.

"Yes, you might be right. Your father and I have discussed this."

"So what are you going to do?"

"I'm not sure. It's a difficult decision. She has been a good, loyal person. If we fire her, I am not sure where she could find work. We would of course be willing to give her a generous leaving wage but I just don't know. I simply don't know."

"I thought I should tell you, that's all. I mean, I was in the kitchen listening to the radio and something came on about Communists and she said . . . well, basically that Hitler was a smart and wise man. You could just tell how much she admired him. It's hard to be around someone who believes that."

"Very hard," Mama whispered.

Three days before the fire, the propaganda machine had already gone into overdrive cultivating fear of Communists. The Red Terror, as it was called, seized the headlines: SA AND SS GRANTED POLICE STATUS IN FACE OF RED TERROR. The article that followed reported that "to protect the German people and all the good citizens of Berlin" against the Communist threat, the formerly private armies of the Nazi Party—the SA, the SS—were officially granted auxiliary police status.

Now a Dutch Communist named Marinus van der Lubbe was arrested and charged with starting the Reichstag fire. All the Nazis needed was a personification of the

Communist evil. Van der Lubbe was the perfect scapegoat. Another headline in a London newspaper that Papa subscribed to shouted, DERANGED DUTCHMAN PERPETRATOR OF REICHSTAG FIRE. The British journalist reported that "A mentally unstable, perhaps slightly retarded young man, Van der Lubbe was said to have been 'discovered' at the scene of the crime." The fact that the reporter put the word "discovered" in quotes was a tipoff that perhaps Van der Lubbe had been set up. German newspapers, even the most liberal, would not dare to suggest such a thing. The following paragraph in the British paper underscored the notion that it was a setup when it reported that a senior Nazi official, upon hearing of the fire, was said to have shouted out "This is the beginning of the Communist revolution."

It was inevitable that the paranoia about Communists would begin to intensify the existing anti-Semitism. But it had still been a shock to me when I stood outside of the pastry shop and saw that sign saying JUDEN WERDEN HIER NICHT BEDIENT. I had turned to Baba.

"I don't get it. I thought it was the Communists they were after now."

Mama said nothing. She just looked at the sign and moved her lips like a child would, trying to sound out words in a primer. I knew what she was thinking: *This simply cannot be.* Then she turned to her dearest friend and blinked rapidly as if to hold back the tears. I noticed that other people slowed briefly as they approached the café, gave a quick glance at the sign, and either rushed on or entered. No one seemed shocked. No one paused as we had. I could not help wondering if we were being watched. Was it perhaps dangerous for us to be standing outside the shop so obviously looking at the sign?

"Yes, the Communists," Baba replied wearily. "And here are the new rules for German people's protections. We have become a police state." She held out a copy of the *Vossiche Zeitung* fresh off the press. The Order of the Reich President for the Protection of People and State was outrageous. The decrees suspended free speech, security of mail or telephone, the rights to assemble. The list went on and on. Seven sections of the constitution guaranteeing individual and civil liberties had been suspended. All these actions were described as "defensive measures against Communist acts of violence endangering the state."

"But I don't see anything about Jews," I said, reading over Mama's shoulder. Actions against Jews would be coming, however. Within a few weeks, Jews would be excluded from holding civil service positions, and the number of Jewish students in schools and universities would be limited. Signs like the one in the coffee-shop window would soon be passed into law.

That day, Mama, Baba, and I had gone to another nearby café. They ordered coffee and I got hot chocolate. While they smoked their cigarettes and drank coffee, I looked at the paper. I turned to Baba's column about the party she had attended the previous evening. "Magda Goebbels wore a stunning Schiaparelli gown. She outshone everyone!" I read aloud. "Baba, I thought you said she usually didn't dress so well?"

"She's improved. I admit I did overstate it a bit. That teacher of yours was there too. My God, that woman practically begged to have her picture taken. I had the photographer take one but made sure the editor didn't use it. I actually feel sorry for Frau Goebbels having to socialize with her husband's mistress. Think of these remarks"—she nodded at the newspaper—"as my social service."

Mama ground out her cigarette, twisting it rather violently in the ash tray. "Stop being stupid, Baba!" I was shocked. I had never heard her speak this way to Baba. "You have to get out! Writing on what Nazi women wear to parties is like fiddling while Rome burns. You have to get out! It's too dangerous for you."

Baba leaned forward, lowering her voice. I wasn't sure if she was angry or what. Certainly what Mama had said was harsh. Baba lifted her chin slightly and blew a thin stream of smoke straight up. It serpentined into the air above the small round table where we sat.

"Listen to me, both of you. I am in the perfect position to help people—not Magda Goebbels. Other Jews. I'll get out in time, rest assured."

The next few weeks would be anything but reassuring.

chapter 30

But there were other forces at work
in the cub, the greatest of which
was growth. Instinct and law demanded
of him obedience. But growth demanded
disobedience. His mother and fear
impelled him to keep away from the
white wall. Growth is life, and life
is for ever destined to make for light.
So there was no damming up the tide
of life that was rising within him—
rising with every mouthful of meat
he swallowed, with every breath he
drew. In the end, one day, fear and
obedience were swept away by the rush
of life, and the cub straddled and
sprawled toward the entrance.

—Jack London, White Fang

On March thirteenth, two weeks after the burning of the Reichstag, Goebbels was officially appointed as head of the Reich Ministry for Public Enlightenment and Propaganda. The next day Rosa arrived at my apartment, having run all the way from school, to announce that Fräulein Hofstadt was leaving for a high government post in the ministry. This did not surprise me.

Goebbels's mistress would not be satisfied with her current employment. There were more glamorous positions than teaching literature to girls at gymnasium.

In the aftermath of the Reichstag fire there had been hundreds of arrests—many Communists, and members of any group that was thought to be a terrorist organization. Some journalists and Jews were also arrested. More decrees to "protect" the German people had been passed. And despite all of this, I felt less safe, and so did the people I came in contact with. Anti-Jewish riots had proliferated throughout Germany and the government did nothing to control them. The pictures in the newspapers were frightening. One did not need a color photograph to imagine the brightness of the orange flames erupting from the roof of a synagogue, or the red blood pouring from the head of an elderly Jewish merchant who had been dragged out of his shop for some unknown reason. But what was almost scarier than the poor man's blood was the SS patrol officers in the picture, standing by with their leashed ferocious dog. It wasn't the dog that had drawn the blood. The dog was actually muzzled. Was this a cousin of Buck or White Fang? When I looked at the picture closely, I thought I saw a kind of terror in the dog's eyes. But the eyes of the on SS officer who faced the camera showed nothing. Not a glimmer of anger, or even madness. Nothing. Nothing at all. They could have been the eyes of a dead man. But I? I felt brutalized as I sat at the kitchen table with the newspaper and a leftover cruller from breakfast, not taking a bite. Hertha was out on an errand for Mama. It was still unclear what my parents planned to do about her. I was staring at the picture when Hertha walked in.

"Something wrong, Gaby?" she asked.

I looked up at her.

"Yes," I said quietly.

Her forehead crinkled up anxiously. "What is it, *Schatzi?*" *How dare she call me Schatzi*, I thought.

"This!" I said, and stabbed my finger at the picture.

She came around and cocked her head to see what I was looking at. "This!" I repeated vehemently.

"Oh, that," she replied casually.

I could have hit her full in the face. I jumped up and glared at her. "That is what you call a chance for things to get better? The chance you dream of, Hertha!"

Hertha took off her apron and set it down elaborately. "Herr Himmel is right. You are—the lot of you—nothing but white Jews!"

And so she left. I was the one responsible for making her go. Quite truthfully I was rather shocked by my own power. Stunned, really. Mama and Papa were relieved, but I could tell a little dismayed, that it had fallen to me to finally do what they considered a task not for a child.

There had been so much turmoil that I had nearly forgotten about Ulla's "situation." That is how she and I referred to it when we talked about it, which was not often. When I inquired she said, "I'm going to tell Mama and Papa soon. Karl wants us to marry in May—that's just six weeks away really. But Karl is very busy right now and so am I, and we just figure we shouldn't get our parents upset before it's necessary." We were both in the kitchen doing dishes. It was the first evening after Hertha's departure. Baba was already on the lookout for a new maid for us.

"But what about Vienna?" I asked.

"Don't talk to me about Vienna!" she snapped. And normally I would have shut up. But this time I didn't. "Well, what about it?"

"There are many more important things," she shot back.

A sudden dread sparked a memory. The posters in the library flashed into my mind, and the booklets promoting "Strength Through Joy," the joy of producing a baby for the Reich.

"What are you doing? Producing babies for Hitler?"

Ulla's hand shot out. There was a loud crack. It was the sound more than the actual smack across my cheek that startled me. I closed my eyes. I actually saw stars exploding on the inside of my eyelids. I didn't feel the sting of the slap—not yet. If I didn't feel it, would it mean it hadn't really happened? I kept my eyes sealed shut until the jittering stars and threads of light that scrambled on the underside of my eyelids bled to a fierce white light, like the white wall of light in the cave of the she-wolf and her pups in *White Fang*.

There were tussles in the den amongst the wolf pups, often followed by the swift discipline of the mother. The quick cuff delivered when a cub would approach the mysterious white light of what it did not even know was the entry to the world outside the cave. I don't know how long I stood there, but when I opened my eyes, Ulla had left the kitchen.

Although Rosa still had to go to school, both Rosa's mother and mine were very good about letting us get together, even on school nights, which in the past was unheard of. So we got to see almost as much of each other as before. Since Rosa was still in school, it was decided that she should keep me up with some of the schoolwork. So it was with Rosa that I now was studying English. Papa taught me mathematics. Rosa and I did Latin together, as well as history and biology. We alternated studying at each other's apartments. One evening I was walking Rosa back to her house from mine. We had gone around the back way so that we were in an alley behind Haberlandstrasse, perhaps two blocks from my apartment, when something caught our eye. Two men were going into the back entrance of an apartment building. Rosa noticed, too.

"Isn't that your father's friend?" Rosa whispered.

"What? Who?"

"You know, your uncle Hessie."

I squinted in the direction she was nodding. It certainly looked like Uncle Hessie, and then the second man turned, and it was my father! They were both dressed in workmen's blue coveralls, the kind of one-piece garments that manual laborers wore. Was this a joke? Were they in some sort of disguise? For what reason?

"Quick!" I whispered. We ducked behind some trash bins in the alley. I soon realized that this was Professor Einstein's building, 5 Haberlandstrasse. A man came to the back door of the building and motioned Papa and Hessie in. We waited and waited for them to come back out, but they didn't. It was becoming late. Rosa had to get home, so we left.

When Papa came home later, I didn't have the nerve to ask him what he had been doing. Mama seemed a bit nervous, and I didn't want to upset her by asking either. It would remain a mystery for another few days.

About a week later, when I came to the breakfast table, Mama and Papa and Ulla were already sitting there. They had very odd expressions on their faces. Mama looked as if she had been crying but was trying to smile. Papa looked confused, to say the least. And Ulla looked like a doll with a painted-on smile.

"Should I tell Gaby, Mother, or should you?" Ulla asked.

"Oh . . . oh!" Mama touched her hair nervously. She turned to me. There was an almost wild look in her eyes, like a bird trying to find an escape. "Well, we have some surprising but exciting news. Ulla and Karl plan to get married."

"Soon," Papa said.

I looked at Ulla. She gave me an almost pleading look. I got it immediately. I was not supposed to know that she was pregnant. I was just supposed to play along like this was all so wonderful. How stupid did Mama and Papa think I was? But I did play along for a while.

"Do I get to be a bridesmaid?" I tried to sound slightly enthusiastic.

"Well, it's going to be a small affair. But, yes, we'll certainly get you a new dress," Mama said, attempting a brightness in her voice that was less than convincing. "We'll have a small engagement party soon so we can meet Karl's parents, Herr and Frau Schenker."

"When's the big day?" I asked.

"It's not going to be a big day," Papa growled. Mama gave him a desperate look.

"It is going to be a lovely, tasteful event. Size has nothing to do with it," she said fiercely.

Size might have everything to do with it! I thought. *It had better be soon, or Ulla is going to have a big belly hanging out.* She was about four months pregnant, at least that's what she calculated. I could just picture her in a wedding dress holding a huge bouquet across her stomach.

Mama continued, "Karl is involved in some activities related to the engineering school at the university so he's quite busy." She had her brown leather date book on the table beside her place. "Let's see, it is now the last week of

March. We thought weather permitting, we would have the engagement party here in the garden in April. The tulips will be up. I hope I can get in the new myrtle I've ordered and two new rosebushes. And then the wedding will be in May."

I nodded dumbly. What was I supposed to say? "Yes, well"—Mama closed her book and pressed her lips together in what was supposed to be a smile—"much to be done." She got up from the table.

"Yes, very much!" Papa said, looking into his plate and rising to leave.

Ulla and I were left alone at the table. She leaned over and took my hand. "Thank you for pretending you didn't know. And . . ." Her voice started to break. "I'm so sorry about"—she swallowed—"slapping you. I don't know what came over me. I wasn't angry with you. It had nothing to do with you."

"You were scared," I said. I am not sure how I knew this, but as soon as I saw the look in her eyes I knew I was right. Ulla was very scared, and it wasn't just about being pregnant. "Ulla, can't you get out of this some way? I mean, you could get rid of the baby. I've heard older girls at school talking about this."

"No! No!" She shook her head. "That's a crime, and Karl would never hear of it." Ulla was breathing hard. She ducked her head, inhaled deeply, and looked down at her hands, which were folded primly in her lap. "I just have to make the best of it." Then she looked up brightly. "Gaby, will you be the godmother?"

"Uh, sure," I replied. I was supposed to be honored and excited, but I was just confused. I liked babies and all, but everything was having to change for Ulla because of this baby.

"Oh, good! That will make me very happy!"

She must have caught my lack of enthusiasm.

"I really love Karl. You have to believe that."

"I do," I replied. But did I?

That afternoon Ulla and I went out on a preliminary expedition in search of a wedding dress for her and my dress for the wedding. Mama was busy with music lessons and more housework. Baba had found us a part-time cook and maid, but we were all doing more of the chores that Hertha had done. Mama said we should go, and if we really liked anything we should get it, as the very next day a boycott of Jewish businesses would begin. We went to Wertheim, which still had the SA men posted at its doors. As soon as we got in I told Ulla what Baba had said last summer to the SA, about dating the Wertheim brothers. I thought Ulla would die laughing. It made me happy. She had been so tense for so long. I had begun to wonder if she had a laugh left in her. We didn't buy dresses that day, but seeing Ulla laugh was worth the trip.

That evening Papa was out late, and Mama and Ulla

and I had dinner, just the three of us, in the music room. It was what Mama called a tray supper. We ate light food—sandwiches and some fruit. We often did this when Papa was out. It was cozy. I tried to imagine a little cradle with a baby in it in the room with us. It suddenly struck me that this little tray supper in the music room had been prearranged in some way. Mama picked up a glass of wine. She rarely had wine when Papa was away from home for dinner.

"Gaby, I thought this might be a good time to explain something to you. It's about Ulla's wedding." I slid my eyes toward Ulla. "Well, this is a little difficult for me to explain but um . . . it seems," Mama said this in an airy almost off-hand way, "that Ulla and Karl are going to have a baby."

It was all I could do to keep from rolling my eyes. Mein Gott, *does she think I was born yesterday? It seems they are going to be having a baby? Like this just happened out of the blue?* Mama had already told me the facts of life. But now, God forbid, pregnancy should be mentioned! And pregnancy before marriage, no less. Mama's reluctance to say the word was ridiculous, but I was prepared to play my part.

"Oh, how exciting. Congratulations!" I cocked my head slightly at Ulla and looked at her with a somewhat disingenuous smile. But I must say I thought I was doing a great job. "When is the baby coming?"

"Well, I don't know exactly," Ulla replied. "Mama, did you call Dr. Steinman to arrange an appointment?"

"Well, that's another little problem. I heard a rumor that

the government is planning to forbid insurance companies to cover treatment by Jewish physicians."

"But Mama, all of our doctors are Jewish, except Schumacher the dentist. What are we going to do if the rumor is true?" Ulla asked.

"Oh, I'm sure we'll find someone."

"I don't want a dentist delivering my baby," Ulla mumbled. Mama gave Ulla a sharp look. This was a bit too clinical for the level of conversation Mama wanted maintained for my innocent ears. A stork delivering a baby, fine. But no reference to an actual medical procedure.

By the time we went to bed, Papa was not yet home. I figured that he had purposely stayed out late so he could avoid any of this conversation.

chapter 31

Of all the creatures that were made,
he [man] is the most detestable. Of the
entire brood he is the only one—the
solitary one—that possesses malice.
That is the basest of all instincts,
passions, vices—the most hateful. . . .
He is the only creature that inflicts
pain for sport, knowing it to be
pain. . . . Also—in all the list he is
the only creature that has a nasty mind.

—Mark Twain, "The Character of Man"

I'm not sure how long I had been asleep after the tray supper, but suddenly I felt someone shaking my shoulder.
"Wake up, Gaby! I have to show you something."

"What? What?" I rose up on one elbow.

"Come here, look out the window," Ulla said.

It was raining—a hard, slanting rain. We went and stood
by the window in Ulla's room, which looked directly down
into the garden. There were two figures hunched over. One
appeared to be digging with a shovel; the other was decid-
edly smaller and held an umbrella over the larger figure.
There was something about the way the umbrella was held
that looked very familiar.

"It's Mama!" I said, turning to Ulla. Ulla nodded.

"What are they doing? It's hardly gardening weather," she whispered. And Mama only gardened in the evening in Caputh.

I knew immediately. It all added up beautifully like an equation. First Mama and Papa were talking about Einstein's house in Caputh. Then Mama asked if Einstein would come back to Germany or if he had left for good. "He has papers here doesn't he?" Mama had asked. Papa replied, "Yes, important ones." And then there was the scene Rosa and I had witnessed in the alley.

"They're burying Einstein's papers," I said.

"What?" Ulla said.

I told her what Rosa and I had seen.

"I bet it's not just papers they're burying," she said grimly.

"What do you mean?"

"Books, too," she muttered.

"What? How do you know?"

"The lists," Ulla replied.

"Lists!" I remembered now Fräulein Hofstadt telling the librarian Frau Grumbach there would soon be a list of banned books.

"What kinds of books are on the lists?" I asked Ulla.

"Well, there aren't actual lists yet," Ulla explained. "Just guidelines about the sorts of books that should not be read. Un-German books."

"But Einstein is German," I protested.

"And Papa is German, too, but his books could be on the lists. He might not be Jewish, but he is considered an adherent to Jewish physics—a white Jew." She paused as if to catch her breath. "And then of course there're authors who aren't German by birth. Nazis have been confiscating their books. Not so much around here. South of here in the Rhineland."

"How do you know all this?" I asked.

She shrugged. "I just do."

"No, tell me Ulla. How do you know?"

"At the university. The German Student Association. They've become very . . . very active."

"Active?"

"I don't know. I try to stay away from it."

"What about Karl? Does he stay away from it?"

I saw tears begin to form in her eyes. I grabbed her hand. "Is Karl involved, Ulla?"

"I . . . I don't think so. I'm not sure."

"What does he say?"

"I try not to ask him about it. It upsets him. He says that Hitler is a fool, that we'll be finished with him in a matter of months. I think he just doesn't want to cause a stir right now."

I looked at Ulla. I wasn't sure if she believed what she was saying or not. I wasn't sure if I believed it.

•   •   •

"I am working mostly now on a new worm-reduction appa-
ratus with a flexible gear coupling for tractors and what we
call the tension ratios for heavy loads. I am especially interested in concentric configurations." It was a week before the
engagement party, and Karl was sitting at our dinner table
telling Papa about his thesis in engineering. Papa was nodding and occasionally asking a question. The conversation
was a bit beyond the rest of us, I think.

Karl had just come back from visiting several farms
in the Rhineland where the Krupp Company had introduced some new tractors for experimentation. Karl looked
handsome. Freshly barbered, he was wearing an English
suit. His tie was knotted fashionably in what some called
the Windsor knot after the stylish Prince of Wales. He had
brought Mama a bouquet of lilies of the valley, Papa a bottle
of scotch, and me a set of hair bows and barrettes. His manners were impeccable. He was gracious and he seemed to
have eyes only for Ulla. He held her hand constantly. He
spoke of the wedding and the apartment he thought he
could get in a suburb near the Krupp plant where he hoped
to work after his graduation. There was just one thing that
I noticed when he arrived at our apartment. Perhaps it was
my imagination. He first shook hands with Papa, then bent
and kissed Mama's hand with as much aplomb as Uncle
Hessie, with what some would call true Prussian elegance.
I was too young to have my hand kissed, so he gave me a
brotherly hug. Because I am short this meant that my nose

was fleetingly buried in the beautiful worsted wool of his tailored suit, and I detected an odd odor. Maybe a cleaning solvent, but it was slightly smoky, yet not the cigar tobacco mixed with wool of Herr Professor Einstein. It was another smoky odor. I couldn't place it.

Later before we went to sleep, I asked Ulla if Karl smoked.

"Yes, all the students smoke. Not me, especially now. It makes me sick."

"Does he smoke cigars?"

"No! Just cigarettes. Only old men smoke cigars. And they are way too expensive for students."

chapter 32

But I reckon I got to light out for the
territory ahead of the rest, because
Aunt Sally she's going to adopt me
and sivilize me, and I can't stand it.
I been there before.

—Mark Twain,
The Adventures of Huckleberry Finn

The weather was beautiful throughout most of April,
and the engagement party was held in the garden in the last week of the month. It looked lovely.
Mama had planted a new variety of daffodil. They were
smaller and very delicate-looking, white with bright orange
centers. They made a gay fringe against the dark stucco of
the wall. The tulips were gorgeous and planted in blocks
of color. Mama always said it was stupid to plant tulips in
rows. They never really made a statement that way, according to her.

And then there was a new rosebush. It was in the corner
where Ulla and I had seen Mama and Papa digging on that
rainy night a few weeks earlier. I shuddered when I thought

of what lay beneath. But I was relieved that it was not yet blooming. The last thing I wanted was for the party guests to go over and smell the roses!

Baba and Hessie and several of Papa's colleagues from the institute and the university had come. Karl had come early, but his parents had not arrived yet. They lived across town, and traffic was often bad.

I was wearing the gray dress that I had bought with Baba last summer. I had yet to find one for the wedding itself. Everyone told me I looked lovely, including Baba who was pleased I was wearing it and promised to help me find a dress for the wedding. I think I did look nice. Everyone told the bride-to-be that she looked lovely too. She didn't. She looked not just tired but haggard. The dress she wore seemed too big for her. She had tried to find something that was not too tight, as her belly was expanding, but she actually looked rather engulfed in the royal blue taffeta. She seemed lost. The best one could say was that the color was a perfect match for her eyes. And everyone did say this. But I doubt if they were looking too deeply into her eyes. Or if they did, they tried to ignore what they saw.

What I saw was resignation, sorrow, and a glint of desperation as well.

"*Aachh! Mein Gott* you look beautiful. The bride absolutely sparkles!" A high voice clawed the air. A large, chunky woman had just arrived and was moving toward us across the courtyard. It was Karl's mother. A diamond and gold necklace squeezed her neck. Her hair was a gaudy orange, and she wore a violent shade of lipstick that made her mouth look like a squashed plum. Her eyes were a turquoise sugary blue. But even from where a stood I could tell that there was no light in them and for some reason they reminded me of marzipan, the painted kind that they used for decorating sweets.

Gerta Schenker looked nothing like her son Karl. A slight man with an ovoid head followed her. He reminded me of a lemon seed. This was Artur Schenker. He was as colorless and dull as his wife was vibrant and garish. I knew exactly what my mother was thinking. *She looks like a bareback rider in the circus!* That was Mama's standard comparison for florid, ostentatiously dressed women. Mama was not very good at concealing her feelings. I could see that she was struggling. She looked straight at Frau Schenker, not daring to steal a glance at either Baba or me—especially not at Baba. If she did, she would roll her eyes and the two of them would burst out laughing.

I was concerned after the introductions to Karl's family, since his mother was actually standing right near the new rosebush Mama had planted where she and Papa had buried the Einstein papers. There was no way, of course, that they could possibly know the papers were under the rosebush, but I was nonetheless consumed with an irrational fear. I was madly trying to think up some way I could get us all to move from this corner when I became aware of Gerta Schenker handing something to Mama.

"Just a little gift," she tweeted in a falsely intimate tone. The gift was flat and wrapped in very fancy paper with gilt sprinkles all over it.

"Unwrap it now, darling. It's very special. I want everyone to see." This seemed a rather self-serving preamble for a gift. Frau Schenker glanced around the garden and motioned other guests to come. Mama untied the ribbons very carefully. She was always so slow opening presents, whereas I tore off wrappings. She handed the ribbon to Papa to hold while she unwrapped the paper neatly. I caught a glint of silver. It was a frame. Then I saw the color drain from Mama's face, and she swayed a bit. Wordlessly she turned the picture around so all could see. It was a photograph of Adolf Hitler.

"Look, it's autographed. Read the inscription," Frau Schenker trilled.

Mama's lips moved but the only sound that came out was "Oh." Then finally, "Why don't you read it, Gerta?"

Gerta took the picture and began to read. "'To Elske and Otto, mother and father of the bride.'"

I did not dare look at Ulla or Karl, or anybody for that matter. I stared straight ahead at the lilac bush, concentrating on the blossoms as Karl's mother read. Their lavender cones, stirred now by a slight breeze, reminded me of scented lanterns. Their sweet, slightly woodsy fragrance wafted across the courtyard. *Mama,* I thought, *say something. Just say it. Say we're not Nazis. Say we can't have his picture in our home.* And I thought if she would just say that, the wedding would never happen. Ulla would be saved from joining this Nazi family.

Mama was now talking, very softly, but she wasn't saying what I wanted her to say.

"I don't think it would work on the piano." She might have been replying to a suggestion of Karl's mother about where to put the picture. I wasn't sure. "You see, I have a baby grand, and the lid is always up. So there is no real room for any pictures." She inhaled sharply, and then her mouth seemed to twitch, and she smiled in a way that I had never seen her smile in my life. "But don't worry," she said gaily, "we'll find a place for it."

Yes, I thought. *The trash bin!* And I was right. The silver frame went out with the trash the very next morning. Ulla was not around, but I was certain that she knew what to expect. It was unthinkable that our family would have such a picture. She had gone to bed immediately following the party, claiming a headache, and off the next morning early on wedding errands.

Of course, Papa insisted we burn the picture.

"You never know, in these times we could be hauled off for throwing out such a picture," he muttered as he took the photo from its frame and then put the match to the glossy portrait. I stood beside him at the kitchen sink and watched as the flame grabbed hold of the edges, singeing them first an amberish brown. Then the color began to darken and spread as the flames licked across that smug, righteous face, with those eyes that were completely insane. Within a matter of seconds there was only a small pile of ashes in the kitchen sink. Just before Papa turned on the faucet to wash them down the drain, I sniffed. "Paper smells different from other things when it burns doesn't it Papa?"

"Yes, I suppose. Different from wood."

That was the smell that I had remembered from the night just weeks before when Karl had come for dinner—burnt paper. The strange chemical and smoky odor that had cut through the fragrance of the lilies of the valley that he had brought Mama, that ash smell that made me ask Ulla if Karl smoked.

"Yes, different from wood," I said softly, and felt my mind shutting down. Something niggled at the back of my brain and I tried to slam a door on it. When I would sometimes have a terrible dream and wake up in the middle of it my first impulse was to turn on the light. Light would dissolve any tatters torn from that nightmare that still might lurk in my bedroom. Now those niggling thoughts in the back of my brain were beginning to squirm. But I wouldn't let them in. Nightmares feed on darkness. Fires feed on oxygen. Cut off the supply and they wither, disintegrate, suffocate.

"Are you all right, Gaby? You suddenly look pale," Papa asked.

"Yes, I'm fine," I said. And I was. I had succeeded in evicting some dreadful tenant from the shadowy corners of my mind. I would remove to the trash bin the rest of the tenant's furniture—the silver frame that Papa said cost at least twenty marks.

chapter 33

The fact that man knows right from
wrong proves his _intellectual_ supe-
riority to other creatures; but the
fact that he can _do_ wrong proves his
moral inferiority to any creature
that _cannot_.

—Mark Twain, "What Is Man"

It was a few days after the engagement party when
Papa came home from his office within an hour after
he had left for it. Mama was out with Ulla. It was
midafternoon, and I was in the kitchen doing the math
problems that Papa had set for me. "The Papa School," as
I had begun to think of my math curriculum, was a lot
more demanding than the regular school. I had completed
what felt like a press march through trigonometry and I
was now beginning calculus, which if I had been in my old
Kaiser Frederick Wilhelm school I would not have started
for at least three years.

Papa came into the kitchen. Barely acknowledging my
presence, he slapped something down on the kitchen table.

"Papa, what is it?"

"Take a look at that." He indicated the papers he had put on the table then he sank down into a chair opposite me. I began reading what was called "12 Theses Against the Un-German Spirit." I skimmed down the pages

The first thesis declared: *language and literature have their roots in the* Volk. *It is the German* Volk's *responsibility to assure its language and literature are pure and unadulterated expression of its* Volk *tradition.*

The fourth and fifth stated: *Our most dangerous enemy is the Jew and those who are his slaves. . . . A Jew can only think Jewish. If he writes in German he is lying.* The screed was written against Jewish writers but apparently one did not have to be Jewish to offend the purity of the German spirit. Many names on the list of banned authors I did not know, but several I did. Jack London! Ernest Hemingway! Mark Twain! None of them Jewish, but all deemed offensive.

"They'll start building the pyres soon," Papa muttered.

"Pyres? For what?" My voice dwindled away.

Papa reached across the kitchen table and took my hand. "Pyres for burning books, Gaby."

"You can't be right. Pyres . . . they burned witches on pyres long ago, four hundred years ago."

"Oh! I'm sure they'll find some witches, too," Papa said, standing up. "I need to discuss this with Hessie." He walked out of the kitchen and I soon heard the front door close behind him. He left the papers on the table. I was afraid to move them. I didn't want to touch them again. Was it just last week that Papa and I had stood at the sink and burned the picture of Hitler? Was it because we had burned Hitler's photograph that now the flames were coming back to haunt us? Had our little kitchen sink fire ignited a larger one? I knew this was irrational. But suddenly the world had become irrational.

One day in early May, Rosa and I met at the southeast corner of the Opernplatz, which was adjacent to the university. We joined a throng of spectators as students in the uniform of the German Student Association and Brown Shirts with swastika badges on their sleeves carried timbers to the center of the stone square. We watched for perhaps fifteen minutes and within that short time the scaffolding for the pyre rose three or four feet.

"How tall will they build it, do you think?" Rosa whispered to me. A robust man standing next to her who wore a monocle and was dressed in a three-piece suit with a gold watch chain spanning his large belly turned to us. "As high as it must be to burn all those Jew and Commie books," he said, smiling pleasantly as if this were the most natural thing in the world to say, as if we had inquired about the weather and was he told us it going to be sunny today. I reached for Rosa's hand and we both turned and left.

But the scaffolding for the pyre was like a magnet. We came back to the square often over the next few days. Perhaps we came with our secret hopes that somehow when we arrived we would find that the building had stopped, the scaffolding had been removed, and the lovely broad stone plaza had returned to normal. No such thing happened. The pyre continued to grow. It spread out as well, like a tumor, a terrible malignancy. I thought of my father's remarks months before. It was the night that Philipp Lenard had visited. He told me about how Lenard had led the attacks on Einstein and Jewish physics. He was trying to assure me. His words came back to me: *And remember things are getting better, I really think so. By spring there will be no more Hitler, just lovely tulips.* I recalled the wistfulness in his eyes.

Now it was spring and the tulips I had helped Mama plant were in full bloom and so were the lilacs. The scent of the linden along the broad avenue named for the fragrant trees was just beginning to tinge the air.

Rosa and I were not the only ones fascinated by the pyre. Every day the crowds watching the erection of the scaffolding grew. Vendors had begun to come to sell hot pretzels and ice cones from pushcarts. There was an odd joviality to the scene, which was strange and uncomfortable and yet we kept coming back. One day when we arrived, the scent of the linden trees was very powerful. The wind was strong and blowing the fragrance across the square. One could even hear the rustle of the heart-shaped leaves. As I drank in the scent of the linden trees and stared at the scaffolding,

I was trying to imagine what the pyre would look like burning and how the smell of the petrol and the flames eating all that paper would eradicate the perfume of the lindens. Just as I was thinking this, the woman next to me who was holding a baby turned to her friend and spoke. "You know, books are actually hard to burn. My son went with a group of engineering students into the Rhineland. They were all part of the German Student Association. They did some experimentations while they were there to explore what was the best fuel for igniting books. Oh, they tried all sorts of things—paraffin, gasoline. He came back reeking of fuel and burnt paper."

And then it came to me, a memory—bitter, acrid, a hot searing blade cutting through the scent of the linden trees. That same odor that I had detected in Karl's beautifully tailored jacket when he had come to our house for dinner the night he had returned from the Rhineland. It was the smell of burning books.

chapter 34

In two weeks the sheep-like masses can
be worked up by the newspapers into
such a state of excited fury that the
men are prepared to put on uniform and
kill and be killed, for the sake of
the worthless aims of a few interested
parties. Compulsory military service
seems to me the most disgraceful symp-
tom of that deficiency in personal
dignity from which civilized mankind
is suffering to-day.

                    —Albert Einstein,
              "The World as I See It"

One day in the second week of May, the phone rang as I was working on some mathematics problems Papa had assigned to me.

I jumped up to answer it.

"Gaby!"

"Rosa! Where are you calling from? It's a school day."

"Yes, it's Wednesday, May tenth." She paused. "Do you know what is happening today?"

"Yes, they are lighting the pyre, but aren't you in school?"

"No. I'm calling from downtown. Meet me at the Brandenburg Gate, on Ebertstrasse near the underground entrance. I'll explain when you get here. Come quick. Make any excuse to get out of the house."

Papa had gone to meet Hessie and Mama and Ulla were out doing wedding things. No excuse would be needed.

When I got off the bus, Rosa was already there waiting for me.

"So what are you doing here?" I asked.

"Hah!" A sharp sound exploded from her. It wasn't really a laugh at all, more of a snarl. "Pays to have connections." There was a bitterness I had never seen before in her gray-green eyes.

"What connections are you talking about?"

"Fräulein Hofstadt. She might have left school, but she has not forgotten us. She works in the office of the Ministry of Propaganda now, and she had three special vans sent to school to take us and the books from the library that were on the list to Opernplatz to witness what we were told would be a wonderful event, an 'affirmation of the German spirit.' She was on the same van I rode in, telling us the great scene we were about to behold like a tour director. "

"How did you get away?"

"Easy. There are hundreds, maybe thousands of people there—students mostly with Gestapo, SA, and SS troops. I just wandered away from our school group."

"So they finally finished the building. I want to see the pyre," I said.

"No, you don't. It's going to be awful."

"I know." I had never told her about Karl, my suspicions that he had taken part in a burning in the Rhineland. I just couldn't bring myself to tell her. It was Ulla that I should have told, but my sister seemed to be in some sort of trance these days, ever since the engagement party. A hundred times a day I had wanted to say something to Ulla. To tell her that she could get out of this marriage. But I watched her and it was as if she had crossed a distant horizon and receded into some remote landscape. Often her hands were loosely clasped over her stomach where this baby slept, oblivious to the world that was disintegrating, the world that it would be born into.

I felt a bitterness steal over me. "But I want to see it anyway!" I took Rosa's hand and yanked it. "Come on."

The Opernplatz was crammed with throngs of students and SA officers. There were vehicles as well, and on top of one an SA officer screamed out instructions to make way for the arriving trucks with their cargos of "filth," by which he meant the books.

It was impossible to see what exactly was happening. Rosa and I were getting jostled and squeezed from all directions. A young man wearing a brown shirt and swastika, the uniform of the German Student Association, came up to us.

"Good girls! You are here. This is the schedule of events!" He shoved a piece of paper into my hands. Rosa read over my shoulder. The torchlight procession was to begin at eleven that evening. The second item on the agenda was band music and singing! Singing as books burned! It was as if the whole world was being turned upside down. After the singing there would be an address by Kurt Ellersiek, president of the German Student Association. And then the minister of propaganda himself, Paul Joseph Goebbels, would speak and then ignite the pyres of books.

"Does your mother know you are here, Rosa?" I asked.

"No." Color suddenly flushed Rosa's checks. "Let's go tell her. And we can see all this from her office. The classics department is right over there." She pointed at one of the imposing neoclassical buildings that faced out on the square. We threaded our way through the crowd toward the entrance where Rosa's mother worked only to be met by Göring's new uniformed Gestapo officers coming down the steps with loads of books in their arms.

"*Achtung!* Make way! Make way!" We had to flatten ourselves against the stone railing. I tried to look at the books they carried but did not recognize any titles.

"Come on, let's go. Mama's office is on the third floor," Rosa said.

She and I ran up the stairs, meeting more officers and students who were dressed in brown shirts with swastika armbands coming down the stairs.

"This is the Classics department," I whispered to Rosa. "What are they burning, *The Odyssey*? *The Iliad*?"

"Who knows," Rosa muttered

At just that moment a book clattered down the stairs. I bent over to pick it up and read the title. *Homeric Odyssey and the Evolution of Justice: A Critical Analysis* by Max Rothberg.

"May I have that, miss." It was not a question but a command. A hand suddenly appeared inches from my nose.

I will hate myself if I give this book to him. I clutched the book to my chest. "I don't want to give it to you," I whispered. My heart was thumping so hard I thought it would jump from my chest. I pressed the book harder.

"What do you mean?" he asked.

I looked up, genuinely confused. He was young. A student. He was dressed in brown. "I mean I don't want to give it to you."

"You don't have a choice."

I backed away from him. He couldn't snatch it, or he would drop the armload of other books he was carrying.

"Yes, I do!" I hissed, then turned and ran up the stairs. Rosa followed me.

"Go left!" she yelled. We raced down a long corridor. "This way! There's a back staircase. We can use it to get to Mama's office."

There was a door with pebbled glass and letters that read DEPARTMENT OF CLASSICS.

"Rosa!" a woman behind a desk who was not Rosa's

mother exclaimed when she saw the two of us. "Rosa, what are you doing here?"

"Is my mother here?"

"No, dear. She had to go to your grandmother's. She wasn't feeling well. And I must say that although I don't wish ill for you grandmother, this is a good time to get out of here." She cast a glance toward the window. "I'm leaving myself as soon as I can. But why are you here?"

"My school brought me."

The woman blinked. "*Mein Gott!* They bring children to this! Well, I think you're safer in here than down there." The woman stood up and walked to the window that looked down on Opernplatz. She shook her head wearily. "Not since the Middle Ages!" That was all she said, then took a wrap from the coat tree, picked up her handbag from her desk, and walked out.

"I guess I'd better call Mama," Rosa said.

Rosa began dialing her grandmother's number.

"Be sure to tell her Fräulein Hofstadt brought you to see the book burning. She'll have to let you leave school now."

Rosa nodded.

"Mama! Yes, it's me. Is Grandma all right? Oh . . . oh . . . yes . . . Mama you'll never guess where I am."

Rosa began to explain. "Yes, Gaby is here. . . . Wait, I'll ask." She put her hand over the receiver. "Mama wants to know if you can spend the night with me, because Grandma's having one of her heart episodes and she needs to stay with her, but if she has to run out for the doctor she wants me there in the building."

I nodded. Then I called my house and Mama answered the phone. I told her I was with Rosa and was spending the night at her apartment. I did not tell her where I was calling from. I suppose Mama thought I was already at Rosa's, and I thought it best to let her believe that. Mama seemed almost relieved in some way that I was spending the night with Rosa. She just asked that I get back the next morning by nine o'clock.

After the telephone call we went to the open window and leaned on the sill, looking down. From this third-floor window, we had a good view. The scaffolding that we had watched being erected was now completely obliterated by the growing pile of books. Behind the pile of books we could see the state opera house. Perched on the triangular pediment of the opera house were three sculptures of the classical muses. They, too, looked down upon what was no longer a mere pile but at the rising mountain of books— literature and volumes of science. I wondered if its peak would reach the toes of the muses.

There was a pale pink light in the sky as the sun began to set. And from the linden trees that lined the broad avenue leading up to the square, a scent wafted toward us. I could imagine those heart-shaped leaves unfurling and trembling in the evening breeze. Everything suddenly seemed so fragile.

"Did I tell you that at Ulla's engagement party, Karl's parents gave us a signed photograph of Hitler?"

"What?"

"Yes, they're real Nazis." My voice suddenly sounded dead and flat as I spoke. "I think he is too."

"How can you be sure? Ulla wouldn't . . ." The words died away.

I turned to Rosa. "I'm sure. I smelled it on him."

"What do you mean? What did you smell?"

"Ashes, smoke, chemicals, the smell of burnt paper. Karl was in the Rhineland visiting farms for part of his studies. And Ulla told me she had heard that books were confiscated from that region."

"Ulla told you that?" I nodded. "Did she say that they burned the books or just confiscated them?"

"Just confiscated. But I smelled that scent on him when he came to dinner after his trip."

Rosa said nothing.

"And then the other day when we were down there . . ." I nodded toward the Opernplatz. "Remember the lady with the baby in her arms who was standing next to me?"

"Sort of."

"She said something about her son who was a member of the Student Association going to the Rhineland, and there was some sort of experimental burning—of books. It all came together for me. Karl's jacket, the smell, the fact that he had been down there too."

"Did Ulla smell it?" Rosa asked. "What did she think?"

I sighed. "Ulla does not allow herself to think or feel anything. I think Ulla has lost all her senses."

"Oh." We looked at each other. It was as if in the space of a few minutes we had both grown old before each other's eyes.

The light leaked from the sky. The pink deepened to lavender and then purple. But it would be hours until the actual pyre was ignited. What did we do during that time? It was like waiting for a funeral to begin. For even though Rosa and I were the best of friends, there seemed to be an awkwardness that had never been there before. We tried to stay very quiet, as we did not want anyone to know that we were still in the office. We did not even turn on a light. Finally an acrid smell cut through the darkness that obliterated the scent of the linden trees, just as I had imagined. Petrol! They were dousing the books now with petrol. Then from a distance we saw the torchlight parade like an immense iridescent worm oozing across the city toward Opernplatz. Swelling in the night were the voices of what must have been tens of thousands of people on the square beneath us as they began to sing.

Zum letzten Mal wird Sturmalarm geblasen!
Zum Kampfe steh'n wir alle schon bereit!
Schon flattern Hitler-Fahnen über allen Strassen
Die Knechtschaft dauert nur noch kurze Zeit!

Die Fahne hoch! Die Reihen fest geschlossen!
SA marschiert mit ruhig-festem Schritt.
Kameraden, die Rotfront und Reaktion erschossen,
Marschieren im Geist in unseren Reihen mit.

For the last time the storm call has sounded.
We are all ready for the fight.
Soon Hitler-flags will fly over the streets.
The servitude will not last long now.

The flag high! The ranks tightly closed!
SA marches with silent, firm pace.
Comrades, shot dead by Red Front and Reaction
March in spirit within our ranks.

More students flooded onto the square. The mountain of books grew higher and higher. I realized I had been holding the *Homeric Odyssey* book the entire time we had been waiting. Now I clutched it closer.

"Look, there he is! On the high platform walking toward the microphones," Rosa said.

"Who?" I asked.

"Him—Goebbels." I had seen him before at the National Theatre, but at that time he was just another high-ranking Nazi out for a festive evening. Now I could see him at work, so to speak. Did he look like a doctor of letters, of literature? Did he look evil? I don't know. What is the face of evil? From my perch I couldn't really see his face, but I did remember it from that night at the theater, and if anything his face had been remarkable for its blandness, its anonymity. I could see his posture now as he stood on the platform, erect, and there was almost a prissiness to his gestures as he waved at the crowd. The singing wound down and he stepped up to the bank of microphones.

"German men and women! The era of extreme Jewish intellectualism is now at an end. The breakthrough of the German revolution has again cleared the way on the German path. The future German man will not just be a man of books, but a man of character. It is to this end that we want to educate you. As a young person, to have the courage to face the pitiless glare of life, to overcome the fear of death, and to regain respect for death—this is the task of this young generation. And thus you do well in this midnight hour to commit to the flames the evil spirit of the past. This is a strong, great and symbolic deed. Here the intellectual foundation of the November 'Democratic' Republic is sinking to the ground, but from this wreckage the phoenix of a new age will triumphantly rise."

At that very moment the first torch was thrown on the books and a claw of fire leapt into the night. There was a huge cheer.

"And now the fire oaths!" Goebbels said. Then one by one members of the German Student Association, and others as well, mounted the platform each holding a book aloft in one hand and stepping up to the microphone. Each student said the name of the author and the particular offense with which the author was charged.

"I commit to the flames the works of Heinrich Mann, Ernst Glaeser, and Erich Kästner, for crimes of decadence and moral decay. We do this to support discipline and decency in family and state." And then the book was tossed into the fire.

"I commit to the flames the works of Erich Maria Remarque for the crime of literary betrayal of the soldiers of the Great War. We do this for the education of the nation in the spirit of standing to battle."

The fires grew fiercer. It appeared at one point that the gowns of the three muses were actually burning! But that was, of course, impossible. They were made of stone. *Stone can't burn*, I thought. The night was torn with flames and jagged cries of triumph, and the air spun with ashes and of course there was the smell, the exact smell I had detected on Karl's jacket, the smell of burning paper. I looked up to find the stars stuttering in the night beyond the flames. Orion was rising. I tried to remember the scent of the linden trees, but the smoke was too overpowering. The heat must have been very intense, for people had backed away to the edges of the square and into the streets surrounding it.

"Gaby! Your sister!" Rosa grabbed my arm as we leaned out the open window.

"Where?"

"Down there, near the statue of the kaiser."

I spotted her. Ulla looked dazed as she had for the last several days. Her hands were lightly clasped over her belly.

"I have to stop her!"

"Stop her from what?"

"Marrying Karl! I'll tell her. I'll tell her that I know what he did in the Rhineland." She couldn't have known, I told myself. She simply couldn't have, or maybe she buried it so deep inside her, beneath layer upon layer of denial. I ran out the office door and tore down the four flights of steps. I could hear Rosa's feet pounding after me.

As soon as I reached the square, I felt as if I were in a boiling cauldron of insane hate. People were shouting. "Heil Hitler!" "Down with obscene Jew literature!" "Slaughter the commies!" Their faces were stretched into horrendous grimaces.

"Ulla! Ulla!" I screamed. Drafts of hot air slapped around me.

"Gaby!" She wheeled around. "What are you doing here?"

I was about to ask her the same question when Karl ran up. I stepped back. He wore the Brown Shirt and swastika of the German Student Association. "Ulla, no!" I called.

"I've got it, Ulla!" he cried out, smiling triumphantly.

She gave a cry and flung her arms around Karl's neck. I didn't understand what I was seeing.

"What? What is happening?" I asked.

"Gaby," Karl said, turning to me, "what are you doing here?"

A fury suddenly roared up in me.

"What is *anybody* doing here?" I screamed.

"I am the captain of the third division of the Student Association."

"You're what?" I shouted in dismay.

"You don't understand, Gaby," Ulla said. "Karl just rescued Papa's book. It took great courage. He did it for me." Her eyes shone with tears.

"But you must be quiet," Karl said, and put a finger to his lips. "This is our secret. I did it only because . . ." I didn't need to hear the rest of the sentence. That was enough. The picture became very clear to me.

"You did it only because you got her pregnant. But why did you join, and become captain no less of the third division of the German Student Association? How many books did you bring to this fire, and to the other fire that I smelled on you, Karl? The fire in the Rhineland?"

"Gaby, don't say that!" Ulla looked at me desperately.

"I'll say whatever I want. I'm not a book. You can't burn me!"

I turned and walked away.

chapter 35

Our task must be to free ourselves by
widening our circle of compassion to
embrace all living creatures and the
whole of nature in its beauty.

—Albert Einstein

The next morning when I returned to our apartment, I was surprised to see Uncle Hessie's car by the curb. I knew I could not tell my parents about what I had witnessed last night. Mama and Papa would surely know about the fires on the Opernplatz. They were still smoldering and there were pictures of the blaze on the front page of every newspaper. But I would not say I had been there.

"Ah, Gaby!" Uncle Hessie came out of the apartment building. "We were about to drive by Rosa's and pick you up."

"You were? What for? Mama said I didn't need to be home till nine."

"This is the weekend your mama and papa planned to go to Caputh to plant the garden and open the house for summer, right?" So it was. Today was Thursday, May eleveth, and since I no longer went to school, I suppose my parents had decided to take advantage of the good weather and leave on Thursday morning rather than Friday night. "Run upstairs, dear. Tell your parents you are here. They wanted to get on the road early."

"Yes, sure," I said. Then I stopped and turned around. "But Uncle Hessie—where are the pansies?"

"The pansies?" Uncle Hessie looked momentarily confused.

"The flats of pansies Mama always buys to take up to plant."

"Oh yes, of course, the pansies. They are already in the car."

When I walked into the apartment I heard Papa shouting. I went right into the study. Ulla was collapsed in a chair, her face blotchy from crying. Papa stood over her shaking his finger.

"This is your last chance. You come with us! We beg you. We'll take care of you and the baby."

"I can't, Papa!" Ulla shrieked.

"Ulla, he's a Nazi!" Mama cried.

"Not forever, Mama. He says that Hitler won't last."

"That doesn't matter!" Mama sobbed. "He is a Nazi. His family are Nazis."

"He is the father of my child, Mama."

Suddenly they all turned and noticed me. They stopped talking immediately.

"We're leaving, aren't we? We're leaving Berlin," I said.

"Just to Caputh," Mama said weakly. But it was a pathetic attempt to lie.

"No, Mama. We're leaving Germany. I know." I turned to Ulla. "Come, Ulla. Please come with us."

She got up and ran to embrace me. "I can't, Gaby. I can't. Please understand."

I did understand. I understood that she didn't really love Karl. She might have thought she loved him. But she didn't. I understood that she was scared to raise the baby by herself even if Mama and Papa said they would help. There was a stigma to being an unwed mother. I knew all of this. I could feel it. I knew Ulla better than Mama or Papa. That is how it is sometimes with sisters.

No one told me I was too young to be a part of this conversation. In fact, Mama and Papa looked at me as if their lives depended on something I might say or do to change Ulla's mind. But nothing could be said.

A few minutes later just the three of us went down the stairs. Ulla stayed in the apartment. I suppose she knew it would be too hard to say good-bye outside, on the sidewalk. I led the way. I had to hold Mama's hand because she was so shaky, and Papa was softly crying. Hessie knew immediately. There were no words needed to communicate the small tragedy that had just taken place in Papa's study. He only said, "Don't worry. I'll look after her." He put an arm around each one of their shoulders and hugged them. "Now, get in the car, all of you."

I soon would discover that the car had been packed not with pansies but suitcases full of clothing that we never took to Caputh. Not shorts and bathing suits. Not holiday clothing, but clothing for everyday life. Mama had probably spent the evening before packing. That was why she was happy I had spent the night at Rosa's. We headed not on Friederich Strasse toward Caputh but instead to the road that went north and west toward Holland. To catch an ocean liner to America, Mama told me. Where? To CalTech? To Princeton? The details weren't important to me. I was too devastated to even think. I only cared about what I was leaving—Rosa, Baba, my sister—not what I was going toward.

I suddenly remembered my Diary of Shame. It was under my bed in the apartment. Maybe someday someone would read it. They might think it was why I left; that I was a better person than I am. But they would be wrong. I didn't want to leave.

I watched Hessie's eyes in the rearview mirror. There was an indescribable sadness in them. It was the despair of the unthinkable, the unutterable, that he was driving us away and we might never see one another again. They mirrored all our grief. Then I couldn't look at those eyes any longer. I felt as if I were breaking in two.

I turned around in the seat and sat up on my knees, gazing out the back window. I could still see Berlin faintly, its buildings rising like a scratchy calligraphy, words in a sentence strung across a page. A page I couldn't quite read.

historical figures

While many of the characters in this book are made up, some are real people. Here is background information on some of the historical figures Gaby encounters:

Josephine Baker was one of the first African American women to gain worldwide fame as an entertainer. A great beauty, singer, and actress, she was born in Missouri in 1906, moved to Europe, and became a French citizen in 1937. She was active in the French Resistance during World War II, for which France awarded her the military honor of the Croix de Guerre.

Vicki Baum, a bestselling novelist, was born to a Jewish family in Vienna in 1888. She wrote more than fifty popular novels, of which the most famous was *People at a Hotel*. In the early 1930s she traveled to Hollywood to supervise the filming of her book as *Grand Hotel*, eventually settling there and becoming a scriptwriter.

Arthur Eddington, a British astrophysicist, helped spread Einstein's theory of general relativity through the English-speaking world. He was the head of the 1919 expedition to photograph the solar eclipse that provided one of the earliest proofs of Einstein's theories.

Albert Einstein, the father of modern physics and best known for his theories of relativity, was born to a German Jewish family in 1879. He became a Swiss citizen in 1901, and much of his most important early work was done in Switzerland. In 1914 he became director of the Kaiser Wilhelm Institute in Berlin and professor of theoretical physics at the University of Berlin. He was awarded the Nobel Prize in Physics in 1921. In addition to his scientific preeminence, Einstein was known as a humanist and a pacifist. In 1933, he moved with his family to Princeton, New Jersey, where he joined the Institute for Advanced Study.

Abraham Flexner, a Jewish educational reformer born in Kentucky, helped found the Institute for Advanced Study at Princeton and worked to bring over European scholars who were at risk from the Nazi regime, including Albert Einstein.

Paul Joseph Goebbels, one of Hitler's most devoted supporters, was a skillful orator and a virulent anti-Semite. He earned a PhD in German literature, specializing in eighteenth-century Romantic drama. Following unsuccessful attempts to become an author, he used his talent for propaganda to become an important member of the Nazi Party, concentrating on attacks against the Jews. He became Hitler's first minister of propaganda and enlightenment in 1933. He is famous for his declaration that if one tells a big enough lie, people will believe it. Although he was not a dwarf, he was sensitive about his appearance, since he was barely five feet tall and had a club foot.

Magda Goebbels, a beautiful socialite, was first married to the wealthy, much older industrialist Günther Quandt. After their divorce, she became involved with the Nazi Party, becoming close to both Goebbels and Hitler. Hitler was a witness for her marriage to Goebbels, and she acted as Hitler's unofficial first lady. Just before the Nazis' defeat, Magda and her husband poisoned their six children and then committed suicide.

Johann Wolfgang von Goethe, born in 1749, was Germany's greatest poet, author, and philosopher. The Nazis tried to package him as a quintessentially German artist and adopted the title character of his *Faust* as an example of the ideal ruthless hero.

However, since Goethe's writing was not concerned with issues of nationalism and he opposed the dictatorship of thought, the Nazis had some difficulty presenting him as their true forerunner.

Heinrich Heine was one of Germany's great Romantic poets. Born to a Jewish family in 1797, he later converted to Protestantism to help further his career. Even during his lifetime, his revolutionary political views made him controversial in Germany, and his writings were sometimes banned. His works were among those destroyed in the Nazi book-burnings. He was buried in Paris. When the Nazis captured that city, Hitler ordered his gravesite destroyed.

Wolf-Heinrich Graf von Helldorf, an ally of Goebbels's and an SA leader, was notorious for harassing and robbing rich Jews. For personal reasons, he later turned against the Nazis and was executed for his part in a plot to assassinate Hitler.

Paul von Hindenburg, born in 1847, was a war hero during the First World War and became the second president of the German Republic. When he was eighty-four years old and in poor health, he was with difficulty persuaded to run for reelection because it was believed that he was the only candidate who could defeat Hitler. Hindenburg disliked Hitler; but being sick, tired, and somewhat confused, he was easily manipulated by the Nazis.

Edwin Hubble was an American astronomer whose work on star spectrums led to Hubble's Law, which demonstrated that the universe is continually expanding. The Hubble Space Telescope is named in his honor.

Erich Kästner was an author, journalist, and satirist. Today he is best known for his children's books, but during the Weimar Republic he was one of the most influential intellectual figures in

Berlin. He was a pacifist and opposed the Nazi regime, but unlike many writers in his position, he could not bring himself to leave Germany. He personally watched his books being destroyed in the bonfire in Berlin. Although the Nazis prevented him from writing, and twice arrested him, he survived the war years in Germany and died in Munich in 1974.

Philipp Lenard, born in Hungary in 1862, was an influential physicist who won the Nobel Prize in Physics in 1905 for his work on cathode rays. Some of his work overlapped Einstein's. He resented Einstein's being given credit that he believed should have been his, and grew increasingly suspicious of Einstein and his followers. He became committed to the idea of a pure German science that would be untainted by what he considered the false ideas of "Jewish physics." He was an adviser to Hitler and became the Nazis' chief of Aryan physics.

Franz von Papen, one of Hindenburg's advisers, was appointed chancellor of Germany in May 1932. He advocated bringing Hitler into the government, believing that then the government would be able to control him. In order to gain the support of the Nazi Party, he lifted the ban on the SA and the SS. After he was forced by his enemies to resign as chancellor, he persuaded Hindenburg to create a new government with Hitler as chancellor and himself as vice-chancellor. He still believed he could control Hitler, but Hitler quickly turned against him and marginalized him.

Joachim von Ribbentrop was an ambitious social-climbing wine merchant. Although he was not a member of the nobility, he persuaded an aunt who had married a nobleman to adopt him so that he could add the aristocratic "von" to his name. As a friend of von Papen's, he was able to assist in the maneuvering that made Hitler chancellor. He became Hitler's foreign affairs advisor.

Leni Riefensthal was an actress and innovative filmmaker. A friend of both Hitler and Goebbels, she made the famous Nazi propaganda film *Triumph of the Will* in 1934. Although she was never convicted of any war crimes, she had ties to the Nazis, and her film career was derailed after the war. She lived to the age of 101, dying in 2003.

Friedrich Schiller, born in 1759, was one of Germany's greatest poets and dramatists. The Nazis claimed Schiller as their prophet and tried to demonstrate that his plays supported Nazi theories. He became the most frequently performed playwright in Germany during the war years. Much of Schiller's work, however, was a plea for liberty of conscience and could not be twisted to the Nazis' purposes, and eventually Hitler banned some of his works.

Kurt von Schleicher worked his way up in the army to become a powerful politician behind the scenes. A friend of both von Papen's and Hindenburg's he was basically conservative but opposed the idea of a military dictatorship. After he broke with von Papen, he helped force him out of office and briefly became chancellor of Germany. Hoping to bring some unity to the government, he reached out to many parties, including the less extreme branch of the Nazi Party. However, after less than two months as chancellor, he was forced out and was replaced by Hitler. He and his wife were murdered in an assassination ordered by Hitler on June 30, 1934, in what became known as the Night of the Long Knives.

•   •   •

The above characters are real. However, three of the fictional characters in this book were based on actual people. Otto Schramm, Gabriella's father, was modeled to some extent on the German astrophysicist Erwin Freundlich. An early supporter of Einstein's, Freundlich led a 1914 expedition that hoped to confirm Einstein's theory of relativity by observing a total eclipse of the sun in the Crimea. However, the expedition was derailed when World War I broke out, and he and his colleagues were temporarily imprisoned by the Russians. Freundlich did not participate in the 1919 expedition that successfully provided support for Einstein's theory, but he was involved in later experiments involving relativity and the orbit of the planet Mercury. In 1933 he left Nazi Germany, becoming a professor in Istanbul and later in Scotland.

Baba Blumenthal was inspired by Bella Fromm, the social columnist for Berlin's liberal newspaper *Vossische Zeitung*. Mrs. Fromm, or Frau Bella as she was known, kept a secret journal that was later published as a book titled *Blood & Banquets: A Berlin Social Diary*. She stayed as long as she could before fleeing the Nazi regime to the United States in 1938. She helped many other Jews escape by obtaining visas, money, and whatever else they needed to get out of Germany. She was born in Nuremberg around 1900 and died in 1972.

Uncle Hessie was based on the dashing Count Harry Kessler, a vibrant figure in Berlin between World War I and World War II. Born into an aristocratic Anglo-German family, he was a diplomat, publisher, and connoisseur of art. He was a friend to a glittering array of people from Albert Einstein to Josephine Baker. The count kept a diary that he began in 1918 with the Armistice that ended the world war and continued until his death in 1937, recording the agonies of his country during the rise of Hitler.

acknowledgments

P eople think of writing as a solitary endeavor, but in truth it is not. It is usually a collaboration between the author, editor, and the many others who assist in guiding writers to wonderful source materials. For this book especially I had the support and the insights of many people.

First I would like to thank Gerhard Kallman, professor emeritus of architecture at the Harvard School of Design. His memories of growing up in Berlin and attending the Humboldt University of Berlin were crucial to my understanding of what was happening at this time when Hitler was rising to power. He experienced it. He lived it and he left just before the most violent waves of anti-Semitism seized the nation. He read my manuscript not only for accuracy in terms of street names and shops that his family frequented but also for the more subtle elements such as the tone of dialogue between parents and children of the social and intellectual strata of the Schramm family. It was because of his acquaintance with Bella Fromm that I decided to create the character of Baba. He also on two separate occasions as a youngster met Albert Einstein. Gerhard shared with me as well his recollections of sneaking into the movie "palaces," as they were called, to see Marlene Dietrich when he was still a lad in short pants. Professor Kallman was in Berlin on his way to a ski holiday the night of the Reichstag fire. "I went anyway," he recalled. "I was just so happy to be finished with exams!" His recollections of these events and people animated the city for me. Luckily his family anticipated, unlike many others, what was in store for Jews and they left in 1934 for Switzerland and then some time after went to England, where he studied architecture.

I must also thank Nadine Lowry. Although Nadine is just fifteen years old, she became my source for translating various German words and expressions that might touch upon the lives of schoolgirls today in Germany. She also described to me certain German Christmas traditions. Nadine is well on her way to fluency in several languages, and I wish her all the best.

Through this entire process my editor, Joy Peskin, although in New York, has been at my side. I cannot express my appreciation first of all for her unbridled enthusiasm for this book from the very start and her wonderful insights that guided me through many revisions and steered me with a light touch around many pitfalls, quagmires, and any other of the words that one can think of for disastrous obstacles and traps that a writer might encounter!

Ashes covers one of the most documented periods in all of history. For Janet Pascal, the production editor, checking the facts of this story for accuracy was a monumental task. With good humor and one of the keenest eyes in the business she slogged her way through this manuscript, finding everything from outright errors to subtle nuances that possibly undercut the authenticity I strived to achieve.

Finally I must give deepest thanks to the Rockefeller Foundation for providing me with an undisturbed month at the Bellagio Study and Conference Center at the Villa Serbelloni through their Creative Arts Residency Program. As much as the quiet and beauty of this special place was appreciated, so was the wonderful and stimulating company of the other visiting scholars and artists who ranged from a composer to a young Filipino poet to an American and a Russian novelist, an African soil scientist, an economist, and a legal scholar. In particular I would like to thank the incomparable director of the Bellagio Program, Pilar Palacio, who made everything so darned easy!

Kathryn Lasky
Cambridge, Massachusetts
2010